PRAISE FOR USA TODAY BESTSELLING AUTHOR JAN MORAN

Summer Beach and *Coral Cottage* series

"A wonderful story... Will make you feel like the sea breeze is streaming through your hair." – Laura Bradbury, Bestselling Author

"A novel that gives fans of romantic sagas a compelling voice to follow." – *Booklist*

"An entertaining beach read with multi-generational context and humor." – *InD'Tale* Magazine

"Wonderful characters and a sweet story." – Kellie Coates Gilbert, Bestselling Author

"A fun read that grabs you at the start." – Tina Sloan, Author and Award-Winning Actress

"Jan Moran is the queen of the epic romance." —Rebecca Forster, *USA Today* Bestselling Author

"The women are intelligent and strong. At the core is a strong, close-knit family." — *Betty's Reviews*

The Chocolatier

"A delicious novel, makes you long for chocolate." – *Ciao Tutti*

"Smoothly written...full of intrigue, love, secrets, and romance." – *Lekker Lezen*

The Winemakers

"Readers will devour this page-turner as the mystery and passions spin out." – *Library Journal*

"As she did in *Scent of Triumph*, Moran weaves knowledge of wine and winemaking into this intense family drama." – *Booklist*

The Perfumer: Scent of Triumph

"Heartbreaking, evocative, and inspiring, this book is a powerful journey." – Allison Pataki, *New York Times* Bestselling Author of *The Accidental Empress*

"A sweeping saga of one woman's journey through World War II and her unwillingness to give up even when faced with the toughest challenges." — Anita Abriel, Author of *The Light After the War*

"A captivating tale of love, determination and reinvention." — Karen Marin, Givenchy Paris

"A stylish, compelling story of a family. What sets this apart is the backdrop of perfumery that suffuses the story with the delicious aromas – a remarkable feat!" — Liz Trenow, *New York Times* Bestselling Author of *The Forgotten Seamstress*

"Courageous heroine, star-crossed lovers, splendid sense of time and place capturing the unease and turmoil of the 1940s; HEA." — *Heroes and Heartbreakers*

BOOKS BY JAN MORAN

The Winemakers: A Novel of Wine and Secrets
The Perfumer: Scent of Triumph

Seabreeze
Shores

USA TODAY BESTSELLING AUTHOR
JAN MORAN

SEABREEZE SHORES

JAN MORAN

SUNNY PALMS
PRESS

Library of Congress Cataloging-in-Publication Data

Moran, Jan.

/ by Jan Moran

ISBN 978-1-64778-050-0 (epub ebook)

ISBN 978-1-64778-052-4 (hardcover)

ISBN 978-1-64778-051-7 (paperback)

ISBN 978-1-64778-054-8 (audiobook)

ISBN 978-1-64778-053-1 (large print)

Published by Sunny Palms Press. Cover design by Sleepy Fox Studios. Cover images copyright Deposit Photos.

Sunny Palms Press
9663 Santa Monica Blvd STE 1158
Beverly Hills, CA 90210 USA
www.sunnypalmspress.com
www.JanMoran.com

1

"*D*o you think the baby's room will be finished in time?" Standing in her sister's beachfront bungalow, Ivy pushed a heavy gray tarp aside and peered through the gaping opening in the wall.

Off the rear of the small house, a partially framed room stood open to brisk sea breezes. Ivy hugged her leopard jean jacket over her lightweight wool pullover. Although it was nearly spring, the air still held a crisp, late winter chill, while sunny rays rendered the ocean a bright aquamarine-blue. Winters along the Southern California beaches felt more like early spring in Boston, as Ivy recalled.

"Mitch promised me the room will be ready," Shelly said, though her frown betrayed her words. "He works on it in the evenings, but he hasn't gotten very far."

Ivy stared at the gaping hole. "It's not very secure. Doesn't that worry you?"

"Mitch thinks it's okay. Summer Beach is pretty safe, but I'm a New Yorker at heart. I make sure to lock the back gate." Shelly crossed her arms. "He hasn't done as much as he'd planned. The coffee crowd at Java Beach keeps him busy."

Lately, Shelly had been working half days at the Seabreeze

Inn as she approached her final months before her first child. But this morning, she hadn't come in, so after serving breakfast and handling guest departures, Ivy had gone to check on her. Shelly had overslept, but Ivy thought she needed even more rest.

Her younger sister eased onto a chair in the kitchen, gathering the folds of a flowing blue-and-white dress around her. Shelly wore one of Mitch's creamy fisherman sweaters over it, and her chestnut hair was piled into her usual haphazard topknot, but the dark circles under her eyes were new.

Instead of buying maternity clothes, Shelly was relying on stretchy yoga wear and flowing beach dresses that she could wear later. Ivy had to admire her unique sense of style.

"Bennett told me he's been offering to help, but Mitch won't let him," Ivy said, recalling the conversation she'd had with her new husband on the beach last night.

Husband. Even after a few months, the word still seemed like a new pair of high heels in her mind—shiny and exciting, but not quite comfortable in that morning-hair relationship she'd had with Jeremy for so many years before his death. Although she and Bennett were still adjusting to each other's ingrained habits, she felt fortunate that they'd found each other again in their mid-forties.

Ivy turned to her sister. "Has something happened between our guys?"

With one hand resting on her curved midsection, Shelly gestured toward the construction site. "I don't know, but Mitch seems determined to do the entire job himself." She paused to yawn. "There's no sleeping while he's hammering out there. I think it's pride; he wants to say he built his first child's room onto the house."

"Be glad that he's a proud father—and willing to help." Ivy glanced at haphazardly placed nails on a two-by-four. While Jeremy had spoiled their daughters, to him, they had been more like possessions to show off. He wanted to be their best friend more than their father. And when it came to pitching in, he always managed to slip out of those duties.

Shelly put her feet up on another chair and eased back. "Between you and me, my husband is more effective in the kitchen or on a boat. When he squeezes in time late at night to work on the room, I hear an awful lot of banging—not to mention some pretty colorful language."

Ivy secured the tarp over the opening. "Maybe this job is a little out of his scope."

"Without any instruction manual at all, I've created a little human," Shelly said, waving a hand. "I thought he could manage a second bedroom. Aren't hammers and nails in guys' DNA?"

Ivy had to laugh. "Why don't you call Forrest? He could have this knocked out in no time with his crew. Problem solved." Their brother usually worked on larger construction projects, but Ivy thought he could find time to help his sister.

Shelly shook her head. "I offered, but Mitch won't allow it. And we're way past me being useful on a construction site. I don't know which was worse—the morning sickness or feeling like I have to pee every five minutes. I have to keep telling myself I can do this."

"Of course, you can." As she spoke, Ivy put away the clean dishes teetering by the sink. "Pregnancy isn't forever. Just wait until you get to hold your baby." Those moments when she'd first held her daughter stood out like treasured snapshots in her mind, as clear and vivid as the days they occurred.

Ivy paused with her hands on the cool tile countertop. A part of her wished for another baby with Bennett, but at her age, with two grown children? That was no more than some ridiculous, romantic notion brought on by Shelly's pregnancy. She finished putting away the dishes and shut the cupboards.

A flush filled Shelly's face. "I *am* excited…and grateful. But this is harder than I thought it would be." She pressed a hand on her stomach and shifted. "Before I met Mitch, I thought I'd never have a family. When we married, I dreamed of having a sweet, Instagram-perfect baby, but the way this one is punching and flipping, we might have created a little troublemaker. This rascal sure made me sick in the beginning."

"Thank goodness that's over," Ivy said, smiling. "You'll love your child no matter what they're like. They come with their own personalities baked in."

Ivy pulled a pair of clean dishtowels from the drawer and looped them over the oven handle. Then she sat at the table, touching her sister's hand in support while studying her.

Despite a rosy bloom in Shelly's cheeks, her bloodshot eyes revealed her weariness. Ivy recalled how tired she'd been in her last months of pregnancy with her daughters. Eager to lift Shelly's spirits, Ivy spoke with cheerful nonchalance. "So, what names have you two decided against?"

Shelly slid a gaze toward Ivy and grinned. "I know what you're doing."

"What?" Ivy asked, feigning innocence.

"You're trying to trick me, and I'm not falling for it. You'll find out the gender and name when this baby is born. We don't want the entire town's input on names—and the Bay family is pretty opinionated, too." She tapped her belly. "You hear that, kiddo? You're going to have a lot to deal with when you arrive. Maybe that's why you're so feisty."

"Can't say I didn't try," Ivy said with a small laugh. "I heard old Charlie is taking bets on the gender at Java Beach." Shelly's decorating scheme didn't offer any clues. She'd decided on seafoam green and sunny yellows with a daisy motif. So they could reuse items for another child, she'd said. Everything she'd bought was stashed in a corner of their only bedroom.

Shelly rolled her eyes. "Charlie would take bets on which way the sun rose if he thought he could make a penny."

"Since you've nixed a baby shower, how about a gender-reveal party instead?" Ivy asked, tapping a finger on the table. At least her sister was smiling again.

"We can't reveal what we don't know. Why can't people accept that we want to do this the old-school way?" Shelly picked a thread from her dress. "Besides, I don't want all the fuss. I saw enough disasters when I was working the party circuit in New York. People got so wound up and forgot they were supposed to be having a good time."

Ivy squeezed Shelly's hand. "Can't blame people for being curious and wanting to be involved."

Although Shelly and Mitch had scheduled an ultrasound to check on the baby's development, they told everyone they didn't want to know if the baby was a boy or a girl. Yet, Ivy suspected they knew but just weren't telling anyone. She smiled to herself. Privacy was precious in a small town where gossip was part of the entertainment. She'd learned that when she and Bennett were dating.

"Speaking of events," Shelly began. "Is everything arranged for our spa week at the inn? I'm sorry I haven't helped much."

"Poppy took the calls and handled everything for you." This was their first spa week, and Ivy was working hard to make it extra special. Filling the inn during the summer season was easy, but the rest of the year took more creativity. "Your Roaring Twenties party sounds like a fabulous idea. We still have time to pull it together."

"I could take guests to the vintage thrift shops in town for costumes," Shelly said.

"That would be fun for them," Ivy agreed. "Let's plan for it and send an updated schedule to guests. It would be fun to have someone teach the dances, too."

Shelly twirled her hand. "Like the Charleston?"

"Exactly." Ivy added that to the endless mental list she kept in her head.

Although the sun still shone, a crisp late afternoon breeze

blew through the edges of the tarp, scattering papers from the table like leaves in the wind. Shelly reached for them but was hampered by her belly.

"I'll get those," Ivy said, reaching down to scoop papers from the floor. "It's pretty chilly in here. Why don't you go into the living room and rest?"

Shelly stifled another yawn. "I could use a nap, but I'm starving again. Those mini-meals don't last long for two."

Ivy plucked an apple from a fruit bowl. "I'll bring you a cup of tea and a snack. The evening's new guests have already checked into the inn, and Poppy can manage until the afternoon wine-and-tea event."

"You're the best," Shelly said, pushing herself from the chair. She grinned and added, "But I'm still not giving up baby names."

Smiling, Ivy turned to fill a kettle, placed it on the stovetop, and adjusted the gas flame. While the water heated, she sliced an apple and a chunk of white cheddar cheese she'd found in the refrigerator and arranged these on a plate with a few nuts. Shelly couldn't eat much at once because the baby was crowding her stomach, so she'd been nibbling throughout the day.

Ivy wished their mother could be here to help Shelly, but she and their father had embarked on their well-deserved, round-the-world sail after Shelly's wedding last summer. Ivy wasn't complaining—she'd do anything for her younger sister —but she was no replacement for Carlotta and Sterling.

A car pulled into the driveway, and a minute later, Mitch charged through the back door. He wore a tattered Grateful Dead T-shirt and held a hard plastic, sand-encrusted kiddie pool in one hand. He leaned it against the wall in the kitchen.

"You're home early," Ivy said, greeting him. "Shelly is resting on the couch."

"My afternoon charter cruise canceled, so I decided to get some work done on the room while it's still daylight." Mitch grabbed an apple from the bowl. Motioning toward the rear, he added, "I bought some bright lights, so I can work better after the sun goes down."

"Forrest would be happy to help you with that," Ivy ventured.

"Shelly and I already talked about that." Mitch frowned and ran a hand over his spiky blond hair. "I might be behind, but I've got this. We still have time. Besides, the baby will sleep in our room for a while anyway. I can work a few hours every night, especially as the days grow longer." He gave her a reassuring grin. "I'll finish the room. I know Shelly wants to decorate it."

"That would mean a lot to her. Cute pool," she added. "The little one will love playing in that."

Mitch's grin broadened. "That's for Shelly. We can fill it with saltwater, and she can have the baby right here in the kitchen. Cool, huh?"

Ivy held a cup in mid-air, shocked at what he was suggesting, although she knew many people did it. But that old thing? It was probably teeming with germs. "You're kidding, right?"

"We've been talking about it. The kid can surf right out." Mitch crunched into his apple and left to see Shelly.

Still trying to process what Mitch had said, Ivy prepared the tea. She remembered what expecting that first child was like—and not really knowing what to expect. Mitch was almost ten years younger than Shelly, and in many ways, his youth was showing. She glanced at the pool and shuddered.

Or was she that out of touch now?

Still, Ivy knew the baby would be fine in their room for a while. Besides, that was their business, she reminded herself, although it was growing increasingly hard to grant them that. As she glanced at the kiddie pool again, her stomach tightened with concern for Shelly. She only wanted her sister to have all the care options available to her if she needed them.

A few minutes later, Mitch ducked through the tarp, a belt

of tools on his hips. He was certainly industrious, and Ivy respected him for that. Still, between running the coffee shop and taking guests out on his boat to see dolphins and whales, Mitch didn't have time for much beyond Shelly and his early morning surf. Expanding the house was an aggressive goal. She hoped he could finish before the baby arrived.

But a kiddie pool? Ivy still couldn't wrap her head around that idea.

And that wasn't all.

As new parents, Shelly and Mitch were underestimating the time an infant would demand. Ivy let out a sigh. She sure had. After Misty was born, she hadn't picked up a paintbrush again until both girls had started school. Even then, she rarely found time. Only this year had she agreed to a special commission painting for a client.

No doubt about it, Shelly and Mitch had a lot to learn about having a baby and raising a child.

And keeping her opinion to herself? That would be her challenge.

Ivy swung through the kitchen with Shelly's tray. "Here you go—your green tea and goodies." She placed the tray on a worn surfboard perched atop bricks.

"I thought I'd have a new coffee table by now," Shelly said, shaking her head. "But it's all about priorities, right?" As she sipped her tea, the house seemed to shudder under the fervor of Mitch's banging hammer, and she winced. "He worked late last night with his new blazing lights."

"That's awfully loud," Ivy said, raising her voice. "Did you get any rest?"

Shelly yelled over the din. "Why do you think I need a nap?" She pressed a hand against her temple. "I really appreciate what he's doing, but I feel a monster headache coming on."

"We have a couple of vacant rooms at the inn," Ivy said, speaking louder as the noise intensified. At least until guests arrived. Her heart was already racing, and she couldn't imagine her sister having to deal with this every day.

Shelly chewed her lip. "How much sleep do newborns need?"

"A lot, if you're lucky." Ivy jerked a thumb over her shoulder. "But not with that going on."

"I can't take this anymore. Let's get out of here." Shelly took a sip of tea before pushing herself off the couch. "Mitch can pick me up later." She rolled her snack into the napkin.

After Shelly told Mitch where they were going, Ivy helped her into the vintage Chevy that Bennett had restored for her. With the white convertible top down in the sun, Ivy punched a button for the heater to take off the chill.

Staring out the window at shorebirds skittering across the sand, Shelly quietly nibbled on her cheese and apples as Ivy drove. As they neared the inn, she broke her silence.

"Hey, Ives?"

"Yeah, Shells?"

"Thanks for rescuing me." Shelly sniffed. "Marriage can be tough at times."

"I know," Ivy said, taking Shelly's hand. "But Mitch really loves you."

Shelly swallowed hard. "That goes both ways. Still, he's driving me crazy building that room. I think he's nervous about the baby, so he's rechanneling his energy."

"He'll settle down after the little one arrives." Ivy remembered how anxious Jeremy had been before Misty was born. "In the meantime, you're welcome here anytime."

She pulled into the car court behind the inn. After Shelly rested, Ivy would talk to her about the kiddie pool Mitch had carted home. Ivy shuddered again. Who knew where that banged-up thing had been?

Their niece met them at the rear kitchen door. Poppy had twisted her blond hair into a knot at the nape of her neck and wore a crisp white shirt with dark blue jeans, loafers, and discreet gold jewelry. She held a hand up to the sun's waning rays over the beach. "That didn't take long."

Shelly twisted her lips to one side. "Mitch is working on the baby's room. There's a lot of hammering, and I've got to get some rest. I haven't slept much in days."

"What about the neighbors?" Poppy asked.

"On one side of us, they're away for the winter. And on the other side is that drummer who's been away on tour. The older man behind us says he just turns off his hearing aid." Shelly turned up her palms. "I'm glad Mitch is doing this, but I wish he'd pick up the pace."

"You can use my room," Poppy said. "I have to set up the afternoon reception anyway."

"Thanks," Shelly said. "No need to mess up a guest room on my account."

"Really, it's no trouble," Ivy said.

Shelly made a face, dismissing the offer. "Got a key on you?" She held out her hand while Poppy fished her key from a pocket of her jeans. Yawning, Shelly pocketed the key and pushed through the kitchen door. "Don't wake me," she called back.

Poppy scrunched her brow with concern. "Was it that bad over there?"

"Mitch means well, but he needs a crew to finish that room," Ivy replied, resolving to talk to Bennett about this situation. "When you have a baby, the first month is a blur. Shelly and the little one will need their rest, no matter what time of the day or night it is. She'll be up at night a lot."

Poppy looked solemn. "I wish Grandma was here for Aunt Shelly."

Ivy wished the same, but she also understood that their parents had interests of their own. "She and Grandpa are having a wonderful time on a trip they've looked forward to for years. They call when they can, and they'll be back soon enough. In the meantime, we're here for Shelly, right?" Ivy rested an arm on Poppy's shoulder. "That's what family is all about. Sunny promised to help, too."

"I should call Dad," Poppy said, folding her arms. "I can't understand why Mitch doesn't want his help."

"That's his choice," Ivy said. Her niece was mature beyond her years, probably because she and her four siblings had roamed the beach on their own as kids.

"But small towns are different," Poppy insisted. "People here take offense if you don't ask for help." Her eyes lit with an idea. "I know Aunt Shelly doesn't want us to plan a baby shower, but can't we surprise her anyway? A lot of people in Summer Beach are asking me about that. They're eager for a party. And she needs more baby stuff than she realizes. One of my friends had a shower last weekend. I couldn't believe how much a baby needs."

Ivy weighed this. Her wild-child sister didn't want anything traditional. "We might upset her."

"I think she'd get over it in a split second," Poppy said, snapping her fingers.

Just then, two of their long-term guests strolled into the kitchen. "Get over what?" Imani asked. She wore a bright yellow cotton turtleneck paired with a full, floral skirt and held a bouquet of pink and yellow snapdragons in one arm. Her golden highlighted sisterlocks were wound into a thick crown.

"A baby shower," Ivy replied, leaning against the counter.

"It's about time," Gilda said, sliding onto a stool at the long center island. Her short, spiky pink hair matched her backpack, out of which poked a furry little nose. A Chihuahua let out a sharp bark. "Even Pixie thinks so, don't you, sweetie?"

"Put me down for flowers," Imani said, reaching into a cupboard for a vase. "I assume you'll have it here."

"Plenty of space in the ballroom," Gilda said, rubbing Pixie's quivering neck and shoulders. "I've been dying to do calligraphy for the invitations. What's the date?"

Poppy shot Ivy a look. "See what I mean?"

Ivy raised her palms. "If we do this, and I'm not saying we will, not a word to Shelly. It has to be a surprise. And nothing that seems too much like a baby shower."

Imani laughed as she filled the vase with water. "I couldn't imagine anything else for your sister. How about the nontraditional? Like birds of paradise and palms."

"Guess that means no calligraphy," Gilda said, ruffling her short pink hair with a sad look.

"I hope you weren't set on doing that," Ivy said.

"I suppose it's just as well," Gilda replied. "I'm on deadline for another magazine article anyway."

"The flower stand is pretty slow this time of year," Imani added. "I can help you plan whatever you think Shelly might like."

"I appreciate that," Ivy said, and she really did. "But I need to think about this. No cutesy baby games—Shelly would hate that."

Poppy's eyes widened. "But those are so much fun—"

Ivy cut in. "Do you want to deal with her hormonal wrath?"

"You have a point." Imani chuckled. "Let us know what you decide."

"I will," Ivy said, feeling a little disappointed that Shelly didn't want to commemorate the baby's birth with a shower. She thought her sister might regret it later. "But we're still on for the Roaring Twenties party for spa week. And you're both invited."

As Imani placed the snapdragons on the center island, she broke into a wide grin. "Costumes, I hope?"

"Absolutely," Poppy said, her eyes sparkling with excitement. "It will be a week to remember."

"And I hope it's a week to repeat," Ivy added, admiring the flowers. They needed the new business at the inn.

· · ·

AFTER MEETING guests who had gathered in the music room for the afternoon tea and wine hour, Ivy returned to the apartment she now shared with Bennett behind the main house. Shelly hadn't come downstairs for the gathering, but Ivy wasn't surprised.

"I'm back," Ivy called out, collapsing on the sofa in front of a fire Bennett had built in the fireplace. For one person, the apartment was plenty spacious, but for two, it had become a little cramped. It was more than the space, though. They were both accustomed to having a place to themselves.

A persistent wintry chill seeped through the edges of the old windows. Built above garages, the apartment was originally meant for the chauffeur, who tended to the former owner's collection of cars. Only Amelia Erickson's cherry red Chevrolet convertible from the 1950s had survived.

Looking around the comfortable living room filled with vintage tapestry-covered furniture and vases of pink stock and English ivy from Shelly's winter flower garden, Ivy thought about all she had to be thankful for.

Not so long ago, she'd been grappling with the death of her husband and his betrayal. She'd had to sell her flat in Boston's Back Bay area and settle for a rented room in a professor's home. When Jeremy secretly withdrew money from their retirement fund to buy this old beach house, Ivy was sure he'd never imagined she might be living here someday with her new husband.

Life certainly had the last karmic laugh on his actions, she mused. Not that she and Shelly hadn't worked diligently to transform the property Jeremy bought as a tear-down for his new girlfriend.

Ivy kicked off her boots, stretched her toes toward the crackling fire, and ran a hand across the back of her stiff neck.

"Looks like you had a long day, sweetheart." Bennett eased next to her and drew his hands across her shoulders, kneading the tension from her neck. "Sorry I couldn't join you for the guest hour this afternoon. The city council meeting ran late with questions about a proposed new development. Did Nan let you know?"

"She did." His hands were warm on her neck. "Mmm. Keep that up, and I'll keep you around forever," Ivy said, relaxing into his arms.

Bennett chuckled. "Wish I'd known this was all it took. Could've saved us a lot of time."

"I think we're right where we're meant to be." After Jeremy's death, Ivy wasn't sure she'd ever marry again, but Bennett was different.

She'd had a crush on him when they were teenagers before she left to attend university in Boston. They'd hardly known each other then, and they were still learning about each other now—and all their little quirks and preferences. They'd married just before Ivy's parents left on their voyage last summer.

Bennett kissed her cheek. "If Shelly is going home, I can take her back before we get too settled."

"Let her be. I think she's down for the night. She told me she hasn't slept much for days."

"Will Mitch come to get her tonight?"

Ivy stretched. "I don't know, but I'm sure they spoke. He planned to work late on the house. It's probably better if she sleeps here."

Bennett took a breath to speak but then seemed to think better of it and glanced away.

Something in his silence stirred her. "You don't agree?"

"If I were Mitch, I wouldn't like it."

"But those two are different. They make up their own rules."

"It's not about rules." Bennett ran his hand over his closely cropped hair.

"Are you concerned about them?"

Bennett raised his brow. "Should I be?"

"Well, no. I mean, I don't think so. Unless you think you should talk to Mitch again about the room addition."

He grinned. "I'll take that as a strong hint."

Ivy bristled at his choice of words. "I'm asking you."

"I told you, I'll try."

That didn't sound as definitive as she would have liked, but she let it go. "Just so you know, Imani and Gilda and Poppy want to surprise Shelly with a baby shower—or a party —let's not call it a baby shower. Please don't let that get around yet, but we'll want you to plan something with Mitch —like working on that room addition."

"You'll have to invite Darla, or she'll feel left out."

Ivy's neighbor wasn't known for her discretion, especially at Java Beach, the hotbed of local gossip in Summer Beach. "Okay, I'll swear her to secrecy and threaten to cut off her banana nut bread supply."

"You're not a woman to cross, Ivy Bay Dylan. Or should I say, Mrs. Mayor?"

Ivy gave an exaggerated shrug, trying not to let him get to her. "Is that the best you can do? Nan calls me her 'First Lady.' I think you should, too," she added in an attempt to tease him. Bennett's receptionist at City Hall was a force in Summer Beach. She and her husband owned Antique Times in the village.

Bennett laughed as he threaded his fingers through Ivy's hair, massaging her scalp. "That's another one you'll have to swear to secrecy."

Feeling the weight of the day, Ivy tried to relax into his touch, but she was still worried about Shelly. Her health, their birth plan, the construction—now, even a surprise party. All this on top of the spa week they'd started advertising before Shelly had known she was pregnant. "I had no idea a baby shower would have to be a clandestine operation."

Bennett waggled his eyebrows. "That's Summer Beach for you. We keep a close eye on our residents. Especially the new ones." A slow smile spread on his face. "How about a glass of wine with me?"

Usually, Ivy would welcome that. As she shook her head, she chewed the edge of her lip. Bennett was the key to bringing Mitch to his senses, and Ivy felt like he'd minimized her request. She had to make sure he would deal with Mitch.

"Not tonight," Ivy said, tamping down her concern. "Baby showers aside, you will talk to Mitch, won't you? I'm worried about Shelly—and the health of her baby. Being older, she's at a higher risk for pregnancy. If anything happened to her, I'd never forgive myself." She blew out a breath. "Neither would my parents. I'm responsible for her while they're gone."

Bennett chuckled and kissed her forehead. "I'm pretty sure they would. And Shelly is a grown woman."

"That's not the point. I'm really concerned about her health."

"I hear you," Bennett said lightly. "I'll try to reason with him. That's the best I can do. You know how proud Mitch is about making his own decisions."

"This is no time for infernal masculine pride," Ivy snapped, feeling her blood pressure rise. "Mitch has got to stop this nonsense and take care of his wife. If he doesn't, I'll make sure she stays here at the house where I can look after her."

Frowning, Bennett pulled back. "Ivy, be careful about getting between them."

"I don't care. I'll do what's right for her."

"Even if it hurts their marriage—and right before the baby is born? This is supposed to be a happy time for them."

"Well, it's not turning out that way. Mitch wants her to have the baby in a kiddie pool filled with dirty saltwater at the house. Do you think that's safe, especially at her age?"

Bennett raked a hand over his stubbled chin. "My sister used a midwife when she had my nephew. She was fine, and so was Logan."

"Well, good for her, but Sunny and I would have died if I hadn't been at a hospital."

Bennett held up his hands. "Okay, I get it, but that decision should be between Shelly and her doctor."

"Exactly. And I think Mitch is influencing her. He wants to say that their baby came out surfing. But this isn't a joke."

"And you think I can fix these problems? I'm not Superman, sweetheart."

"I'll say." With fear for her sister pushing anger through her veins like molten lava, Ivy pushed up from the couch. "Mitch looks up to you like an older brother. You could talk some sense into him," Ivy said, punctuating her words with a finger. "Otherwise, Shelly is staying right here."

As Ivy charged into the bedroom, she heard Bennett call to her, but she didn't stop. It was late, she was exhausted from work and worry, and her husband wasn't taking this situation as seriously as he needed to.

She peeled off her clothes, wriggled into a nightgown, and slid into bed, pulling the covers over her head. Bennett opened the door, but she ignored him. The responsibility she felt for Shelly in her parents' absence was a heavy burden.

If Bennett didn't understand the seriousness of this situation, then she had other things to consider. Yet, a small thought crept into her mind. Had she been too hard on her husband?

2

𝒯he next morning, the sun rose in a clear blue sky. After the buffet breakfast in the dining room, Ivy washed the dishes by hand and put them away. She'd been thinking about installing a dishwasher, but one wouldn't be enough anyway. Besides, this old house had plenty of other repairs that took priority. Fortunately, the twin refrigerators in their vintage turquoise glory were still humming along. Gert and Gertie, she'd named them. She swiped a rag over their handles. Gratitude, that's what she needed more of.

Although a new dishwasher wouldn't hurt either.

Voices floated up from the lower level where Pages Book-shop had landed after the earthquake a few months ago. Remembering that Paige, the proprietor, liked her morning tea, Ivy filled a kettle with water and put it on the stove.

Waiting for the water to heat, she thought about Bennett. He had left for City Hall early that morning. They had barely spoken this morning, and they'd both avoided talking about last night. She folded her arms over her sweater and jeans.

Bennett knew what he needed to do.

Ivy adjusted the flame under the tea kettle on the stove.

She brought out a mug that read, *Life is better in Summer Beach*. Bennett had brought it home from City Hall.

Turning over her troubling thoughts about Mitch, she decided she would talk to Shelly and offer her one of the guestrooms until Mitch completed construction. He couldn't expect her to put up with that madness at this stage of her pregnancy.

Ivy had a lot to discuss with Shelly once her sister was awake and alert.

The kettle began to whistle. Pushing aside her thoughts, Ivy poured a cup of tea. She wanted to speak to Paige about the spa week at the inn. She thought the bookseller might like to share a few stories with the group that was arriving soon.

The inn had been full this past summer, but Ivy had to find ways to fill empty rooms in the off-season. Winters were mercifully mild in Summer Beach; flowers still bloomed, the citrus was plentiful after the new year, and the beach was blissfully quiet. On many days, the sun warmed the pool area for a few hours, although the sun set earlier. This season was perfect for beach visitors who wanted to escape the summer crowds. Now she understood why some residents thought this was the best time of year.

Ivy nestled a couple of oatmeal cookies she'd made next to the mug of tea and started downstairs to see Paige.

Fortunately, Summer Beach residents were still supporting the bookseller. Now, when people strolled up the front walkway, they were just as likely to be shopping for books as checking into the Seabreeze Inn. Ivy liked that.

Paige brought fresh energy to the old beach house. As a result, new people were discovering the inn. That benefit worked both ways, and Ivy was pleased that Paige had expanded her clientele since her temporary relocation. Guests of the inn usually paid a visit to the bookshop, too.

As she cleared the last step, she heard Paige speaking to a

new guest who had checked in yesterday. Despite decades as a bookseller, her enthusiasm for books never waned.

"You'll love these stories," Paige said as she tucked three novels into the woman's blue-and-white striped beach bag.

"I like discovering a new series," the woman said. Sunglasses were perched on her head, and she wore a white windbreaker. "I'm here for a week, but I'm a fast reader, so I might be back soon. What's your name?"

"I'm Paige with an *i*," the older woman replied as a smile lit her bright blue eyes. Her thick silver hair glinted in the sunlight streaming through high clerestory windows.

"I'm so glad you're here," Ivy said to the guest. "I'm sure Poppy told you about our morning walks and yoga, and we're also having a spa week. You're welcome to join us for our speakers. On the schedule is a physical therapist who'll share strengthening exercises, a local wellness writer to talk about mental calm and clarity, and a cafe owner for healthy cooking ideas." She'd asked her friend Marina Moore, who owned the Coral Cafe, to demonstrate in the kitchen.

"And my sister Shelly will take you on a tour of her organic gardens and hothouse. This is a new tradition at the inn."

"That sounds interesting," the woman said. "Looks like I came at just the right time."

The bookshop occupied an area demarcated with rugs, potted palms, and bookshelves, many of which were fashioned from reclaimed objects, from a worn surfboard to the bow of a small dinghy. Pages Bookshop had been an institution for years in Summer Beach. The damaged building that also housed Paige's apartment above the shop was being repaired. A local contractor, Axe Woodson, was in charge of the restoration—as well as the new theater company that had been his long-held dream.

Ivy wondered if Mitch would let Axe help. He was a good friend of Bennett's, too.

Just then, more footsteps sounded on the stairway, and Ivy turned. "Celia, you're here early." She had once stayed at the inn when her home was damaged in the Ridgetop fire, and now she contributed her time and funds to the school music program. Many of her proteges practiced their performances in the music room at the inn.

"I'm only picking up books Paige ordered for me," she said, tucking her long dark hair behind an ear.

Immediately, Ivy was concerned about her. She looked paler than usual, and Ivy thought she might have lost weight.

Paige nodded to Celia and discreetly slid her books into a bag, but not before Ivy saw the titles. They were about couples counseling and planning for divorce.

Celia looked embarrassed, but Ivy rested a hand on her shoulder. "If you need to talk, I'm always here for you."

"I just don't know what to do about Tyler."

Ivy hardly knew what to say. The couple had troubles in the past, but Ivy thought they were past that. "Counseling is a good idea."

"If I could ever get him off that boat." Celia bit her lip. "He needs a different hobby."

Ivy had heard rumors about parties Tyler had on the boat when Celia was busy. She didn't like what he was doing to her friend. "Call me later."

"I'll see you one afternoon this week in the music room." Celia paid for her books and hurried back up the stairs.

Ivy watched her go, wondering what she could do to help her. She and Paige traded a sad, knowing look. She didn't like to see anyone's marriage fall apart.

After Celia and the new guest left, Paige gestured to Ivy. "I discovered a book I thought you'd like."

"And I brought you a cup of hot tea and my oatmeal cookies," Ivy said, sliding the mug onto a counter. "It's a little chilly down here."

"Thank you, dear." Paige pulled a cornflower blue sweater

that matched her bright eyes around her shoulders. "My old place was pretty drafty, so I simply layer my clothing. In the afternoon, beautiful rays filter through the window and warm the space."

Reaching down, Paige pulled a slim volume from under the cash register area and handed it to Ivy. "Here's something very special for you. I thought you'd want to see it."

"Is this from Amelia's library?" The musky scent of aged paper rose from the small book, which seemed to make it even more fascinating.

"It is." Paige nodded toward the tall bookshelves that lined one wall. Recently, they'd found boxes of old books concealed under the stairway. "It's been calling out to me."

"Not whispering?" Ivy smiled. Locals called Paige a book whisperer because she had the uncanny ability of choosing just the right books for patrons, often ones they would never think of selecting.

"Fairly screaming, this time." Paige nodded toward the shelves. "I think our Amelia might have had something to do with it."

"Please don't spook the guests," Ivy whispered, repressing the urge to shudder. She smoothed her hand across the cover. "*Gift from the Sea*," she read. Somehow, it seemed familiar. "I think my mother had a copy of this."

"It's been popular for many years. It's a collection of essays—meditations on life, you might say."

Footsteps clattered on the stairway, and her sister's voice rang out. "Come on, Ives. What's wrong with acknowledging the obvious?"

"We don't have a resident ghost," Ivy replied, bristling at the thought. "Much as you two would like to think. And I'm glad you could finally join us, Shelly." Although she tossed out that comment, she was glad her sister had some rest away from the construction site her home had become. She hoped Shelly would agree to stay longer.

"I'm feeling a lot better." Shelly pulled her thick fisherman's sweater around her shoulders.

Paige nodded toward a feather duster. "I clean those shelves every morning, along with mine. This book seemed to be edging off the shelf over the past couple of days. It was quite insistent." Paige exchanged a knowing glance with Shelly.

Ignoring the insinuation, Ivy opened the book. "Oh, look. The author inscribed it to Amelia Erickson." Ivy read, "To my dear friend, Amelia, from Anne Morrow Lindbergh."

"That has to be worth a few bucks," Shelly said, easing into a vintage wingback chair.

Ivy arched an eyebrow toward Shelly. "It's something to be treasured. Not everything of value has a price."

She flipped through the book, pausing to read a few lines and admire illustrations of shells that caught her attention. *A moon shell, a channeled whelk, an argonauta.* Turning back to Paige, she asked, "Wasn't this author married to Charles Lindbergh?"

"She was," Paige began, lifting her chin. "But she was also a talented pilot in her own right. Charles might have been lauded for that historic Atlantic crossing, but Anne flew later missions with him as a co-pilot and navigator. She was the first licensed female glider pilot in the country—and only the tenth person overall, mind you. History has largely forgotten her aviation efforts."

"Go, Anne," Shelly said, brightening. Her eyes had taken on their usual sparkle again.

"I wish she were still with us." Paige sighed. "Her aviation career began only a few years after some women had won the right the vote in these United States," Paige said. "Mind you, many of our sisters wouldn't gain that right until years later. A travesty, that was."

A sobering look crossed Shelly's face. "In the grand scheme of history, that was only a minute ago. Sometimes I forget that." She quirked her lips to one side. "Maybe that explains Mitch's lizard brain. Men are still adapting."

"It might," Ivy said, heartened at Shelly's observation. "I'm so glad you got some rest last night. It's important for you and the baby."

"Junior will be fine," Shelly said with a wave of her hand.

"We'll make sure of that." Ivy turned a page in the small book. "Like Amelia, it sounds like Anne also had a fascinating life."

Paige went on, "She and Charles set many flight records together and mapped out commercial routes that are still flown today. She was yet another woman who kept her husband on track. Not that she didn't make errors in judgment as well."

"Haven't we all?" Shelly motioned to her belly. "I waited so long for Ezzra that this is considered a geriatric pregnancy. So what happened to the Lindberghs?"

Paige continued thoughtfully. "Sadly, they suffered so much with the kidnapping and death of their first child that Charles could almost be excused for his later indiscretions with a number of women and his somewhat misguided views. For all his fame gained for flying across an ocean, I doubt he was very well informed as a young man. Anne's wisdom seemed borne of pain mixed with her exhilaration for life on several fronts—aviation, writing, and motherhood. Together they lived through the highest of highs and the lowest of lows."

Ivy thought of Jeremy's affair; she hadn't known about it until after he died. Thankfully, there wasn't a whiff of that in her relationship with Bennett. He was so different, and she was having to adjust thoughts that had long ago become automatic for her. Jeremy had expected her to run the house, look after the children, and not bother him with details.

On the other hand, Bennett had asked why she wasn't

involving him in decisions now that they were married. Somewhere on that spectrum, there had to be a happy compromise.

A twinge of guilt tensed her shoulders. Maybe she'd been a little short with him last night, but she'd only asked for him to talk to Mitch. Couldn't he do that for her?

Nodding toward her and Shelly, Paige added, "In Anne's writings, you might both find some illumination for the stages of life we women go through. She once said that every twenty years, our lives change. Anne wrote this book in her late forties; she'd taken a holiday by herself on Captiva Island, which is just off Florida's Gulf Coast. She used shells she found on the beach to represent the stages of a woman's life."

"I'd like to read that, too," Shelly said thoughtfully, then brightened with curiosity. "Darla mentioned that you used to fly, Paige."

"I used to." Paige flicked her hand with modesty. "In the second world war, my mother joined the women's division of The Royal Canadian Air Force. She learned to fly and served in support roles. Ferrying planes, training, that sort of thing. Mother insisted I learn to fly, and at the time, I was thrilled to do it. But I flew for the fun and thrills."

Ivy gazed at Paige, whose brilliant eyes sparkled with her zest for life. "I'd like to hear more about that."

"I loved it," Paige said, straightening her shoulders. "Soaring through the skies in a small craft was marvelous—until persistent inner ear issues grounded me."

"Did you grow up in Canada?" Shelly asked.

Paige smiled. "A little here and there. Mother married a fellow pilot from California—a friend of a friend—and he found work with Hughes Aircraft in Los Angeles after the war. That's how we landed here."

Ivy nodded at that; aviation and aerospace were major industries on the west coast. "I heard that Lindbergh's Spirit of St. Louis plane was actually built in Southern California."

"San Diego," Paige said, smiling. "But investors from St.

Louis had the naming rights. Old Charlie is always sharing stories about that at Java Beach. Ask him about that sometime —his father was on the engineering team. And word has it that Amelia and Gustav also invested in early aviation efforts. Maybe even for Lindbergh or the Ryan Aircraft Company, which built his airplane specifically for the transatlantic flight."

Ivy thought about the residents she'd met in Summer Beach. Many of them had fascinating backgrounds, including the inn's former owners, Amelia and Gustav Erickson, who had been prominent investors and renowned art collectors in their day.

Ivy glanced around the lower level, which Amelia had sealed after hiding a cache of masterpiece paintings. Only recently had Ivy managed to clean and use this space. If just one of the paintings she and Shelly had discovered here hadn't been rescued from theft during the war, Ivy could have sold it. That would have paid for a lot more of the necessary renovations in this cavernous old beach house the Ericksons built. But for now, authentic shabby chic would have to do.

"This might be a good read for the book club." Ivy closed the old volume, resolving to read it.

"What an excellent idea," Paige said, a smile playing on her lips.

Shelly stretched and turned to Ivy. "I'll help you finalize the schedule for spa week if you'd like."

"If you're up to it," Ivy said. She turned to Paige. "By the way, I wanted to tell you about our plans for the week."

"Poppy already did," Paige said. "I'll create a display with books on wellness for guests to browse, and I'll feature your guest speakers' books." She paused in thought. "I think Marina should write a cookbook for the cafe. I'll have a talk with her about that."

Taking the book Paige had given her, Ivy started up the stairs. Pausing, she added, "Are you up for a walk, Shelly?" It was important for her sister to get exercise, even if she wasn't feeling like it. And Ivy wanted to speak to her away from the inn.

"Since I slept through the morning guest walk, I suppose I should." Shelly pushed herself up from the chair. "Mitch said something about low tide and the weird El Niño weather effect today."

Paige nodded. "That's quite something to see. The low tide often uncovers hidden treasures. Maybe you'll find a gift from the sea as well."

"I'd rather find a gift from Amelia," Shelly said. "Then I could hire someone to finish the room addition before giving birth. Not that I don't appreciate Mitch's dedication, but it's so nice to sleep in a quiet home. I took that for granted."

"Isn't it?" Ivy smiled, hoping Shelly would be amenable to her idea. Maybe that would motivate Mitch, too.

As Ivy climbed the stairs with the book in her hand, a strange sensation tickled her neck. She'd lived here long enough that she was aware of a presence of some sort, although she still didn't want to admit it. Yet, unlike Shelly, Paige didn't seem like the type to stretch the truth.

AFTER CHANGING into their beach shoes at the back door, Ivy and Shelly set off toward the beach at the farthest edge of town. Ivy liked this stretch of sand, which usually had fewer people than the wide sandy beach by the village. Here, the breeze was usually bracing, and the waves were wilder, crashing onto the shoreline with the untamed force of nature. Only the most experienced surfers tackled these waves, but today, even they had steered clear of the tempestuous low tide conditions.

Ivy stooped to pick up a spindle-like shell about the length of her palm from a tide pool. Turning it in her hand, she ran her fingers over smooth knobs that studded the swirled, chalky exterior, which was shaded with gray and brushed with rosy pink at the tip of its spiral.

"That's beautiful." Shelly paused to inspect the shell. "Wonder what kind it is?"

"Flint calls this a Kellett's whelk. That's a sort of sea snail." Their brother was a marine mammalogist, a biologist who loved the ocean and had collected shells from childhood. As a young girl, Ivy used to go with him on beach expeditions.

With the receding tide, the shoreline stretched farther out on the beach, exposing creatures and items usually underwater. Ivy brushed damp sand from the shell's graceful whorls and thought about the book Paige had shared with her. Flipping through the pages, she'd noticed a chapter on the channeled whelk that had a small illustration of a shell similar to the one she'd just found.

If Ivy believed in signs—that was Shelly's domain—this would be one. Still, this was quite a coincidence.

She handed the shell to Shelly. "Here's our first gift from the sea today." She recalled a line she'd seen in the book. "One is free, like the hermit crab, to change one's shell."

Shelly peered inside. "No one home." After admiring the shell, she handed it back to Ivy. "Living here, it's funny how we can take all this beauty for granted."

"When I stop to think about it, I'm in awe of all that's happened since we returned to California."

Shelly placed a hand across her stomach. "And of what is yet to come."

Ivy slid a look toward her sister. "Getting excited?"

"And a little nervous." Shelly blew out a breath. "Guess that's normal, huh?"

"I think so." Detecting a note of trepidation in her sister's voice, Ivy stole another scrutinizing look at her. Shelly had always been the first one to embrace new ideas and plans, whereas Ivy liked her lists and life in order. If anyone could adapt to the uncertainties children flung at you every day, it was Shelly. Ivy was sure of that, even if her sister wasn't.

Ivy held up the shell. "This will make a good home for a hermit crab eager for a change. We should probably return it to the sea."

Shelly nodded, and Ivy cast it over the water.

As they strolled along the water's edge, she turned up the collar of her jacket against the cool mist and shared thoughts on their spa week plan. This was the first of several such weeks they would host. This time, they would offer an array of experiences to see what resonated with guests. In the future, they were considering other specialty weeks, too.

"Maybe one for healthy meal planning and preparation," Ivy said. "Poppy suggested a week for people who are interested in writing memoirs. We could ask a writing instructor to teach."

Shelly nodded. "I could lead sessions on gardening. We could probably involve Leilani from Hidden Garden, too. So, are we ready for everyone?"

Ivy ticked off items on her fingers as she picked up the pace. "The pool heater is working now, and Poppy volunteered to lead water aerobics. I've been making reservations for facials and other treatments for guests. Do you feel up for gentle yoga classes?" Poppy had alternated in leading sessions with Shelly, but she'd taken over more in the last couple of weeks.

Shelly twisted her mouth to one side. "I want to try."

"Have you spoken to Mitch today?"

"I woke up about five this morning and called him before I went back to sleep."

"Is he okay with your staying here?"

"I guess so. He seemed pretty tired." Shelly turned her face into the ocean breeze. "He hadn't planned to surf this morning, which is why he wanted to work so late. He said low-tide surfing is risky around here."

They walked on until Shelly paused again to rest, drawing a hand over her rounded belly. "It won't be long now."

"This is what you dreamed of for so long," Ivy said. As she spoke, Shelly's gaze darted to one side.

"Can I tell you something?" Shelly added, "If you promise not to mention it to Bennett or anyone else."

Ivy turned away from the ocean toward her sister. Maybe this was the talk they needed to have. "Of course."

"Is it normal to be a little scared of how our lives will change? I love Mom, but she was a professional baby machine —I don't know how she managed five of us. I worry about handling one." Shelly sucked in her lower lip. "What if I don't turn out to be such a great mother? I've wanted this baby for so many years, but honestly, I wasn't exactly studying childcare all that time. I've never even changed a diaper. What if the reason Mitch is nervous is because he doesn't have confidence in my abilities?"

"Has he intimated that?"

"Not exactly." Shelly kicked the sand.

Ivy's heart went out to her younger sister. "Oh, sweetie, I don't think that's the case at all. And it's normal to get pre-baby jitters. I'll help you in any way I can. And that includes making sure that—"

"No offense," Shelly said, cutting her off. "But a lot has changed since you had your children. And I've already arranged for a doula to help me. Not that I don't appreciate what you're doing, but she understands all the natural child-birth methods I want. She's very knowledgeable and supportive."

"I'm hardly ancient," Ivy said, feeling slightly taken aback. "And babies haven't changed. You still love them the same way. As for the natural…" Ivy heard something and started to turn.

From the corner of her eye, she saw the rising water and gasped. "Oh, no—" A swift wave nearly swept her from her feet. In front of her, Shelly stumbled, and Ivy's heart leapt. *She mustn't fall.*

"Grab my hand," Ivy called out, planting her bare feet in the sand against the long, low-tide waves rushing out to sea in response to insistent gravitational pulls. Ivy struggled to keep her balance against the ocean's force, greedily stealing golden sand from beneath her curled toes.

Screaming with laughter, Shelly stretched her fingers toward her sister with one hand and cradled her curved belly with the other. "Paige was right—this is crazy," she yelled over the roaring tide. "Come on. Let's get out of here." Shelly turned and raced ahead.

Suddenly, Shelly tripped and tumbled to her knees. The strong magnetic pull of the ocean swept her onto her side as it receded.

A larger wave was rushing toward her flailing sister. In an instant, Ivy's survival instinct kicked in.

Her sister. The baby.

"I've got you." Leaping after Shelly, she caught her under the arms and lurched back with her, away from the water's unrelenting force. As Ivy grappled for a toehold, she lost her balance and landed on her bottom. Shelly flopped on top of her like a great pregnant dolphin. With the breath knocked from her lungs, Ivy coughed, gasping for air.

The water drew back, but Ivy saw another, larger wave bearing down on them. Gritting her teeth, she tightened her grip on Shelly.

3

The wave crashed onto the shore, barely missing Ivy and Shelly, and rushed back to sea, swiftly capturing everything in its path.

"Wow, you had some hold on me," Shelly said. With awkward effort, she rolled off Ivy and extended her hand to her. "I had no idea you were so strong. You sure got us out of the path of that wave. Are you okay?"

"The baby," Ivy replied, sputtering as she expelled saltwater and scuffled to her feet. Her jeans were soaked to her skin, and her sweater was covered with sand. Although the sun was high in the sky, a brisk chill pierced the wet denim. She shivered, as much from the whoosh of adrenaline as from the cool air.

"I think Junior is fine," Shelly said, rubbing her stomach. She gathered her cotton skirt in her hands and wrung out the soggy hemline. "But this big old belly throws me off balance."

Ivy glanced at her sister's foot in alarm. "You're bleeding."

"It's just a small cut," Shelly said, winching slightly. "The saltwater will be good for it. I'll slap on a bandage when we get back to the inn." Shading her eyes against the sun, she nodded behind her at an object partly obscured by sand. "That's what I tripped on. What is it?"

Grayish green kelp had snagged against what looked like part of an old beam protruding from the sand.

"I have no idea," Ivy said, peering at the strange object. "But I've never seen the tide this low here. I'll take a closer look." Wary of the encroaching waves, she started toward the water's edge.

"I'm right behind you, Ives."

Ivy whirled around. "I'm not taking a chance with you again. Stay clear of the water."

"You don't have to be so bossy about it," Shelly said, shrugging a shoulder.

Glaring, Ivy pursed her lips. "I mean it. If anything happens to you, I have to answer to Mom and Dad and Mitch —and the entire family."

"Is that all you're worried about?" Shelly flicked her hand toward the strange protrusion. "Go," she said in a cool tone. "I promise I'll stay on higher ground."

"Come on, don't be that way. I'm only looking out for you. And you'd complain if I didn't care so much."

"But you hover," Shelly shot back. "You're almost as bad as Mitch."

"At least I'm not tearing holes in the house. And who just saved your—" Stopping herself, Ivy just shook her head and started toward the large object. They were both on edge today.

Ivy peered at the object. Whatever it was, it was old. Barnacles, sea anemones, and other sea organisms had colonized the rusted surface. Angled against rocks, the straight beam stretched under the water, submerged for an indeterminate length. Peering farther, she saw another parallel edge lifting from the sand.

Ivy realized what it was. She hurried back to Shelly, who

was standing on a sun-warmed stretch of sand, her hands on her hips.

Arching a brow, Shelly asked, "So, what is it, Sherlock?"

Ivy rubbed her hands together to warm them. "It looks like an old craft. I guess you can't see it unless the tide is low."

Shelly's eyes sparkled. "You mean, a shipwreck?"

"Of some sort. I wonder if anyone has seen it before."

"Maybe some of the old-timers have. I'll ask Darla. She knows everybody's business."

Ivy lifted her chin to the chilly sea breeze and the salty air that prickled her cheeks. Their neighbor had become Shelly's *de facto* mother-in-law. When Mitch had landed in Summer Beach years ago, he'd run a coffee stand on the beach before scraping together the funds to open his Java Beach coffee shop. Ivy suspected Bennett wasn't the only one who might have helped Mitch in those early days. Every day, Darla still made her way there.

Mitch had taken a liking to Darla's crusty exterior, determined to get to the softer heart he said he'd always known was there. It had taken some time, but Ivy had discovered that, too.

"We'll find out." Shelly poked Ivy. "Come on before I bleed out on the beach."

Ivy sucked in a breath. As she inspected Shelly's toe, she shook her head. "It doesn't look that bad."

"Got you." Shelly's eyes twinkled with mischief. "See, you still have that older sister guilt from that time you insisted I was fine after I fell off my bike when I was five, and Mom and Dad had to take me to the doctor for stitches."

Ivy shook her head as they started back to the inn. "The butterfly bandage worked fine until they got home. Will you ever forget that?" Shelly was seven years younger, so Ivy had always felt responsible for her. But she'd been a child, too. Ivy wouldn't make that mistake again. "You'd better get a tetanus shot for that."

"I'll check, but I'm pretty sure I'm up to date. I just hope I don't go into labor with you around."

Ivy bumped her sister with her shoulder. "You know I'd be your best hope."

"Only if I'm drowning," Shelly said, laughing. "And I doubt if I'll drown in a kiddie pool."

Ivy prayed her sister wasn't serious about that. "Hey, I've studied first aid. But it's Mitch I worry about. He's liable to freak out when you go into labor."

"I have faith in him. He'll figure it out fast."

"Like the house?"

"Okay, you're right about that." Shelly thew out her hands. "I wish Mom and Dad were here."

Ivy understood. Their father would insist on helping Mitch, and their mother would dote on Shelly. She nudged her sister. "Got your hospital bag packed yet?"

"I have time." Shelly shrugged. "But I'm seriously considering a home birth."

There it was again. Ivy blanched as an old memory swept to the surface. "Please, don't do that."

"What happened to you with Sunny was rare."

"But lots of other things can happen." Ivy shuddered as she thought about that birth. She came close to losing her second child—and her own life. Thankfully, her medical team had acted swiftly. Never had she been so relieved to be in their hands.

Shelly poked Ivy in the ribs. "Lighten up, will you? Women have been having babies without hospitals since Eve. Mitch thinks it's a cool idea. We'd fill a plastic wading pool with saltwater, which is very hygienic. The baby could emerge into the sea," Shelly said, sweeping out her arms. "Mitch says it will be a surfer from day one."

"You're serious?" Ivy stopped and pointed back to the rusty beam engulfed with organic matter. "That's hardly hygienic. Yuck, bacteria on that thing, for sure." She shivered against the breeze in her wet clothes. "Mitch might think it's cool, but if you're going to do a water birth, please don't wing it. Engage a professional, at least."

"I'm talking about that with my new doula. Or maybe I'm just having you on," Shelly said with her quirky smile. She shrugged out of her hoodie and draped it over Ivy's shoulders. "Here, this is the least I can do for you after saving my life."

Ivy sighed. Even now, she couldn't always tell when Shelly was kidding. "Don't be so dramatic...but thanks. Aren't you cold?"

"This kiddo is like an internal heater. I can't even sleep with a blanket on anymore. I toss the covers onto Mitch."

Ivy smiled at a memory. "At a friend's restaurant, she used to let me stand in her walk-in freezer. But that was Boston in the summer. Sticky hot and sweltering. Winter babies are better."

"It should be spring by the time this one comes."

Ivy raised an eyebrow. "You look like you could have it any day now. Are you sure it's not twins?"

"Don't even say that around Mitch. He'll start hyperventilating. In our birthing classes, the couple next to us is having twins. He was so unnerved, he wanted to move—as if twins could be contagious."

"And he seriously wants you to give birth in a plastic wading pool? It's not even a new one."

"It might be fun."

Ivy looked doubtfully at her sister. "That's not a word I would use for labor. How about excruciatingly painful?"

"And joyous," Shelly said. "That's what you've been telling me."

"I'm just worried about you." Ivy drew out a long breath. "You and the baby need rest, so I've been thinking..." She hesitated, unsure of how Shelly would take this.

"So have I," Shelly said. "If a room opens up, maybe I could..."

Ivy jumped on her sister's thought. "Stay at the inn while Mitch is finishing the room? Of course," Ivy replied, vastly relieved when Shelly smiled at the idea.

"You're not fully booked?"

"You can always stay with Poppy."

Ivy would move into the attic rooms with Bennett if she had to. Even without plumbing up there.

"It felt so good to sleep last night," Shelly said, peeking from beneath her lashes. "Is that selfish of me?"

"Not at all." Ivy put her arm around her sister. "Any time you want to talk, I'll be right there."

"If a room opens up, Mitch can stay there, too, right?"

"He's welcome; he's family."

Ivy had to admit that Bennett was right about that; she didn't want to come between Shelly and Mitch. But Shelly needed more care than Mitch could provide right now. He had to understand that.

Ivy glanced back at the barnacle covered beam protruding from the sand. She had an odd feeling about it, although she couldn't explain why. "Poppy can look after the inn a little longer. How about we change clothes and have coffee at Java Beach? We can finalize plans for the spa week."

"We have coffee at the inn," Shelly said. "And I doubt if anything you have would fit me in my current state. Besides, I have to pick up clothes at home." She slid a suspicious glance toward Ivy. "Why the sudden urge to go to Java Beach?"

"You were the one who told me about the new coffee drinks Mitch is testing," Ivy said. "I've had that on the brain ever since. Poppy can handle the place for a while." Shelly should tell her husband about her decision in person.

Ivy didn't want any hard feelings from Mitch right now, and she wanted to be there to defend Shelly if she had to.

"You should tell Mitch about your decision right away."

Shelly nodded. "I hope he's cool with it."

"I don't see why he wouldn't be. It's for the best."

And yet, Ivy was concerned he might think she'd come between them. She quickened her pace.

Maybe she had.

*a*s Bennett approached Nailed It, the hardware store next to Java Beach, one of the owners called out to him.

"Hi, Mr. Mayor," Jen was struggling to lift a large patio chair into a customer's van.

"Need some help with that?"

"I won't say no," Jen said, letting Bennett take the wrought-iron chair. "With the sun breaking through the clouds, we're having an early run on patio furniture."

"That's good. But where's that husband of yours?"

"George is visiting our furniture supplier in Mexico," Jen said, hitching up her blue jeans and sweeping her long high-lighted hair from her face. "The artisans there do such beau-tiful work—we wanted to arrange our shipments early this year. I can usually manage fine on my own. But these pieces are heavier than I realized."

Turning to her customer, Jen introduced them. "Bethany, this is Mayor Dylan."

"Welcome to Summer Beach. It's always good to see young people moving in." Bennett positioned the chair in the van so it wouldn't topple over. While he was doing that, Bethany told him about the old beach house she was renovating that she had inherited from her grandparents.

"There, that ought to do it," Bennett said as he finished securing the patio furniture. He stepped from the van.

"Where are some good local places for coffee or a glass of wine?" Bethany asked.

Bennett jerked a thumb over his shoulder. "Java Beach is the best coffee shop in town, and Spirits & Vine serve up fine wines and a great ocean view."

Bethany thanked him and got into her van.

Bennett found that by walking around the village and speaking to shopkeepers and local residents and visitors, he could learn more in a morning about people's concerns in Summer Beach than in a month of sitting behind his desk at City Hall. Dusting off his hands on his khakis, he turned to Jen. "Is business going well for you and George?"

"Couldn't be better, but the city trash collection has gotten a little sloppy. They've been tossing trash cans around, not caring where they land. One hit a customer's car the other day. Thankfully, it was an old car, and the owner was forgiving, but what if it had been a new vehicle?"

"I'll see what I can do about that. Thanks for letting me know." Bennett would have to talk with the contractor again. He suspected the staff needed more training—and a lesson in courtesy.

Jen drew her brows up with concern. "Anything more on the old airfield development?"

"That's in Boz's hands right now," Bennett replied.

Jen shook her head. "I can't see how a new shopping center would be good for any of the shops here."

"I'll sure keep that in mind." Her worried expression told him everything he needed to know.

Bennett moved on to Java Beach, where locals and a few

visitors were lounging over coffee and Mitch's fresh muffins. He raised his hand in greeting. "How's the java business?"

"Hot today," Mitch said with a wink. "Folks are beginning to return to open their summer houses. As soon as it starts to feel a little warm, they stream back."

"Can't blame them. All good here?"

"You bet," Mitch said, stifling a yawn.

"Looks like you could use a shot of the dark stuff you're peddling."

"I'll have an espresso with you," Mitch said, stepping up to the stainless steel espresso maker. "I just picked up this cool La Marzocco machine at a restaurant supply auction." The machine gurgled and steamed, filling two small cups. Mitch pushed it across the counter. "See how you like it." He tossed back his own and began to make another one.

Bennett took a sip of the hot brew. "That's rich." Recalling Ivy's request, he added, "How's the room going?"

"Pretty good," Mitch said.

Bennett grinned. "Is that why you're having a second shot?"

"I worked too late on it," Mitch replied, shrugging. "It happens."

Stroking his chin, Bennett said, "Seems like once I get into a project, it takes longer than I expect. It's not uncommon to run into all sorts of unanticipated problems."

Mitch let out a sigh. "You've got that right."

"Do you need a hand on that?"

Mitch threw down the second shot. "Nope, I'm good."

"You sure?"

Mitch pressed his lips into a thin line, and he shook his head. "Since this is the third time you've asked me, I'd think you'd know that by now." His tone was biting, which was unlike Mitch.

Bennett held up his hands. "Hey, buddy, I didn't mean to upset you."

"I don't know why everyone thinks I need help doing this. Like I'm some imbecile who can't figure out how to build a room onto my house."

"No one thinks that," Bennett said, surprised at his friend's short fuse. "I'm not judging you. But just saying, if you need a hand, I'm here."

Abruptly, Mitch swiped the empty cups from the counter. "I'm needed in the kitchen." Squaring his shoulders, he turned around.

Bennett watched his friend stalk away from the counter. He'd never known Mitch to act rude, but something was troubling him. Was it the pressure of having his first child? Or business concerns? Or maybe he and Shelly weren't getting along. Perhaps there was more to her spending the night at the inn than the inconvenience of the construction project.

He hoped their marriage wasn't in trouble, but you never knew what went on between two people. He had other friends who had separated or divorced, like his old neighbors on the ridgetop, Tyler and Celia. They were back together at the moment, but rumor had it that he was considering another long trip on his boat, and that could spell trouble between them. Tyler needed more in his life than the boat. In Bennett's opinion, retiring young had left Tyler floundering.

But it was Mitch and Shelly he was most concerned about. Bennett had made a promise to Ivy that meant a lot to her, and now it seemed he couldn't keep it. Unless he simply showed up with his tools, Bennett didn't know what else to do.

Glancing through the kitchen, he saw the stiff pitch of Mitch's shoulders.

He could do that—and possibly lose a friend. But how could he explain this to Ivy?

Bennett never regretted their marriage for a moment, but adjusting to one another's habits had been challenging. He didn't recall Jackie having so many cosmetics in the bathroom, not that Ivy even wore much makeup. For the life of him, he couldn't figure out what all those little porcelain pots of cream were for. *Skincare*, Ivy told him. Shouldn't just one do the job?

Still, whatever was in those little jars was clearly working because Ivy was beautiful in his eyes. He pared down to the necessities and stuffed his things into a bottom drawer. They only had so much room in the apartment unit above the garage. Still, he told himself it was all they needed right now.

Bennett dug into his pocket and tossed a few bills onto the counter for the coffee. Considering the mood Mitch was in, he didn't want to be accused of freeloading. With the baby on its way, the guy could probably use every bit.

Maybe that's it, Bennett thought. Mitch might be short on cash. Compared to the busy tourist season in the summer, winters were lean. Most business owners knew to set aside money for the slow period. He'd counseled Mitch on that when he'd helped him start Java Beach a few years ago. He also knew the younger man could be sensitive about discussing finances.

Sure enough, as Bennett pushed through the door on his way out, he heard Mitch calling after him. "Hey, you forgot something. I'm not taking your money."

Bennett ignored him and strode down the sidewalk toward the next shops he wanted to visit.

As he walked, he thought about the tenants in his home on the ridgetop. The couple's lease ended this summer, and they'd asked Bennett to help them find a home for their family. He and Ivy could move into his house, where they would have a lot more room.

Surely Ivy would appreciate living away from the inn. And Jackie had put a lot of personal touches into the house, from the hand-stenciled kitchen to the sponge-painted walls in the living room. After Jackie died, he hadn't wanted to change a thing. To do so seemed disrespectful to her memory.

Ivy's paintings would look nice there, he imagined. The damage from the fire had been completely repaired, so the house was ready to move into. Once the couple living there found a home, Bennett would surprise Ivy with the idea. They could move right away. While it was an average-sized home for Summer Beach, the views across the Pacific Ocean were astounding. And they'd have a lot more room than they had in the apartment above the garage. Bennett had moved into the inn only because his home had sustained damage in the Ridgetop fire.

Pausing on the sidewalk, he opened the door to the Laundry Basket and held it for a woman and her daughter who were leaving. There was so much he wanted to do for Ivy if she would only let him. The independence he'd admired in her could be frustrating now that they were married, yet he trusted she would relax into their partnership soon. A new home was just what they needed.

Behind the counter, Louise, the proprietor, greeted Bennett with a broad smile. He stepped inside.

They spoke about business, then Louise leaned across the counter. "When are you and the new missus taking that honeymoon I heard you're thinking about?"

"Now where would you have gotten that idea?"

Louise's cheeks flushed. "Teresa at Get Away said you were looking at booking a honeymoon. So, what will it be? Paris or Hawaii?"

Bennett chuckled. There were few secrets in this town. Instead of telling her which way he was leaning, he replied, "Ivy needs to be here for Shelly and the baby."

"Better hurry then. It's liable to be a long postponement."

"Why do you say that?"

Louise's brow creased with surprise. "I imagine Ivy will be helping Shelly after the baby comes. Especially without their mother. Now is the best time to go—not that I'm trying to rush you into anything. Just being realistic."

Bennett hadn't thought about that. As much as he'd like to whisk Ivy away for a long, indulgent honeymoon, neither of them could be away very long right now.

If Ivy would go at all.

Yet, once the summer season was underway, the inn would be fully booked, and he'd be busy with Summer Beach visitors. As it was, he had a lot of city business pending. Still, they could use the time away.

As Louise stuffed an order of clothes into a laundry bag, she glanced through the front window. A man was charging toward the door of the Laundry Basket. "Here comes trouble."

Bennett looked over his shoulder. It was the developer who'd been pestering him about the old airfield and a potential development project for a large discount shopping mall. Aaron Macallan was a lean, angular man with a perpetual smirk on his face that indicated he thought himself superior to everyone around him. Bennett knew that superiority complex was a result not of Aaron's success but his father's. The son had been dispatched to Summer Beach to make quick work of this deal. And from what Bennett had heard, probably to keep Aaron out of his father's way.

Aaron pushed open the door. "I left a message at your office," he said without greeting Bennett. "Didn't think you'd be out doing menial tasks like collecting your laundry during the workday, especially with our deal at such a crucial stage."

Bennett wasn't having any of Aaron's demeaning remarks. "We're both here, aren't we?"

"The mayor is on his monthly walkabout," Louise interjected. "It's how he keeps up with everyone in Summer Beach."

"How quaint." Aaron's tone had a sarcastic edge. "When you return to the office, how about checking on my rezoning request? It's critical."

"You can do that yourself." Bennett was cordial yet firm. "Check in with Boz. Zoning is his department."

Aaron tilted his chin and positioned his hands on his hips —a stance that seemed calculated to intimidate. "Look, we don't have much time left on our option."

"Your nearing expiration of an option term on that land is not the city's emergency." After having led the city in an expensive legal fight to block Ivy's former husband from demolishing the old Las Brisas del Mar estate for a high-rise resort, Bennett was accustomed to such intimidation. He was having none of it from this newcomer who only wanted to make money off Summer Beach. Aaron didn't care about their residents or their quality of life.

Aaron responded with a snort. "You need us. This development will generate huge sales tax on purchases that this little town obviously needs."

Sizing up Louise, Aaron added, "I'm sure you would welcome new customers. Unlike some who want to keep Summer Beach in the past." With disdain, he glanced around the modest cleaners, blind to the charms of Louise's potted plants and photos of happy customers on their special days.

Color rose in Louise's cheeks. "I have a good business just as it is. And I trust our mayor and Boz to do what's good for Summer Beach. You'd be wise to listen to them, young man."

Bennett ran a hand across his chin, hiding his amusement. Louise didn't let anyone patronize or intimidate her.

Aaron turned to leave. "I'll see you at City Hall, Ben."

"It's Mr. Mayor to you," Louise called after Aaron with disgust.

Bennett nodded to Louise. "I appreciate that. We'll deal with him."

The developer wanted the city to earmark funds for the development. Bennett had to consider if the advantages would offset costs for the community. If only there was another buyer interested in the old airstrip land.

"Nan told me about that discount mall plan of his." Louise tossed a laundry bag into a large cart. "I think it would bring in too much traffic on our narrow roads. I've seen the crowds those shopping centers attract. Locals would have a hard time getting in and out of town, especially on the weekends. And where will all those people who work there live? I think that would drive up rental prices in Summer Beach. It's hard enough to find a place here for our own folks this close to the beach."

"Good points, Louise. What's the sentiment around town?"

She touched the bronze-covered relic of a cash register she still used. "While it might offer some benefit to my business, I doubt if it would be much. However, discount stores would put a lot of village boutiques out of business."

That was as Bennett suspected.

"Those business owners are my friends, and I'll stand by them," Louise continued. "If someone wants a cheap designer purse, there are plenty of other places to shop. What's a few dollars more when people spend so much money on vacation? People come to Summer Beach because it's unique. We have to keep it that way. If the village shops close, major chains will move in, and then the town will look the same as every other place."

"We'll bear that in mind," Bennett said thoughtfully. An influx of shopping tourists would help some—even the Seabreeze Inn—but would damage others. But she was right about the chain stores. He'd had several contact him.

As he left the shop, he set his mouth in a grim line and resolved to discuss this matter with Boz. The former owner's heirs were pressing hard for a resolution in order to sell the property, but Bennett was determined to do what was best for the city.

What they needed was another plan, but he didn't have any ideas. Not yet anyway.

Bennett continued his walk around the village, stopping at an appliance store next. In each store, everyone agreed with Louise. As he approached Antique Times, a new item in the window caught his eye. Curious, he stepped inside.

"Hi, Arthur," he said, greeting a man in a Hawaiian shirt. Nan, Bennett's receptionist at City Hall, had met Arthur in England on holiday. They had bonded over antiques and had been married for years now. Besides running the antique shop, they also oversaw the historical society.

The two men caught up on happenings around town, and Arthur agreed with Louise about the new shopping center. "The scales should tip in favor of the community. Isn't there anything else that could be done with that land?"

"All it takes is money," Bennett said. What they were talking about was no small sum, and the city didn't have the funds for the purchase. "The land hadn't been for sale, so the city didn't have much notice."

He swung around. "That tandem bike in the window, is it in working order?" Many people placed old bikes in their yards to hold baskets of flowers as a garden element.

Arthur's face broke into a smile. "It could use a bit of care, but she'd be a sweet ride. You don't see many bicycles-built-for-two anymore—at least, not like that one. It's a classic."

Bennett thought about how much fun it would be to cruise around Summer Beach with Ivy on that. Intrigued with the idea, he moved closer to get a better look at the bike.

He had another surprise planned for Ivy that he'd spent quite a bit on. It was something he knew she needed, although it wasn't very romantic.

Yet, a vintage bike like this didn't come around often.

After inspecting the frame and gears, he stepped back, considering it. He could manage the repairs. Maybe a new paint job, too. "What's your price, Arthur?"

Arthur smiled. "If it's for Ivy, I'll give you a special deal. She sends a lot of guests to the shop."

Bennett ran his hand over the frame again. Would Ivy really like it? He wasn't sure.

Still, they needed something to bring more play into their lives. Maybe this was it.

5

*I*vy stepped inside Java Beach with Shelly and glanced around. The coffee shop was a vintage, mid-century beach throwback. Vintage Polynesian travel posters covered the walls, and fishnets filled with old oars and colorful buoys hung from the ceiling. Beach reggae music played in the background. This is where Ivy and Shelly met Mitch the first day they'd arrived in Summer Beach.

Over the past year, Mitch had expanded the outdoor seating area, which simply meant adding more beach loungers on the back of his sandy lot that looked out to the ocean. People liked to sip coffee with their toes in the sand and their gaze on the horizon. It was a beautiful way to start a day in Summer Beach.

"You just missed Mayor Bennett," Darla called out, seated at a nearby table inside. Her short, royal-blue hair and silver-studded sun visor reflected the sunshine from a nearby window, which stood open to the ocean breeze.

Ivy greeted her neighbor. "I see enough of him at home," she said, joking.

Frowning, Darla asked, "Has the bloom on the marriage faded already?"

"Never," Ivy replied with confidence. Her spirits lifted. If Bennett had been here, he must have spoken to Mitch about helping him finish the room addition.

"Is Mitch around?" Shelly asked.

Darla angled her chin toward the kitchen. "Your grumpy hubby is back there. Tell him to cheer up before he comes out. It's bad for business."

Shelly arched an eyebrow. "And you wouldn't know anything about that, would you?"

"It wasn't me this time," Darla said, holding up her palm. She jerked a thumb toward the front door.

Bennett. Ivy wondered what they'd had words about. Maybe their talk didn't go as planned, but she couldn't understand why it wouldn't have.

"I'll go cheer him up." Shelly squeezed behind the counter and disappeared into the kitchen.

Ivy chatted with Darla about the new plantings Shelly had planned for spring. Her sister often planted the so-called leftovers in Darla's yard. The older woman was fairly active, but gardening wasn't one of her strengths, so Shelly made sure her yard looked nice, too.

A few minutes later, Ivy looked up. Mitch approached with two tall mugs of icy cold coffee. Shelly slid into a booth and winked at her. Ivy excused herself from Darla to join Shelly.

"Two of today's house specialties," Mitch said, sliding a pair of tall, frothy mugs onto the table between Ivy and Shelly. "And an extra scoop for my wife," he added, kissing Shelly on the cheek.

Ivy was relieved to see that Mitch was in better spirits. She admired the concoction in front of her. "This looks more like a fabulous dessert."

Mitch grinned. "Life is short; have dessert every day."

Ivy didn't need any more padding around her middle section, although it was too yummy-looking to resist. She'd catch up on her goals during spa week. Taking a sip, she smiled. *Or not.* "This is heavenly. What do you call it?"

"Tiramisu coffee," Mitch replied. "French vanilla cold brew, a scoop of homemade mascarpone ice cream, and whipped cream with a dusting of powdered chocolate. The ladyfinger cookies are for dipping into the coffee. I'm trying this out for the new summer menu."

"It would be even better with a shot of Amaretto," Shelly said. "After the kiddo comes, that is."

Looking a little sheepish, Mitch turned to Shelly. "I'm glad you got some sleep last night. It was probably just as well you slept at the inn because I had to rip out what I'd done earlier. Mismeasured, I guess. But I sure missed you last night."

Shelly smoothed her hand over his. "So did I, babe. You'll hurry to finish the room? With all the summer tourists, you won't have time to work on it again until fall. By then, our kid will probably be a real screamer."

"Neither one of you will get any rest then," Ivy said, grinning. Sometimes humor was the best way to make an impression.

Mitch furrowed his brow and nodded with reluctance. "I'll finish as fast as I can. I know our baby will need that room."

Watching them, Ivy let out a little breath of relief. At least Mitch understood the urgency now. Something Bennett said must have gotten through to him. Ivy hoped this job wouldn't take much longer. While Shelly needed rest, she also needed Mitch. Ivy knew how easily love and intimacy could slip away, and she never wanted that to happen to Shelly.

Mitch glanced down at Shelly's bandaged foot. "What happened there?"

Shelly wiggled her foot. "A monstrosity sticking out of the sand attacked me this morning. It was some kind of rusty old thing the low tide uncovered, and it sliced my toe."

"You've got to be careful on the beach," Mitch said. "Did you clean the wound well?"

Beaming at him, Shelly nodded, and he rubbed her shoulders.

Ivy was relieved to see the tenderness between them. She liked Mitch for Shelly, and she prayed the baby would bring them closer together. Although he'd known how eager Shelly was to have a child before she turned forty, Mitch had sought counseling to overcome his fear of becoming a father before the wedding last summer. His father had been abusive, and he worried that he might have inherited that tendency.

Ivy appreciated that Mitch didn't want to put his children through what he'd had to bear as a child. That was an important step in his healing and support of Shelly, yet Ivy knew that changes of that magnitude didn't happen after a few sessions. Mitch was still a work-in-progress.

As we all are, she thought ruefully.

Mitch kissed Shelly again. "I have to get back to work, but I'll see you at home."

"Are you working on the room tonight?" Shelly asked.

Mitch nodded. "I have to finish."

Shelly twisted her lips to one side. "Then I'd better stay at the inn again. The baby and I need to sleep, honey."

Mitch's face fell. "If that's what you think you need."

"Will you pick me up when you're finished?"

"It might be pretty late again." Mitch ran a hand through his spiky blond hair. "I'll see how it goes." He hurried back to the kitchen.

Pressing her fingertips lightly against Shelly's forearm, Ivy leaned forward and whispered, "I think that embarrassed him."

Shelly sighed. "I don't know what else to do. I can't take all that noise."

"Maybe that will spur him to ask for help."

They sipped their coffees and talked about the spa week, while people stopped by the table to ask Shelly how she was doing. Charlie, a grizzled old retiree who took small bets on sports teams, also approached them. He'd once taken bets on the odds of Ivy and Bennett's marriage, but for the most part, he was harmless.

Charlie hitched up his jeans. "So, when are you and Mitch going to announce the big gender reveal?"

Frowning, Shelly crossed her arms. "And just how is that any of your business, Charlie?"

"That will be on the baby's birthday," Ivy said, nudging Shelly's knee under the table. "They're doing this the old-fashioned way."

"Aw, shucks," Charlie said. "I'm just trying to schedule a payday."

Shelly slapped the table. "I like your honesty, Charlie. I promise you'll be the first to know outside of family."

"Everyone is family here," Charlie said, chuckling. "Word travels fast at Java Beach."

"That was sweet of Mitch to be so concerned about you," Ivy said after Charlie left. She was glad to see Mitch looking after Shelly's well-being. Ivy had to have faith that he would shape up for her sister.

Looking pensive, Shelly sipped her coffee. "If that's really part of an old shipwreck out there, I'd love to know more about it. There might be sunken treasure down there."

Ivy gave her a doubtful look.

"Really," Shelly protested. "That happens all the time."

Ivy started to reply, but a memory occurred to her, and she snapped her fingers. "Now that I think about it, I recall reading something on that."

"Where?" Shelly asked, leaning across the table.

"Remember the letters between Amelia and Gustav that we found under the stairway?"

"Between the baby and the move and the landscaping at the inn, I never had time to read them."

"I've read a few. Amelia wrote to Gustav about a vessel

that wrecked nearby. I just figured it had been removed a long time ago."

"What else can you remember?"

"I think Amelia called it the *Lucky Lady*." Ivy tried to recall the details. Her curiosity piqued, she added, "We should look at those letters again."

"Let's walk back and do it," Shelly said, pushing off from her chair. She placed her hand on her stomach. "With all this kicking and flipping going on, the kiddo must be excited, too."

When they returned to the Seabreeze Inn, Poppy was at the front desk giving a young couple restaurant recommendations. "I think you'll enjoy the Coral Cafe," she said, jotting directions on a notepad and seeing them to the door.

Poppy turned back to Ivy and Shelly. "You two look like you have a big secret. What's going on?"

Ivy grinned. "I just remembered that Amelia wrote about a ship that had crashed on a nearby shore. Maybe it's the same one that Shelly stumbled over this morning."

"That would've been a long time ago," Poppy said. "Why would people leave a rusty old vessel there for so long?"

"I have no idea," Ivy said. "But now I'm curious about it."

Poppy's eyes glittered. "Okay, count me in. It's pretty quiet around here, so let's go find those letters."

"It's not like we have to tear down walls or anything this time," Shelly said with a laugh.

"I'm all for anything that doesn't require restoration," Ivy said.

One night soon after she and Shelly had moved into the old house, Ivy had tried to nail a calendar to a wall in the kitchen. When the nail hit a brick wall behind the drywall, she and Shelly took crowbars to the wall to find out what it concealed, which was how they discovered the lower level.

The exterior landscaping had been mounded around the house to hide it. In the end, they'd found a cache of rare paintings that had been stolen during the second world war. As it turned out, the Ericksons had stored them for safekeeping, but they were long forgotten in Amelia's haze of Alzheimer's. In the end, Ivy returned the paintings to their rightful owners.

Since then, it had been costly to restore what years of neglect had inflicted on the house. She often wondered if she'd ever get ahead in this old structure. At least Bennett was understanding and pitched in with minor repairs when he could.

By necessity, Ivy had become more proficient with the tools her brother had given her, and Shelly found she had a knack for resolving the plumbing issues that sometimes plagued guests. They couldn't afford to call a plumber or handyperson for every minor repair.

"I stashed the letters in the library," Ivy said, leading the way.

Inside the paneled library they used as their office now, Ivy pulled a carton from the bottom of a bookshelf and placed it in the middle of the round table. They all gathered around.

"Let's divide these letters. I don't recall which one had details about the ship." Ivy removed the lid. She dug into the pile and passed some to Shelly and Poppy. The letters were written on thick stationery that still held a faint scent of violets.

"Letter writing was such a lovely art," Poppy said, touching an embossed wax seal on an envelope. "Look at the attention to detail. I wish I had someone to write letters like this to."

"You still could," Ivy said, but the truth was she didn't write letters anymore either. Maybe she would, just to surprise someone. She reached for a pair of leopard-print reading glasses and slid them on.

"These are amazing literary relics," Shelly said as she opened the first one and scanned it. She pressed a hand to her chest. "Listen to how they address each other. 'My dearest heart,'" she read. "How sweet is that? No one will ever read the love texts that Mitch and I exchanged in the beginning. They weren't exactly Shakespeare, though. More like, *Hey babe. Love you.*"

"Few are," Poppy said. She drew her hand over the yellowed pages. "Look at this beautiful script. Not many people write like this anymore."

"They used fountain pens," Ivy said. "Those made the writing look so romantic. Without texting and instant messaging, they had to be deliberate in expressing their thoughts."

Poppy sighed. "My generation is missing out on that."

They continued, scanning letters in the stacks. After a moment, Ivy said, "Here it is. Listen to this." Adjusting her glasses, she began reading.

The Lucky Lady *broke free from her anchor in this last winter storm. Save providence, she might have crashed on the shore of Las Brisas del Mar, but as it was, she lodged against those treacherous rocks on the shoreline just south of us. Since it was a Tuesday, there were no guests aboard. However, I daresay none would have made the drive or chanced flight in the torrential downpour we have had for days now.*

"So that storm we had last year was nothing new," Shelly said.

Ivy nodded. "It's a testament to how well this house was built and maintained that it's withstood the winter storms." She continued reading.

A few staff were on board, but they were rescued and brought safely to shore. Of course, I offered them shelter, much to the chagrin of Mrs. Keller, who is an otherwise worthy housekeeper. Fortunately, the bedrooms were still set up after the holidays, so our surprise guests are quite comfortable, indeed. With Mr. Buckley in the carriage apartment, I feel quite safe, so there is no need for you to curtail your business trip. Given the weather, the journey would prove quite difficult. I shall keep you informed, my treasured love.

. . .

As Ivy lowered the letter, Shelly said, "So that's what happened."

"I wonder what kind of the boat the *Lucky Lady* was," Poppy said.

Ivy removed her glasses. "Let's ask around. Who has lived the longest in Summer Beach?"

"We could start with Arthur and Nan," Poppy suggested. "They had all that old information about this house. Maybe they know something about the *Lucky Lady*, too."

"That must've been big news back then," Shelly said.

Ivy nodded thoughtfully. "That event probably made the newspapers in Los Angeles. We need to find out more about it." She checked the time. "We've got guests to tend to, so we can search through these letters later."

"And I'll ask Auntie Google," Poppy said. "She never sleeps. Sort of like you, Aunt Shelly."

"That's not funny," Shelly said. "And I'm spending the night again. Hope you don't mind sharing your room. Just like we used to when the inn was full in the summer."

"Which it will be again for spa week," Ivy said. "Our first guests are arriving tomorrow."

"We're not quite full anymore," Poppy said. "While you were out, we had a cancellation in one of the Sunset suites. From that woman who was bringing her dog. It seems the dog needs surgery, so she canceled for the week. If it's okay with you, Shelly can take her room. It's pretty quiet back there."

Shelly's face bloomed with relief. "If another guest comes in, I'll move back in with Poppy."

"You got it," Ivy said. "You'll be more comfortable, and Mitch could join you."

"I don't know if he will." Shelly shrugged off the thought. "But I want to hear more about this shipwreck. Maybe there was treasure on board. I wonder how far down we'd have to go to get inside the wreckage. If only I could scuba dive in this condition."

"I can dive," Poppy said. "All my gear is at Mom and Dad's house. Or I can snorkel around and have a look."

"I don't think there's much left of the boat," Ivy said. "No one is going down there in the shape that thing is in." She shuddered, thinking about the rust and sea creatures that had taken up residence on the part of the vessel they could see. Who knew what was farther under the sea or how far down it went?

"We could probably get a good look during low tide," Shelly said, her eyes brightening.

"Especially not then," Ivy said. "The current is stronger than people realize. And I am not diving into that yucky mess to rescue anyone. Did you see all the barnacle and kelp tangled up on that skeleton?" She shuddered at the thought of tearing through all that.

Of course, Ivy knew she'd be the first to dive in if she had to—she'd rescued a few people from murky waters during her lifeguard days when she was younger.

Shelly rose from the table. "I'm calling it right now. There's something we're meant to find. I can just feel it."

A shiver flowed through her, and Ivy gave a wry laugh. "Right before spa week, here we go again."

6

*I*vy turned the key in the door to a lower-level unit behind the main house. The Sunset suites had been the maid's quarters in Amelia Erickson's day.

"You'll get a good night's rest back here," she said to Shelly. After refurbishing the four separate units, Ivy found these were ideal for families and those who brought cherished pets. She picked up Shelly's overnight bag and stepped inside.

"I can still carry a bag," Shelly said, following her.

"Why take a chance?" Ivy shrugged off her sister's comment. Shelly's preference for independence could be annoying sometimes, but Ivy recognized that trait in herself, too.

Usually, Ivy was proud of her self-sufficient nature, but Bennett had pointed out to her on more than one occasion—as gently as he could—that she was part of a team now. When she was married to Jeremy, he'd spent so much time traveling for business that she'd learned to manage everything herself. Not unlike the military wives she'd known and admired. She prided herself on being able to handle the children and the household on her own, but this phase of her life was different. She wanted a partnership in her marriage.

Yet, Ivy didn't always know how to embrace that. Communicating with Bennett was sometimes like trying to speak a new language—she had to think and translate her thoughts to the new situation before she spoke.

Ivy realized she wasn't always successful. But then, Bennett was adjusting, too. Their exchange the other night still bothered her. Before they married, they each had their separate space. Now, they had to be considerate of each other 24/7, and that included making plans. While Ivy wasn't entirely used to that, she was trying to work on it.

Ivy placed her sister's bag on an old tapestry-covered bench at the foot of the bed. She surveyed the room, which they'd painted white and outfitted with a pair of marine-blue, slipcovered wingback chairs, a fluffy white duvet, and Ivy's hand-painted beach pillows. Near French doors to a patio stood a wrought-iron bistro set they'd found downstairs and restored. One of Ivy's seaside watercolor paintings graced the wall.

"I'd forgotten how nice these rooms were," Shelly said, absently rubbing her belly. "This one is crying out for flowers, though. I'll cut some today for these rooms."

"Your daffodils look like they're ready," Ivy said.

Shelly glanced from the window toward the garden. "Daffodils are harbingers of spring. I planted an assortment of winter flowers we can clip. However, this year, I have a particular affinity for daisies." She sat on the bed, bounced a couple of times, and smiled. "It's good to be back here. I can get more work done in the garden now. I need to harvest lemons and mandarin oranges, and then—"

"Low branches only," Ivy cut in. "You're not getting up on a ladder like you did last year. Call me for that, or ask Jamir. He's a lot taller than you are."

"Geez, you're bossy." Shelly flicked away her comment with a wave of her hand. "He's usually in school or helping his mom at the flower stand. I'll ask Poppy for help, but only if I think I need it."

"Be smart, Shelly. Especially this close to your delivery date. It's only a few more weeks."

"I guess so." Shelly bit her lip and nodded with reluctance.

Sensing her sister's need to talk, Ivy eased onto the bed next to her. "Everything okay?"

Shelly drew a breath. "I have to do as much as I can now." Her words spilled out while tears rimmed her eyelids. "I need to see Leilani at the Hidden Garden to buy spring plantings for the inn. I've hardly worked on the garden at my house, although I have some vegetables and herbs that I started in the greenhouse, but how can I do that as long as Mitch is trampling the area with his construction material? And now, the spa ladies will be arriving, and once Mitch is finished, I have to prep the baby's room. But I also have to tend to my birthing plan…and the plumbing issues here…" Shelly heaved a sigh. "I wish Mom were here. She'd know how to organize my out-of-control life."

Ivy bumped Shelly's shoulder. "You always tease me about my lists, but I can help you. Some, anyway. As of now, I'm taking over the unclogging of sinks and toilets around here. I ordered this fancy gizmo that should clear out the old pipes."

"I appreciate that." Shelly nodded and wiped her eyes. "I watch you buzzing around every day tending to guests and keeping this place in good repair. You don't have much time to deal with me anymore. Besides, you have your Mr. Darcy to watch over."

Ivy smiled at the nickname Shelly had given Bennett after they'd read *Pride and Prejudice* a few months ago in Paige's book club. "He's a grown man and can take care of himself."

Shelly shot her a look beneath her damp lashes. "That's what they all say, but I know better now. Do you have any idea how much laundry a man can generate? And it's full of sand."

"Mitch is a surfer," Ivy said gently. "Why didn't he continue doing his own laundry? He's capable."

"I offered one time, and bang—it became my job. Besides, he cooks for me."

"He has to eat, too. If you think that's a fair exchange, okay. Otherwise, talk to him." Still, Ivy saw the distress on her sister's face. She recalled the mess she and their brothers were on the beach when they were young. "Or bring your laundry here. Lizzy can do it while she's changing the linens. We'll pay her a little extra, so that's off your mind for a while."

Shelly smoothed her hand over the snowy duvet. "It's not that I'm ungrateful for what you're doing for me, but I really do miss Mom."

This wasn't the first time Shelly had said this; she seemed stuck in a loop. Ivy slipped an arm around her sister. "I know, sweetie. But Mom and Dad deserve this trip, too. At their age, this might be their last one. You didn't know you were pregnant when they left. Doesn't she call you when they pull into a port?"

"Yeah, but that's not often." Shelly hesitated, fiddling with a loose thread from her dress. "Ives, I'm a little scared. I've been reading articles online about what can go wrong when you have a baby."

Her sister's fear sliced through Ivy. She stroked her hand. "Your medical team is well informed, right?"

"But you had so much trouble with Sunny. At the time, I didn't even realize that you and the baby could have died."

"You were only a teenager," Ivy said. "And I was on the other side of the country." Even though she hadn't talked to Shelly much about what had happened, Ivy had been frightened, too.

"Mom flew out to be with you, didn't she?"

"Yes, she did, after I gave birth," Ivy said softly. An edge of competition existed between all of them—including Forrest, Flint, and Honey. She didn't want Shelly to compare their experiences, but it was clear she held that thought in her mind.

"The youngest kid always loses out," Shelly said.

"We all thought you had it the easiest," Ivy said. "Mom and Dad were so strict with Honey. By the time you came along, they were a lot more lackadaisical in their parenting approach."

Shelly only sniffed, so Ivy went on. "Sweetie, I love you, and I'm here for you. So are Flint and Forrest. No one will let anything happen to you." *If we can help it*, she thought to herself. As optimistic as she wanted to be for Shelly, she knew that every childbirth carried a health risk, which was why she wanted Shelly to have the best care possible. "You're happy with your doula, right?"

"I like her, but I'm worried if something goes wrong."

"You shouldn't spend your time being afraid of things that probably won't happen. And when it's over, you'll forget most of that." She smiled with confidence. "I'd do it all again a hundred times. Holding Misty and Sunny after they'd been born was the most incredible feeling I've ever known. You'll feel more joy than you've ever known."

Shelly grinned. "A hundred times?"

"Maybe just once more." Ivy wondered where that came from. But now that the idea had entered her consciousness, she rather liked it. She smiled at herself for thinking that. Wouldn't Bennett be surprised?

"I've longed for a child of my own. But I still have to learn how to change a diaper."

"Piece of cake," Ivy said. "Speaking of cake... Remember when we were flying to Summer Beach from Boston, and I was having one of the worst days of my life? I was desperate to sell the house and dreaded talking to my old high school crush." Bennett had been the real estate agent partner assigned to sell the house when her first choice retired due to health problems. "That visit was my final, frantic effort."

"Bennett wasn't too happy to see you either," Shelly said, curving up one corner of her mouth.

"And what did you do?" Ivy chuckled. "Only kept me waiting at the boarding gate while you ran around buying fancy cake pops to cheer me up. I never forgot that, Shells."

"Worked, didn't it?" Shelly grinned. "And look what your crazy idea of turning this old house into an inn has brought us." Her eyes regained a little of their sparkle. "That was the day I met Mitch at Java Beach. So, where are my cake pops?"

"There might be some in your future." Ivy hugged her sister, praying she could reignite Shelly's zany spark for life. When her sister was determined, she was unstoppable, but she could also curl up and let worry inhibit her actions. Ivy recalled how the final weeks of pregnancy were sometimes unbearable in terms of waiting and discomfort.

Smiling now, Shelly rubbed her belly. "Thanks for the talk, but I need to rest for a little while."

Ivy rose and made her way from the room, shutting the door softly behind her. As she crossed the garden pathway that Shelly had created with tropical plantings, she wondered how soon her parents would reach the next port. She needed to talk to her mother.

When Ivy neared the pool area, she saw a woman in a large-brimmed hat and a *Life is Better in Summer Beach* hoodie.

The woman lifted her hand in greeting. "You must be Ivy. Poppy at the front desk told me you would be around. I'm Gayle, and I'm here for the spa week."

"We're so glad to have you," Ivy said, greeting her. Gayle looked to be in her early thirties. Her blond hair was pulled into a ponytail beneath her hat, and she wore the latest style of denim jeans with kitten-heeled booties.

Gayle's eyes sparkled with curiosity. "My friend told me about this old house, and I've read about all the treasures you've found here. That must have been so exciting. Paintings and jewels—did you get to keep anything?"

"We wish," Ivy replied with a smile. She fielded this question a lot. However, the publicity had helped fill the inn. For that, Ivy was grateful. Had it not been for that, she might have lost the house to Jeremy's unpaid tax liens. When a flash of pity dampened Gayle's inquisitiveness, Ivy quickly added, "But it's been fascinating. Is there anything I can do to help you get settled now?"

"Poppy took care of everything. I'm so happy to be here. I've always wanted to explore this old house. When I heard you and your sister had turned it into an inn—and you were having a spa week—I just had to come."

"We have a late afternoon mixer every day in the music room so you can meet other guests and have an appetizer before you go out for dinner. Won't you join us later today?"

"Poppy told me about that, so I'll be there. My friend should be arriving soon. She's flying in from up north. We wanted to come today to get an early start."

"Then I'll see you both later."

After leaving Gayle, Ivy saw she had just enough time to work on a new seascape commission for a couple who had admired her paintings at the inn. They had specifically requested a vivid turquoise sea with bright sunshine and colorful umbrellas—a typical summer day in Summer Beach. After that, she would change for the afternoon reception.

As she crossed the veranda to the light-filled studio she'd set up with a view of the ocean, she thought of how good it was to feel busy again with a full week ahead. While she had welcomed a brief reprieve after the summer tourist season, too much of a lull wasn't good for her pocketbook. She'd started and finished several paintings in the fall, and the holiday season picked up a little, but she'd been eager for more activity after the new year.

Inside her studio, Ivy opened a window to listen to the sound of the ocean while she worked. She slipped on her painter's smock, which was one of her father's old white shirts that she'd salvaged from a donation bag when she was helping her parents pack the house before they left on their journey.

This frayed, paint-splattered shirt made her feel close to her dad. It made her feel as if he were encouraging her while she worked. Photos of Sterling at the helm of his boat and of her mother on the beach lifted her spirits, too. She imagined them thinking of her and her siblings and their children thousands of miles away under the same sunny skies.

Ivy glanced at the framed images on the shelf. "I'll email a photo when I'm finished. I think you'll like this painting."

Carlotta and Sterling had sold some of Ivy's artwork at the art show they'd had on the grounds of the inn, and she had been pleased with the prices they'd fetched. Her parents had traveled the world for years to buy crafts from local artisans. Carlotta and Sterling had supplied those to top department stores and were far better at sales than Ivy was, but she was learning. She felt good about gaining this commission, and it wouldn't take her much longer.

As Ivy worked, the ocean provided the soundtrack, and she was quickly lost in her brushstrokes. The smell of paint and sea breezes usually calmed any anxiety she brought into the studio, paving the way to a sense of clarity and purpose.

She thought of the little book Paige had given her. She'd read a few pages early this morning while showering, and as she dabbed her brush in a deeper shade of teal to add dimension to the waves she was painting, thoughts filled her mind. A passage that Amelia Erickson had noted came to mind.

Channeled whelk, I put you down again, but you have set my mind on a journey, up an inwardly winding spiral staircase of thought.

Ivy stepped back to check her work. Often her mind was an endless swirl of thoughts and things on her to-do lists. Write a check for Sunny's tuition, check on Misty in her new apartment in Los Angeles, answer guest questions, replace light bulbs in rooms, plan new events for guests...and find time to spend with Bennett.

As much as Ivy loved her family and the inn, she needed this solitude in her day as much to create as to sort out the thoughts in her mind—or to simply escape from it all for a blissful hour. She'd been sure to include a painting class on the spa week agenda.

When the timer she'd set went off a little while later, she was so immersed in her work that the chimes surprised her. As she cleaned her brush and hung up her painting shirt, her mind filled again with the duties of the day.

And at the top of that list was Bennett.

Ivy hated when things weren't quite right between them and wondered if this was a sign of deeper issues. Maybe instead of worrying about Shelly's marriage, she should examine her own. She thought of poor Celia, and what she was going through with Tyler. Ivy never wanted her relationship with Bennett to deteriorate in such a way.

Even though she was irritated with Bennett's lack of influence over Mitch, she'd have to find time to talk to him. The sooner, the better.

7

*A*fter leaving City Hall, Bennett drove the short distance back to the inn. He'd never imagined that this grand dame of a home would someday be his residence. It was Ivy's property, and he made no claim on it, although he was as attentive as she was to its need for repairs and maintenance.

The old house gave him a chance to keep his tools in use, he told himself with a chuckle as he parked and eased from his SUV. Still, it would be nice for them to have their privacy —Ivy could be called away at any moment for a clogged drain or a tripped electrical circuit breaker. Surely she'd prefer to have someone else handle that. If Bennett was there, he helped her handle the issue, which he didn't mind, but he often saw exhaustion etched on her face.

She had been through so much in the past few years. He knew what is like to grieve for a lost mate. Even though Jeremy had been far from perfect, Ivy had toiled to make their marriage work. She had felt the loss, but perhaps more poignantly, for her daughters on the loss of their father. Added to that were her financial difficulties, losing her home, and stumbling into this mammoth project of a fixer house. If he could make her life easier by giving her the comfort she deserved, he would know he had succeeded.

As he stepped from his vehicle, he remembered the bike in the back. Checking to make sure no one could see him, he lifted out the long bicycle and stashed it under a moving blanket to one side of the garage where Ivy wasn't likely to find it. She needed fun in her life, too. Her laughter could light up his heart. Despite the inevitable challenges in life, he hoped they would laugh every day for as long as they lived.

Bennett loved planning for his new bride. The bike, a honeymoon, and soon, something even more. He was waiting for just the right moment to surprise her about moving into his home. As he closed the garage door, he thought about how active their lives were here with interesting guests visiting.

After Jackie died, his home on the ridge had become unbearably quiet—to the point where he dreaded going home except to sleep. Being of service to others in Summer Beach, first through his real estate practice and then as mayor, served him as well. Now, Ivy would light up his home again, and he could hardly wait until he could share it with her. It had been a happy home with Jackie, and it would be again.

Making his way toward the main house at the inn, he heard strains of music wafting across the patio. Someone was playing the piano in the music room—most likely another of Celia's students from the school music program she and her husband supported. Some of the older students were now playing at Spirits & Vine on the weekends for the brunch crowd.

Celia and Tyler had moved to Summer Beach after he retired early from a technology company in the Bay area. People like them kept the community vibrant and thriving, though Celia was the one who'd become involved with the community. Tyler wrote the checks and said that was enough, although Bennett suspected it wasn't. A man needed a purpose, and Tyler hadn't realized that yet.

Bennett stepped into the wood-paneled music room, where Ivy was greeting new guests. A low fire crackled in the fireplace, chasing away the late afternoon chill in the air. She turned slightly, and Bennett caught his breath.

Golden rays poured through the open doors, casting a shimmery sheen across Ivy's face and illuminating her green eyes. Coppery highlights shone in her rich brown hair. The graceful tilt of her head and the genuine, heartwarming smile on her lips still affected him—just as it had so many years ago when they were timid teenagers on the beach. How different their lives would have been if they had actually acted on their crush and connected, yet perhaps they weren't ready then.

He smiled to himself. It was probably better this way. Today was their time: the prime of their lives. They had each sustained heartache in their lives, and now they were wiser and more patient because of it. Bennett was grateful for every day he was given on this earth because he knew how fleeting that time could be.

As if Ivy sensed his presence, she turned toward him, and her face lit with a smile. Yet, when he lifted his chin toward her, a flash of concern shadowed her face. After a quick, tight smile, she turned her back.

With a sinking feeling, Bennett recalled the words they'd had last night.

Celia stood just on the other side of her, and the two women were speaking intently. Celia's dark hair was brushed from her forehead into a ponytail, revealing distress on her face.

Tyler, Bennett thought. He wondered if the rumors he'd heard about her husband were true this time. Celia gave so much of herself to the music program and the kids. Tyler didn't deserve her.

Bennett looked around. Mitch, who usually brought cookies and stayed to see Shelly, was nowhere around. Maybe he'd received a whale-watching charter this afternoon.

More likely, he was working on the room addition. Bennett pressed his lips together. He had to find a way to help Mitch move that project forward.

He'd promised Ivy.

Imani noticed him. "Good afternoon, Mr. Mayor. We've missed you lately."

"I've had a lot of work at City Hall."

"Anything you can talk about?"

"The owners of the old airfield are entertaining an offer. We're having meetings on that—you and other residents are welcome to attend." He would appreciate her input. Imani had been a practicing attorney in Los Angeles before moving to Summer Beach and opening Blossoms.

"Sounds important."

Bennett spoke to her for a few minutes, although he kept Ivy in his field of vision. She didn't turn around again.

She was definitely upset with him. This should have been easier, but he'd resolve the problem. As mayor, that's what he did every day. So why couldn't he manage that with Ivy?

"Excuse me," Bennett said when there was a lull in the conversation. "I need to see my wife about something. Good to see you."

Ivy was moving toward another guest when Bennett crossed toward her. "Hi, sweetheart. How was your day?"

She took a breath to speak but then seemed to think better of it.

Bennett reached out and clasped her hand. "I missed you today." That was true; he often thought of her during the day and always looked forward to seeing her after work. Before he met Ivy, he filled his days simply because he had nothing else to do. But since he'd married, it seemed that his receptionist Nan understood, too. She pushed him out the door every afternoon, saying, *Go see your wife, Mr. Mayor.* Which he gladly did.

Lowering his voice, he said, "I didn't like the way we left that conversation last night."

Ivy's face softened a little. "Neither did I."

"If you've greeted everyone you need, we could take a walk on the beach before dinner." There weren't many people here this evening.

Glancing over her shoulder, Ivy hesitated. "With the spa ladies arriving, I don't have very long. Another guest is flying in soon."

"Shelly and Poppy are here. Couldn't they handle that check-in?" Bennett didn't want to leave this until they were both tired and easily irritated. Maybe that's what had gotten them into this situation.

"I suppose they can."

As they wove through the room of guests, Ivy whispered to Poppy. A moment later, they were outside, their toes in the sand. Bennett took Ivy's hand and breathed in. As the sun slipped beneath the horizon, it flung a paintbox of pinks and corals across the clouds.

They'd made it. Ivy looked relieved, though her brow was still drawn with tension. "Would you like to head toward the marina?"

"Actually, I want to show you what the tide revealed this morning." She started in the opposite direction. "Although I don't know if we can still see it."

"What was that?"

"Shelly stumbled on what we think are the remains of an old ship. Amelia referenced it in one of her letters. It might be part of the *Lucky Lady*."

"That was an old gambling ship. It was anchored off the coast during Prohibition in the 1920s and washed up on the shore during a storm. It's only visible when the tide is low during certain weather conditions. Was Shelly hurt?"

"It was a minor episode, but that sure scared me."

Bennett detected anxiety in her voice. "Shelly is pretty tough. You shouldn't worry so much about her."

Ivy bristled at that. "Besides the difficulty that I had with Sunny's birth, I think that what you went through with Jackie during her pregnancy would be enough for you to understand my worry."

Bennett gulped at Ivy's words. "Does it feel like I've been minimizing your concern?"

"It does."

It pained him to realize she thought he'd done that. Maybe he had.

"I...I'm sorry for that." He squeezed her hand. "I do understand."

She cast her gaze toward the sea and sighed before turning back to him. "And I'm sorry for bringing up Jackie. I know that was a devastating loss for you."

"It's okay. That was a long time ago." More than ten years now, Bennett recalled, though it seemed like a lifetime. While the ache in his heart had subsided, he still remembered his first wife with tenderness.

Ivy slid her arm around him, and he nestled her to his side. For a moment, they watched the deepening shades in the wide sky while the tide rushed toward them and then drew back in an endless magnetic loop. He could feel the tension draining from her body.

Ivy looked up at him and offered him a tentative smile. "Shelly and I went to Java Beach today, and Darla said we had just missed you. Did Mitch agree to your help?"

"We talked, but he was busy. I don't know if I made much headway, but I promise I'll get through to him for Shelly's sake."

Telling her about their argument was pointless. He would get through to Mitch. Even if he had to call others for help. Forrest and Axe would be the logical choices. He wondered if Tyler was any good with tools, though he doubted it.

"There's no way she can get enough rest with that racket. This is about her health."

He rubbed her shoulder. "I know how important this is. I'll do everything I can to support them."

"I appreciate that."

Bennett let out a sigh. This was the beginning of the return to normalcy between them, that is, if there had ever been such a thing. He laughed softly to himself.

"What's so funny?"

"I was thinking about how we're so wrapped up in everyone else's life here at the inn. Living on the property is convenient, but I had another idea."

Ivy arched an eyebrow. "Go on."

Here's my chance. He drew a breath and plunged ahead. "The family that rented my home wants me to help them find a house to buy in Summer Beach. Since my place will soon be vacant, I thought we could move in. The views from the ridge are amazing, and we'd have a lot more privacy."

Ivy sucked in her lower lip. "But the inn is my home."

"It's *your* home," Bennett said gently. "I want to share mine with you. You haven't been inside, but it's really nice. Our relationship wasn't to that point before the fire."

"We didn't have a relationship until you crashed in the room next to mine." Ivy allowed a small smile. "Well, not a good one, anyway."

Bennett took that as a positive sign. "It's a great place, and I think you'd really like all the artistic touches. Jackie hand-painted stencils in the kitchen and sponged painted the—"

"Hold it right there." Ivy stopped on the beach. "I'm sure it's lovely, but I'm not moving there."

"I think it would be good for us."

"For you, maybe."

Suddenly, Bennett realized what he'd done. "Of course, I'd want you to make the house your own. You probably don't want Jackie's artwork in your home."

"It's not that," Ivy said. "I never knew her, and I'm certainly not jealous. I would want to make the house my own, but I don't want to leave the inn. Without living on-site, managing it would be difficult. Everything that happens needs immediate attention for guest comfort."

"That doesn't leave much time for us."

"You knew this before we married."

"I didn't see everything then. Now, when people call you in the middle of the night, they're calling me, too."

"Those *people* are our guests." Ivy crossed her arms. "So, you're saying you didn't sign up for this?"

"Not at all," Bennett said quickly. "I'm just proposing more privacy for us. I want you to myself for a few hours a day." He drew his hand tenderly across her cheek. "Ivy, I love you. Is that so wrong?"

Ivy touched his hand. "I understand, but I really love the inn, too. You might have a beautiful home, but I love waking up in mine—with you. Having Sunny in the house and room for Misty when she visits means a lot to me."

"The girls are welcome, too." How could he have been so short-sighted?

Ivy shook her head. "It doesn't seem possible right now."

"Okay." Still, he had to find a solution. "You have your home, and I have mine. How do we put them together in a life that makes sense for both of us?"

Her expression took on a shadow of sadness. "I thought we already had. And I thought you were happy living at the inn."

Trying to lighten her spirits, he grinned. "You have to admit our quarters are a little small for the two of us. I'm afraid my stuff gets in your way." The apartment over the garages was fine for one person, but they seemed to be bumping into each other all the time now.

"No, it's me. I can pare down. I'll store things in the attic."

"It's not that."

"I've taken over the bathroom, haven't I?"

"Just a little." Bennett smiled. "You were used to Amelia's large bedroom and bathroom." After they married, they chose the apartment because of the living area and balcony that overlooked the beach. Admittedly, they did have a little more privacy outside the main house.

Ivy looked miserable. "I don't know how to solve this problem."

"I didn't mean to make you unhappy," Bennett said. "I only thought you'd be excited to have a home of our own, but I see that's not the case. And I can see why."

"I like where we are."

"Then we have no problem that we can't live with." Bennett swept his arms around her. Marriage was a series of compromises. This one was entirely manageable—especially if it meant Ivy was happy. "Look at what we have. We live in a beautiful home on the beach. What could be better than that?"

The tautness in her face relaxed, and she smiled up at him. "I've worked so hard for this home, and I'm so glad you understand." A smile played on her lips. "Still, your idea was thoughtful. Your heart is in the right place."

A wave of relief swept through Bennett. He had also planned to surprise her with his plans for a honeymoon getaway, but something in his gut told him to save that for another time. She would want to be a part of that plan.

They walked on a little more in comfortable silence until Ivy paused and gestured ahead. "I think the remains of the barge were about here, but I don't see anything now."

Bennett nodded toward the ocean. "The tide is going in the other direction, so we won't. Some folks call the *Lucky Lady* a ghost ship, but it's hardly even that anymore. Just the skeletal remains. They haven't surfaced in a long time, so you caught them on a rare occasion."

Ivy's shoulders dropped. "Do you think there is anything in the hull beneath the surface?"

"I imagine the barge was stripped by fortune hunters a long time ago."

"That's probably just as well." Ivy heaved a sigh. "Why is the *Lucky Lady* still here?"

"As I understand, there was no one to claim her. There's another gambling barge that still rests off the coast of Coronado Island in San Diego, the *Monte Carlo*. When the tide is out, that one is often visible, too."

Ivy stared out to sea. "I can't explain it, but I feel like there's something about that vessel calling to me."

Before Bennett could ask why, he heard the low roar of an engine overhead. Looking up, he could just make out a small aircraft in the waning light. The Coast Guard flew that low in policing the shoreline, but this wasn't a path that private craft would usually take.

Beside him, Ivy stared up. "That plane is getting awfully close."

As Bennett watched, his breath caught in his throat. The plane was losing altitude too quickly, and it was headed directly toward them.

"The pilot's in trouble," he shouted against the sputtering plane and the roaring sea. "Watch out!"

With his heart hammering, he grabbed Ivy and tried to gauge where the plane would set down. Would they attempt a water or beach landing?

When the nose dipped toward them, Ivy screamed.

Suddenly, the aircraft banked hard toward the dunes. The pilot might have seen them.

"Oh, no," Ivy cried, pressing a hand against her heart. "It's going down. We have to reach them. Come on."

Ivy began running toward the sand dunes, and Bennett was right behind her.

"I'll call it in," he yelled, pulling out his phone. Though he and Ivy were both trained in first aid, he dreaded what they were going to find.

They climbed a dune and slid down the other side. As they scrambled to their feet, they saw the plane drifting precariously before thudding to the ground.

"Let's go," Ivy yelled.

Bennett raced after her, knowing they had to reach them as fast as possible.

8

*S*parks flew into the air as the small aircraft bumped along broken concrete overgrown with weeds. Ivy pulled up, watching. With her adrenaline pumping, she clutched Bennett's arm. "What is this place?"

"It's the old airfield. Hasn't been used in decades."

She'd heard people talk about the airfield in town, but she had never seen it behind the dunes and overgrowth. Surprised it was so close, she'd also expected more, but a place like this was easy to overlook.

Her heart was racing, and she prayed that whoever was on board would make it out safely. Instantly, she cast aside all thoughts about what she and Bennett had been talking about.

The plane jerked to a halt, and Ivy took off again, pounding across the broken pavement. She needed to reach the occupants in case the plane caught fire. The smell of the engine filled the air.

As Ivy approached the aircraft, the door burst open. A slender pilot nearly tumbled out, regained her footing, and climbed shakily from the plane.

"I've got you," Ivy said, reaching out to support her.

"Have to get away…from the plane," the younger woman managed to say in a wavering voice.

Ivy saw the woman's knees buckling, and she hoisted her up. "Put your arm around my neck and hang on." Half dragging her, Ivy hurried away from the plane.

Bennett met her midway from the plane and scooped up the woman. "Help is on the way," he said, rushing ahead.

They stopped a safe distance away from the plane, and the younger woman sat down on the old tarmac, clutching her knees. "That was as close as I've ever come to crashing." Her shaky voice was flooded with relief.

Ivy got a better look at her. The woman's short black hair was matted with perspiration, and the pupils in her dark blue eyes were dilated. "You might be in a mild state of shock." Ivy pressed her thumb on the woman's wrist and counted. As expected, her heart rate was elevated.

In the distance, the sound of a siren split the still air. Ivy lifted her chin toward Bennett. "The mayor called for help."

The woman looked confused. "The mayor?"

"This is Bennett Dylan, and he's the mayor of Summer Beach," Ivy replied, nodding toward her husband. She wanted to keep the woman alert and speaking. "I'm Ivy. What's your name?"

"People call me Piper." She grimaced. "And that was a fairly sound Piper Cherokee."

Bennett leaned in. "What type?"

It took Piper a few moments to answer. "A vintage model 172. Engine trouble. I was almost there, too." She pressed a hand to her head. "I'm a little dizzy."

"Did you hit your head when you landed?" Bennett asked.

"I-I'm not sure."

Gently, Ivy brushed aside the curly dark fringe that framed Piper's face. A trickle of blood oozed from a wound. "Looks like you might have a small cut. The paramedics will take care of that. Where were you heading?"

Piper named the town next to Summer Beach, which had a small private airport.

Ivy rocked back on her heels. Another ten or fifteen minutes, and Piper would have made it. "Do you have friends or family there?"

Piper thought for a moment before shaking her head. "Not there. I'm meeting a friend in Summer Beach."

An emergency vehicle turned onto the old runway and headed toward them. Bennett stood and waved his arms.

Against the flashing red lights, Ivy leaned toward Piper. She recalled what their new guest had said. "Are you meeting Gayle at the Seabreeze Inn?"

Piper started to get up. "You know her?"

"Easy, don't move." Ivy touched Piper's shoulder to keep her seated while the paramedics brought their equipment. A second fire unit pulled along the aircraft. "I run the inn, and we've been expecting you. Gayle told me her friend was flying in tonight, but I thought she meant on a commercial flight."

Bennett greeted the emergency team.

Two paramedics knelt beside Piper. "We'll take it from here," one of them said, who introduced himself as Noah. With warm brown eyes and an engaging smile, he worked quickly and efficiently to assess Piper's condition while trying to put her at ease.

Piper was still shaken. She reached out and took Ivy's hand. "Can you stay with me?"

In Piper's muddled expression, Ivy saw the signs of a young woman who needed a friend. "Of course. And once Noah clears you to come back to the inn, we have a comfortable room ready for you. Gayle will be there, too."

Noah asked a few questions about what happened as he took Piper's vitals, and she answered, explaining that the plane had developed engine trouble.

Bennett knelt beside them. "I'll call Poppy and ask her to tell Gayle that you're here with us."

With her gaze darting between them, Piper frowned. "I don't want her to worry."

"She'll worry more if she doesn't hear from you," Ivy said, stroking Piper's hand.

"I can't believe you saw me go down and came to help," Piper said while Noah cleaned the cut on her head and bandaged it. She glanced at the plane, which was sitting slightly askew, and shuddered. "That was really close."

"You're lucky we were just over that dune." While Ivy stayed with Piper, she heard Bennett on the phone making arrangements with Poppy. "And it was fortunate that you saw this abandoned airstrip."

"I remembered it was here." The color was coming back into Piper's face, and her voice was gaining strength. "Lucky Lindy used to fly in here. Charles Lindbergh."

"We've just been talking about him." Ivy smiled, musing about the coincidence. She was relieved that Piper appeared less confused now.

Ivy went on. "I found a book that his wife, Anne Morrow Lindbergh, wrote and dedicated to the former owner of the inn. They might have all been friends."

Looking out across the pavement in the waning light, she scanned the old airstrip, which bore the ravages of time and weather. The surface was cracked and weeds grew through the fissures. Kids had left chalk drawings, and bicycle tire marks swirled around the pavement. A small, two-story wooden structure with boarded windows sat off to one side.

Trying to keep Piper engaged and alert, Ivy nodded toward the tire marks left by others. "Look, you're not the only one racing down this runway."

"That's funny. Great place to skate, too." Piper chewed her lip. "My old plane is usually more dependable. I hope she's okay."

"*You're* okay," Noah said as he checked her. "And that's what counts." He was a nice-looking young man with thick brown, sun-streaked hair brushed back from his temples. Ivy knew he surfed with Mitch sometimes. Noah gazed at Piper with obvious admiration. "You must be a good pilot to have dropped her in here with engine failure...and no running lights to guide you."

Piper's eyes focused on him, and she gave a self-conscious grin. "I'm not too bad."

"You're being modest," Ivy said. "That looked like an expert move to me."

The fire chief made her way toward them, and Bennett met Paula midway. After conversing with her, Bennett brought her to speak with Piper. Ivy released the young woman and stood up.

She felt the light-headedness that went along with the surge in adrenaline she'd felt clambering over the dunes and racing toward the plane. Her worst fears were that the plane would crash or catch fire. Thankfully, neither had occurred. If it had, their spa week would have started in a somber mood. She let out a long, slow breath of relief.

Bennett put his arm around Ivy's shoulders. "I was pretty impressed with your quick actions."

"Anyone would have done the same," Ivy said, warming to his touch. She appreciated having him there with her.

With admiration shining in his eyes, Bennett angled his head toward her. "Not many people race toward disasters to help. That's just one more reason I love you."

Blinking back a surge of emotion, Ivy turned into his embrace. Their earlier disagreement seemed minor now compared to what might have occurred had Piper not been so skilled.

Just then, a pair of headlights shone toward them in the gathering twilight.

Ivy looked up. As Bennett's SUV drew near, she saw her blond-haired daughter Sunny at the wheel with Gayle in the front passenger seat. When Sunny stopped, Gayle slid out and raced to her friend.

"Thanks for coming and bringing Gayle," Ivy said, hugging her daughter.

Sunny beamed at her. "Poppy is tending to another guest, and Shelly is pretty tired, so I volunteered." Her green eyes were wide, taking in everything around them.

"I'm glad you did." Ivy was proud of her daughter for taking responsibility. "It was a miracle the pilot wasn't hurt."

Sunny was dividing her time between working at the inn and an animal shelter and taking her final college classes. Although she was nearing graduation, she had added classes in hospitality and nonprofit management to explore her options, and Ivy had supported that. Her older sister Misty was narrating audiobooks and had a part in a new television series, but Sunny was still trying to find her way.

Watching Piper, Sunny scrunched her face with concern. "Is she going to be okay?"

"They're releasing her now, and it looks like she'll be coming back with us. I suppose she'll have to tend to her plane later." Ivy put her arm around Sunny's shoulder. "Come on, let's see what else she needs."

Piper was smiling now as Noah tended to her. He'd been asking her a series of questions, and he seemed satisfied with her answers.

When Piper looked up, Sunny asked, "Is there anything you need from your plane?"

"My purse and travel bag, and a gift that I brought for Gayle. I sure appreciate it." She turned up a corner of her mouth in a wry half-smile. "I don't usually make an entrance like this."

"We'll get your things," Bennett said, nodding at Sunny. "You can come back with us now. The plane should be safe enough here. Chief Clarkson will have a patrol check on it during the night, but there's not much traffic out this way."

Piper nodded in agreement. "Since I'm here for a week, I should have time to get it repaired or towed."

Noah seemed to pick up on that. "Mind if I check on you at the inn to make sure you're doing okay?"

"I'd like that," Piper replied, sounding pleased at Noah's attention.

Bennett and Sunny set off for the plane. He climbed in and brought out Piper's suitcase and handed her purse and a gift bag to Sunny to carry. Ivy was happy that Sunny was eager to help tonight. While she was still the more mercurial of her two daughters, she seemed to be on a better course than when she was part of a wild crowd of friends back east.

Sunny and Bennett started back to the SUV as Ivy walked with Gayle behind Piper and the paramedic to the vehicle. Gayle was shaken, too. Ivy surmised that they were long-time friends.

Ivy watched the paramedic help Piper into the SUV. He seemed to be taking extra care of her.

After Noah settled Piper in the front seat, he fished a card from his pocket. "Call me anytime if you want to talk. You'll probably feel more banged up the second day. If there's anything you need, I live pretty close to the inn."

Piper touched the wound he'd bandaged and gazed at him. "I'll let you know. And thanks for helping me. I'm feeling a lot better now."

Ivy smiled at the sweet exchange; it was clear that Noah and Piper were attracted to each other.

As Bennett walked Ivy to the car, he put his arm around her. "Is that the way we were when we were young?"

"We were much younger back then," Ivy replied, leaning into him. "And we were both reticent about expressing our feelings."

"Glad we got past that." When she didn't respond right away, he added, "We have, haven't we?"

Ivy smiled up at him. "I think so. And I appreciate your

understanding about the house. I know it's a lot to ask you to give it up for a garage apartment, but I promise I'll find a way to give you more space—and find more privacy for us."

That wasn't too much for Bennett to expect; she could manage that for him, although she wasn't sure how she could conjure more space in a garage flat.

A breeze kicked up from the ocean, and Bennett brushed a few strands of hair from her face. "My fragile male ego was in overdrive, but we'll figure it out." He nodded toward Piper and Gayle. "You'll probably want to get them settled when we return."

Ivy paused by the car door. "Piper needs rest. Gayle is here to look after her, and Poppy and Sunny can make them comfortable."

Bennett paused with his hand on the door. "Sounds like you have a free evening."

With the light of the surrounding emergency vehicles illuminating his face, Ivy took a step toward him. "I might have something else in mind tonight."

Bennett touched a finger to his chest. "Would that have anything to do with me?"

Ivy smiled. "It has everything to do with you." Piper's close call this evening had eased the tension between them, at least for now. Besides, she enjoyed flirting with her husband. "Come on, let's get this crew back to the inn."

Bennett chuckled and opened the door for her. Everyone piled into the SUV after them.

Inside the vehicle, Piper was talking about how she remembered the old airstrip.

Ivy nodded toward the boarded-up, two-story building they passed. "That must have served as the air traffic control tower."

Piper leaned forward. "Actually, I heard that's where the smugglers watched out for the authorities."

"Cool," Sunny said, chiming in. "What were they smuggling?"

"Booze, mostly," Piper said. "It was during prohibition, and some gangster leased this property and built the private runway to bring in cargo."

Ivy turned in her seat. "I wonder if that had anything to do with the *Lucky Lady*? That was a gambling barge anchored a few miles out. My sister stumbled over the remains when we were out for a walk earlier."

Piper grinned. "I'll bet it did. Must have been pretty wild back then."

The fine hairs on the back of Ivy's neck bristled, and she sensed there was more to this fascinating story. Amelia Erickson seemed to know what was going on. As they drove the short distance to the inn, Ivy wondered who in Summer Beach might know more about the *Lucky Lady*.

he next morning, Ivy rose early and led the beach walk for the spa guests who had arrived, and Shelly taught a relaxing yoga class. Piper slept in, and Ivy figured she was still feeling quite shaken from her emergency landing.

Afterward returning, Ivy met Shelly in the kitchen. "How was yoga?"

"A little modified to allow for my extra guest," Shelly replied, tracing a circle on her belly. "But it felt good to stretch and breathe. Especially after a full night's sleep. Except for a few punches in the middle of the night from junior."

Ivy laughed as she arranged muffins in a cloth-lined basket. Shelly still wasn't letting on if the baby was a girl or a boy, but she'd given up trying to coax that information from her. "Enjoy those uninterrupted nights of rest while you can."

"I decided I'm going to love every minute of the entire messy life of this little one," Shelly said. "At my age, this might be my only chance. With Mitch being so much younger, I worry that he'll want more children, and I won't be able to have another one."

Ivy dusted crumbs from her hands over the sink. "As Mom always says, don't borrow trouble."

"What does that even mean?"

"Basically, you never know what life is going to serve up to you, so don't worry about it."

Shelly wrinkled her nose. "Speaking of trouble, did you know the sink in my room is leaking? I put a bucket under it this morning."

"That's my job now," Ivy said. It was probably minor. "I'll look at it later."

Shelly quirked a grin. "If I can teach yoga, I'm sure I can still manage a pipe wrench in my condition. Maybe the kiddo will learn through osmosis. We could use another hand around here."

"You're on. If it's not one room, it's another. At least it didn't happen with a guest."

Ivy could barely keep up with repairs, but they would manage. They always did. She hoisted the tray and carried it to the dining room, where they served breakfast every morning. Shelly followed with the coffee creamer and honey.

The room was beginning to fill with more spa guests, and Ivy and Poppy welcomed them with lighter fare than usual. Along with a selection of ruby red grapefruit harvested from trees on the property, they served homemade yogurt and granola. Mitch had delivered muffins made from a heart-healthy recipe without white flour or sugar. He had promised to include healthier options all week. They were so good that Ivy decided to keep that option on the breakfast menu after spa week.

Gayle and Piper arrived toward the end of breakfast, and Ivy seated them. "How did you sleep after your ordeal last night?"

Piper grinned. "We uncorked the wine I'd brought for Gayle, and after one glass, I was out."

"Until Noah called this morning to see how she was doing," Gayle added. "He's going to meet us in the village after our massages."

Piper's cheeks flushed pink. "Except for my near-crash landing, I think we're going to have a great time this week."

"I'm happy to hear that." Ivy gave them a schedule of the week's events. "We'll introduce everyone at the afternoon mixer. It's a social hour we host before everyone departs for dinner in town."

"These muffins are fabulous," Gayle said. "We're foodies, so we have to explore the town and find some great restaurants."

Ivy was pleased to hear that. "I've arranged spa selections at several restaurants. The Coral Cafe is a fun, casual place on the beach while Beaches is fine dining with an ocean view. The Starfish Cafe also has spectacular views from a hillside garden."

"I was so relieved to learn this wasn't one of those starve-yourself bootcamps," Gayle said. "We just wanted to relax with a healthy holiday by the beach—and a good dose of pampering."

They chatted a little more about the week ahead. Afterward, Ivy cleared the dining area with Shelly and Poppy.

"Piper is lucky to be here," Shelly said as she picked up the empty muffin basket. "I wish we'd found some casino treasure on the beach. I would have to stumble over some worthless piece of junk, right?"

"At least there's a good story behind it," Ivy said. "I wonder how the Ericksons were involved in all that?"

"Maybe that's how they got good alcohol and wine," Poppy suggested. "How much bathtub gin could you drink? Besides, I heard that stuff was lethal."

"I once read that you could buy wine with a doctor's prescription during Prohibition," Ivy said.

Shelly laughed. "Or get religion. The pastors and rabbis were still allowed to serve wine. Hell, I'd be there for that."

Ivy swatted her sister. "That's what they were trying to avoid, silly."

"Oops." Shelly clamped a hand over her mouth, but they all laughed. "Hey, why don't we ask Nan and Arthur? They run the historical society."

Poppy picked up a tray of dishes. "I've got some photos of our spa week kick-off to post on social media, so why don't you two go to Antique Times? I'll be here to check in guests if they arrive early."

After washing dishes, Ivy and Shelly called ahead and then strolled into the village in the morning sunshine to see Arthur. The door to the antique shop stood open.

As they stepped inside Antique Times, the scent of old wood and Nan's vanilla potpourri wafted through the air. Ivy loved this antique shop; it was like stepping back to a time when everything was made by hand. She trailed her fingers over a dainty, polished inlaid desk and imagined writing letters on it.

A middle-aged man in a bright Hawaiian shirt looked up. Arthur had arranged the purchase of a vintage chandelier from Ivy when she and Shelly had first arrived and needed money for renovations. A smile creased his face. "Ladies, what a pleasure. Since you called, I've started research on the *Lucky Lady*."

"This might sound crazy," Ivy began. "But I feel there's a connection between that old barge and the Ericksons. The barge, the inn, and the airstrip—are like puzzle pieces. I wish we could fit them together."

"Nothing crazy about that," Arthur said, running a hand over his smooth head. "Tony Diamond supplied the carriage trade with fine spirits and entertainment during Prohibition. The *Lucky Lady* was a hot spot, and a lot of Hollywood celebrities made the trek here. People who worked the casino lived in town, and many people stayed overnight at the Seal Cove Inn. There wasn't much else here."

"Except the old inn," Shelly said. "Our Las Brisas del Mar."

Arthur leaned across the glass counter. "She was one of the first homes here and certainly the grandest. I've heard the Ericksons had stocked so much wine in the cellar that it lasted throughout Prohibition. Fourteen years."

Shelly's eyes widened. "That must have been quite a collection."

Arthur chucked. "Curated by a live-in preacher-sommelier-chauffeur who supposedly held services in the ballroom or by the pool in the summer."

"The original multi-hyphenate entrepreneur," Shelly remarked.

"His sermons frequently coincided with the cocktail hour before dinner." Arthur tapped his chin in thought. "I believe his name was Buckley."

"Bingo," Shelly cried. "We just read about him in one of Amelia's letters."

"That explains that bar and the wine racks on the lower level," Ivy said. "So tell us more about the *Lucky Lady*."

"I'll do better than that." Arthur's eyes twinkled. "I'll show you." He stepped around the counter and led them toward the rear storage area. "We don't get many calls for this type of antique. It's so large that I keep it back here." He swung open the door and gestured toward one wall.

"A roulette wheel," Shelly cried. "Look, it says *Lucky Lady* on it."

Arthur brushed dust from the wooden device. Behind it leaned a newer roulette table. "When she crashed on the shoreline, people rushed to see what they could find. Old casino relics surface here from time to time." He smoothed his hand over the old brass and polished wood. "I used to spin one like this in my misspent youth. One summer, I worked at the casino in Monte Carlo."

"Imagine the fortunes won and lost on the spin of that wheel," Ivy said. "That must have been some vessel."

"It was an old one, even then," Arthur said. "You were lucky to see it."

"Or unlucky." Shelly crossed her arms. "It sliced my toe, so this better be worth it."

"It's a good story, I promise." Arthur cleaned his glasses on his shirttail as he spoke. "Today, some people call the *Lucky Lady* a ghost ship, but she was just an old gambling barge, similar to the one that crashed against the rocks on Coronado Island."

"Bennett mentioned that," Ivy said.

"That one is also visible sporadically, usually when an El Niño weather effect displaces more sand than the usual low tide."

Ivy shivered. "Any ghosts around there?"

"Not that I've heard of," Arthur replied.

Before Shelly could go off on that favorite topic of hers, Ivy said, "I'd never heard of gambling ships. Were they legal?"

"Not unless they were three miles or more off the coastline. Last I checked, the law is twelve nautical miles. That's almost fourteen miles, so you don't see small gambling barges anymore. It's no longer economically feasible to transport people that far."

Shelly perched on a nearby stool. "But it was then?"

Arthur chuckled and adjusted his glasses. "During prohibition in the 1920s, a few unsavory sorts acquired old barges and ships and anchored them just outside the three-mile marker. Of course, that law was changed because of these vessels of iniquity. Ships of sin, as they were known."

"That's what Piper was talking about," Ivy said.

"Piper?"

"The young pilot who had an emergency landing on the old airfield last night."

"I heard about that rescue this morning at Java Beach," Arthur said. "That must have been quite a landing."

Shelly leaned forward to inspect the old roulette wheel,

which was made of wood. "Tell us more about the *Lucky Lady*. Spill it all, Arthur."

"With pleasure," Arthur said, touching the old device. "The *Lucky Lady* had been a salvage ship, and she'd been put out to a watery pasture on retirement. The new owner—a rather shady, larger-than-life fellow who went by the name of Tony Diamond—acquired her and towed her out past the three-mile limit. There, he could do whatever he wanted. Tony outfitted her with a casino, featured nightly entertainment, served alcohol, and offered lodging. All sorts of—shall we say, *indiscretions*—probably occurred."

Shelly let out a low whistle. "A real den of sin. Like Vegas, right?"

"This was before Las Vegas was built up," Arthur said. "Legend has it that the *Lucky Lady* drew a fast crowd from Los Angeles. Many top Hollywood actors were known to have frequented the bar and casino. At that time, Summer Beach was little more than a few houses on the beach. Tony ferried everyone out to the *Lucky Lady*. It was quite an operation."

"So he needed an airstrip," Ivy said.

"That's right." Arthur went on. "Tony Diamond put in the private airstrip. He called it the Seabreeze Shores Airfield." Arthur smiled, clearly relishing these historical details.

"Seabreeze...how about that?" Ivy laughed. "Still, that's a pretty fancy name for a stretch of pavement."

"When exactly was Prohibition?" Shelly asked.

"In the United States, it lasted from 1920 to 1933," Arthur replied. "Rumor has it that Tony Diamond imported the finest Canadian whisky and the strongest Mexican spirits. Likely he flew in the booze and smuggled it onto the *Lucky Lady*, where he could serve it and charge whatever the market would bear. Or brought it in by boat. Supposedly, some fine bottles bobbed to the shore after the *Lucky Lady* broke free and crashed in the storm."

"Was anyone hurt?" Ivy asked.

"According to an article I found, the storm occurred on a night they were closed, so there was a lean crew," Arthur said. "They made it to safety and fled the law, leaving behind all the fancy trappings. At the shop, Nan and I have received all manner of items from the vessel over the years. Besides this roulette wheel, we've had a blackjack table, a pair of barstools, and engraved glassware. They fetch a good price as part of Summer Beach history. We've had some old photos, too."

"I'd love to see them." Ivy shook her head, amazed at the story. "I don't understand why the remains of the craft were left on the beach. It's a real hazard."

"I agree," Arthur said. "But at the time, the country was in an economic depression, Tony Diamond had skipped the country, and clearing wreckage wasn't high on anyone's list. Once the *Lucky Lady* crossed the three-mile line, she was an illegal vessel, and no one would claim her. So there she rested in her watery grave."

Shelly drummed her fingers on the table. "Since it was a casino ship, was there any money onboard? There had to be a safe, and I bet the crew didn't have access. It might still be in the vessel."

"I doubt it," Arthur said. "Beachcombers picked apart the skeleton of the old vessel, salvaging whatever they could. But you're correct. In fact, it's a theory that resurfaces from time to time. Supposedly there was a vault with the house money and other treasures that people left behind. It's also rumored they had a safe full of silver dollars and gemstones smuggled in from South America."

"See, I knew it," Shelly said triumphantly. "Was anything like that ever found?"

Arthur shook his head. "Not to my knowledge."

"Guess if I'd found that, I wouldn't advertise it," Shelly said.

"What a fascinating story." Ivy thought about how

different Summer Beach was then. She wished she could have seen her old home in its heyday and met the people who'd passed through its doors. "I wonder what became of Tony Diamond?"

"Disappeared—many believe he fled to Mexico," Arthur said, lowering his voice. "Some say he lived out his years in South America, but as far as anyone knows, he left no heirs. After a number of years, his wife was granted a death certificate. Eventually the airstrip land was sold."

Ivy felt that odd prickling sensation on her neck again. "That land...it looked like kids have been playing there. What a great area that could be for families."

"And close to the inn," Shelly added with a quizzical look.

Ivy rubbed her neck, trying to banish the peculiar feeling. "I wonder if the Erickson's ever visited the *Lucky Lady?*"

"I doubt it was their kind of scene," Shelly said. "Weren't they pretty conservative?"

"I wouldn't be so sure," Arthur said. "The *Lucky Lady* was lavishly decorated and drew all sorts of people. Tony Diamond had first-rate entertainment there."

Shelly slid a look toward Ivy. "Do you think there might be a connection?"

"I can't imagine what it would be." Ivy shivered. *Maybe it was only a draft.* "Like you said, it probably wasn't their style."

"Or maybe they hit the gambling tables on the *Lucky Lady*," Shelly said, laughing. "And brought all their friends. Imagine, this might have been Amelia's lucky roulette table."

"It's possible," Arthur said. "They were young then."

Ivy thanked Arthur, and before they left, Shelly snapped a few photos of the roulette wheel to use in one of her videos chronicling life in Summer Beach for her blog and video channel.

During their walk back to the inn, Shelly stopped as they turned onto the street that led to the beach in front of the inn. "Hold up a minute," she said, cradling her belly.

When Ivy saw the concern on Shelly's face, her senses went on alert. "Is something wrong?"

A moment later, Shelly breathed out. "The kiddo is shifting, I guess. I get a strange feeling when that happens." She rubbed her back. "I can't exactly explain it."

Ivy watched her sister. "Anything that seems out of the ordinary you should talk to your doctor about. When is your next appointment?"

"Next week, but I can call her office."

Ivy tried not to frown, but she was worried. "Maybe you should do that."

"Since I'm a geriatric mother, right?"

"You should take care of yourself at any age. Look at Mom; she's sailing the high seas right now."

A wistful look crossed Shelly's face. "I wish I could see her. I didn't realize how much I would miss her. But I know this is their dream."

They started off again, and Ivy kept a close eye on Shelly.

When they returned to the inn, Poppy met them in the foyer. "What did you find out about that rusty old menace on the beach?"

"A lot." As Ivy conveyed the story, Poppy's eyes brightened.

"A local organization called this morning about renting the ballroom for a fundraiser," Poppy said. "They're not sure what kind of event yet. Maybe Arthur would let us borrow the roulette wheel for a casino night or work out a good deal on it."

An idea sparked in Ivy's mind. "We could use it for our Roaring Twenties party this week. I'll ask him about that. Speaking of events, have the spa guests arrived?"

Poppy closed the registration book. "Everyone is here. The kickoff is in an hour. Is there anything else you need for me to do?"

"Make sure everyone has a copy of the week's agenda," Ivy replied. "Mitch is sending his organic sugar-free cookies to go with our selection of herbal teas. Almond-butter cookies with honey and raisin bars made with applesauce. Nature's sugar."

As Ivy made her way to her apartment over the garage, she couldn't help but feel she was missing something. She didn't even know what she might be looking for; it was just a feeling she had—as if fate had set a chain of events in motion.

As she climbed the stairs, a thought occurred to her. *Amelia's letters.* Perhaps there was more information in them.

It couldn't hurt to have another look at the box of correspondence.

Ivy opened the door and stood in the entry, already thinking about what she could do to this apartment to give Bennett more room. Or could they add a room as Shelly and Mitch were doing? Yet that would cost money she could use elsewhere in the inn for repairs.

Ivy walked through the unit, considering all options. Even though she'd drawn a line, unless she could make Bennett more comfortable here, she might have to consider his offer.

10

*T*he spa week guests sat on Adirondack chairs gathered around a larger firepit that Bennett and Mitch had built last summer on the sandy portion of the property near the beach. The flickering orange flames were just enough to chase the chill from the air as the sun inched toward the horizon, bathing the setting in golden hues. The ocean was a rich aquamarine-blue today, gently caressing the shoreline. Ivy thought she couldn't have painted a more relaxing picture.

This was the perfect beginning for their guests.

"Welcome to a week of relaxation and rejuvenation," she began. "I hope you've all had a chance to glance at the activities ahead."

"I'll be up for yoga tomorrow," Gayle said, nodding to Shelly.

"That's great. Poppy and I will alternate," Shelly said. "I'm pacing myself for obvious reasons."

As they went around the small circle, the women talked about what they were looking forward to and what they wanted to do in Summer Beach.

"Not wake up to an alarm clock," one woman said. "And read some good books on a beach lounger."

"Come visit me at Pages Bookshop on the lower level," Paige said, nodding toward her. "I have a nice selection set aside, from wellness to fictional escapes."

Another woman added, "I'll do that. I need to make some changes in my life, and I want to approach those decisions with a calm mind."

A few women around the fire nodded in agreement. Ivy knew that feeling all too well. Most women of a certain age did, she suspected, although seismic shifts could happen at any time.

"I want to try painting," Piper said. "I've seen so much beauty from above, and I'm determined to capture that feeling on canvas."

"Work hard, play hard," Gayle added, touching her wine glass to Piper's.

"I can't wait to see what you have in mind." Ivy smiled at the younger woman. Piper had recovered from her ordeal, and she seemed intent on putting as much effort into a week of relaxation as she did into her flying.

The conversation shifted to the changes people wanted to make in their lives. Some were contemplating career changes while others were looking for relationships—or getting out of them. One woman was considering a long-distance move to be closer to her grown children.

At a lull in the conversation, Piper stretched her hand toward the fire. "I'm at a crossroads myself. I've been working with my family in the Bay area, but I want to do something on my own. If we each have a destiny, how do we discover what it is?"

"That's a good question," Ivy replied. "I don't know how to answer that, other than sometimes a new course of action just feels right. I had a flash of insight the first time I saw this house. It was awfully downtrodden; it needed saving, and so did I. A new life was calling to me—if I were brave enough to risk it."

A deep voice sounded behind her. "I hope you still think that was a good choice."

Ivy turned and smiled. "And this is my new husband, Bennett, who is also the mayor of Summer Beach."

Bennett reached down to kiss her cheek. "I just wanted to say hello to my lovely wife and welcome you all to the inn and the community. It's a great place to unwind."

From the corner of her eye, Ivy could see Piper watching them closely. She'd seen Noah walking her back to the inn before the afternoon gathering, their heads bent together as they talked and laughed. It seemed the two had immediately connected. Ivy hoped they wouldn't break each other's heart at the end of the week, yet sometimes life opened a pathway to change. She wondered if it might for Piper.

As others talked, Ivy thought about the old airfield. This was the property people were debating in town about what to do with. Not many wanted a discount mall. She could just imagine a different use for it. When she caught Piper's eye, she leaned forward. "You mentioned that your family is in real estate development. I was wondering what you might know about developing community spaces."

Piper inclined her head. "We've built some as part of larger communities. Why?"

Ivy went on to share thoughts about a Summer Beach park with her. It was a wild idea, but she just couldn't get it out of her mind. "People are already enjoying those old runways, but that space could be so much more."

On her walk this morning, she'd seen a couple of young moms with babies in strollers and toddlers on bikes, learning how to ride. Ivy thought of the parks in Boston where she'd often taken Misty and Sunny. There had been so much to do there. Summer Beach had the village and the beach and a few neighborhood parks, but it could use a larger one.

Piper seemed intrigued, and they went on to talk about the idea until the embers grew cool.

The evening around the firepit turned into a happy bonding experience for all the guests. By the time they separated to go to their rooms, many had already made plans to meet for yoga or the morning beach walk, or later for lunch or by the pool. Friendships were blossoming.

Maybe even love, Ivy thought, glancing at Piper as she walked ahead of her. She had gained even more insights into Piper this evening, and she admired the young woman who seemed determined to make her mark somewhere, though not necessarily at her father's company.

When Ivy returned to the apartment above the garage, Bennett was strumming his guitar on the balcony. Candles flickered beside the cushioned love seat that faced out to the sea. Shelly had filled this area with potted plants, creating a sweet retreat for them. Ivy glanced around. If Shelly could make use of the space on the balcony in such a clever way, surely Ivy could do the same inside. She eased next to Bennett.

As he made room for her on the small wicker sofa, he said, "Looks like an interesting group you have for the week."

"They are," Ivy said, reflecting on the conversation this evening. "I learned that Gayle is an angel investor. She's helped fund several prominent startups in Silicon Valley. Another woman is a top interior designer in Beverly Hills, and her friend decided to pursue a lifelong dream of acting. She's made a career of playing grandmothers on television shows, and she's in two series."

"They sound creative. I'm sure they found you interesting as well." While he listened, he strummed a few chords.

Ivy shrugged off the compliment, although she was proud of what she'd achieved here at the inn. "There is another woman who is trying to decide what to do with her life once her children leave for college. You should have heard the suggestions."

"And how is Piper?"

"She's doing much better now." Ivy slipped off her shoes and tucked a leg under her. "We had a fascinating conversation about the old airfield."

Bennett stopped strumming. "You did?"

Ivy nodded. "It's so close to this neighborhood and is within walking distance to the village. I think it has possibilities for community use. Like a park."

"If only the city had the money." He put down his guitar and slipped his arms around her.

Ivy warmed to his touch. "I'm glad you came by and met our guests, if for no other reason than to let the ladies know this handsome hunk wandering around the inn is my personal property."

Bennett threw his head back and laughed. "If I said something like that, you'd object."

"I most certainly would," she said, nudging him. "We each have free will, and I respect you."

His eyes sparkled in the candlelight. "Speaking of free will, I will if you will."

"You're teasing me now," she said, smiling at him. Despite the early bumps and potholes in their relationship, Ivy was growing to love Bennett more every day. Learning to live together as adults set in their habits was a challenge, and Ivy knew they would both have to work at it.

Bennett rubbed her shoulders. "I have a pot of hot chocolate on the stove. I thought it sounded good on a cool night like this. We can wrap ourselves in blankets, listen to the ocean, and watch the stars."

"A man who can read my mind. Need some help?"

"Nope." Bennett wrapped a blanket around her. "I'll be right back."

Ivy watched him walk away. The little things Bennett did

showed how much he cared. Anticipating how she might feel at the end of a long day, preparing little treats, and making the ordinary seem special. His consideration of her and his generosity of spirit still surprised her.

Or was he about to spring something on her? She chuckled to herself. *Relax*, she told herself. Bennett wasn't like her first husband.

After spending so many years with Jeremy, Ivy was finally beginning to realize just how selfish her first husband had been. She had been the giver in the relationship, attending to his every need in the house. Now, being on the receiving end was a little foreign to her, but it was a delicious new experience.

A few minutes later, Bennett reappeared with two mugs. "Just the way you like it...a dollop of whipped cream, a sprinkle of cinnamon, and a peppermint stir stick. Mitch taught me this one." Bennett grinned and sat down beside her, pulling the blanket around them. He tapped his mug to hers. "This is the life, isn't it?"

"I think life is as good as we decide it will be."

"Agreed. Barring any unforeseen tragedies. But look what can come afterward."

"We are fortunate."

Kissing him lightly, Ivy thought about the conversation around the fire pit. "I wonder...why is it that once you've chased the proverbial wolf from your door, it's easy to forget that the lull in between is the time you should be happy. Instead, it seems we find things to complain about—as if we feel guilty for having a patch of the good life." She paused to sip her hot chocolate.

"Wise thoughts," Bennett said. "I've found that gratitude can help put everything into perspective."

"So, what are you grateful for?" Deciding to tease him a little, she smiled up at him through her lashes. "Besides the obvious, which is me."

Bennett threw his head back and laughed. "I'm very grateful we found each other again. Even though we don't always agree. I believe love wins in the end."

"So do I." Ivy leaned into him and thought about the few pages she'd read in her book this morning. "Life is a series of chapters, and one is not necessarily going to be the same as the one that came before."

Bennett hugged her close to him. "Do you forgive me for not thinking about how you might feel about leaving the inn? I was caught up in the idea of providing a home for you."

"Of course, I do. And maybe I'm a little obstinate sometimes."

Bennett chuckled. "A little?"

She swatted him playfully. "Watch it."

"That's your strong suit. Just one of the many, many things I love about you."

"Why do I feel like you're buttering me up?"

Bennett raised his gaze to the night sky. "I don't know about this living together idea. You're figuring out all my angles."

Ivy narrowed her eyes. "I knew you were up to something with candles and hot chocolate."

"That's called being romantic."

"And I love it." Ivy grinned at him. "So, what's on your mind?"

"Remember that fancy honeymoon we've talked about? Although I can't offer Paris right now, how would you feel about a drive up the coast after your spa week? I thought you might need a break then, and Carmel and Monterrey are beautiful. It wouldn't take you away from Shelly for very long. The drive is a day each way, so no more than a week, or maybe ten days if you want to visit San Francisco or the wine country while we're that far north."

The trip sounded wonderful, and Ivy was tempted, but she shook her head. "I really want to be here for Shelly. Especially since our parents are away." They'd discussed taking short weekend trips, but it was difficult to find the right time to go.

"You said she still has time."

She shifted, feeling slightly irritated. How could he not realize being there for Shelly was so important to her? "True, but you want me to leave while Shelly is still dealing with a torn-apart house? I'd have to take up a hammer before packing for a trip."

"I'm working on that. I promise it will be complete before our trip."

"I'd appreciate that." She pressed her lips together.

Bennett was quiet for a moment. "I've considered all this. Next week would be a good time to get away. Before the baby and the summer rush. Once the baby arrives, Shelly will need you even more. As much time as you need to spend with her then, I'll understand."

Ivy inclined her head. She supposed he had thought this through after all. "That sounds awfully logical."

"I want you to be there for her," Bennett insisted. "Just as I plan to support Mitch. He doesn't have anyone else, and welcoming a new life into the family is a rare, beautiful event."

Ivy felt torn. She and Bennett could benefit from a special trip to honor their marriage. Shelly and Mitch still talked about how wonderful their honeymoon had been. Bennett should have that with her. Shelly needed her as well, but maybe not for every minute of her pregnancy. The baby would arrive when it was ready, and it wasn't ready quite yet.

"I want us to do that," Ivy said, growing more tempted. "I'm a little concerned about the timing, but I promise to think about it."

"That's all I ask." After putting his hot chocolate aside, he picked up his guitar and strummed it.

If Bennett was disappointed, he hid it well. Still, Ivy could sense it in the set of his shoulders, even if he was handling this like an adult.

Like the man she respected and admired.

And loved very much.

At that moment, Ivy realized she still had much to learn. How could she be available for everyone else and put her marriage first, too? She sipped her hot chocolate as she listened to Bennett's soft tune and thought about the trajectory of her life.

In Boston, she'd spent most of her time looking after the girls and the house and Jeremy. He hadn't wanted her to work outside the home, and now she understood why. When he wanted his wife, she was there waiting for him.

Now, as an innkeeper, strangers were often in line before her husband. Ivy wondered how other women blended their family, husband, and career. What was that phrase about women having it all, just not all at once? That was assuming a woman had a choice in the matter. In her case, she'd be better off taking juggling lessons.

And Shelly wondered why Ivy lived by her lists. Her sister would soon find out.

As she leaned her head back against the loveseat, enjoying Bennett's music, she wondered how she could make her life work. Somehow, it seemed easier when she was younger.

Maybe she was set in her ways after all.

THE NEXT MORNING after leading the beach walk, serving breakfast, and cleaning up afterward, Ivy welcomed a local author who was giving a talk downstairs about wellness and healthy living. Paige had ordered books and the author would sign them for guests.

As Shelly hung a dishtowel to dry, she asked, "Are you going downstairs to listen to the presentation?"

"Not this time. I have work to do."

Shelly twisted her mouth to one side. "Mitch wants to talk, so I thought I should see him."

"How's the progress on the addition going?"

"I hope that's what he wants to talk about." She gazed out the kitchen window.

Ivy heard the loneliness in her sister's voice. "You two miss each other."

"Even though we see each other every day, it's not the same as sleeping and waking together. But I needed rest."

"And you still do." Yet, Ivy understood the need for the emotional intimacy that came from being together. Shelly needed that as much as she needed sleep.

"I'll look after the spa guests," Poppy said. "They're off to the Coral Cafe for lunch, so they'll be gone at least a couple of hours. I can go with them."

"You don't mind if I delegate that to you?" Ivy asked.

"I wish you would." Poppy raised her palms and spoke earnestly. "For example, not all three of us need to make breakfast and clean the kitchen every day. We can take turns in teams of two. Sunny has time after class, even though it would be an hour later. Dirty dishes can wait a little while, and that gives you and Shelly time to do other things on your off days. And it gives me chunks of time to do more marketing for the inn and for my other clients."

"Even with the mountain of dishes we always have?"

"I'm used to it," Poppy replied with a resigned smile.

Ivy gazed at Poppy with admiration and wondered why she hadn't thought of that herself. Yet, her mind was always stuffed with myriad details about managing the inn and making repairs. "That's genius. I knew I should've listened more in college."

"I didn't learn that there," Poppy said, laughing. "I've been thinking about ways we could be more efficient, especially with the new baby coming and Shelly taking time off. We'll have to shift it a little then."

"Let's create a schedule and try this." Ivy was impressed. This might be the answer she was looking for.

Poppy reached into her pocket and drew out a piece of paper. "Already done."

After deciding on their new schedule, Ivy carried her laptop into the wood-paneled library. She opened her computer and began typing an email to her parents. While they had a hand-held radio for emergencies at sea, they didn't carry a satellite phone as they were so expensive to use. They would be in port soon enough, she imagined. They would find a cafe or hotel lobby to check their email before making calls to the kids.

Hi Mom and Dad, I hope you're having a great time. I don't want you to worry, and Shelly is in good health, but she's a little overwhelmed at the prospect of motherhood so close at hand. I'm trying my best to reassure her, and everyone here is looking out for her, but could you try to check in more? It would mean a lot to her. I guess there's some comfort only a parent can offer.

Ivy chewed her lip, feeling a little guilty about asking her parents to do this while they were on their dream holiday. Carlotta and Sterling were checking in, but she sensed Shelly needed more support right now. After hovering a finger over the send button, she finally tapped it and sent the email.

If Poppy could find a way to manage life more efficiently and effectively, Ivy could, too. Maybe she didn't have to be on call for everyone all the time.

That was much easier to say than do, she realized.

Ivy glanced at an antique clock ticking on a bookshelf. With Poppy's new plan, she still had time to spare. There on the bookshelf, the box of Amelia's letters seemed to call to her again. Eager to discover if she could find out more from them, Ivy rose to retrieve the carton. She wasn't sure what she was looking for, but she knew it was there.

Ivy swept a hand over her forehead. That crazy thought made no sense to her, but she still felt compelled. Chuckling at herself, she reached inside for another stack of letters. The answer was there; she just didn't know the question yet.

11

"Would you hand me that wrench?" Bennett asked his brother-in-law.

"Sure," Dave replied, passing the tool over the bicycle frame.

Bennett had arrived at his sister's home in Summer Beach early this morning as he'd arranged with Dave. He'd forgone his usual sunrise run, telling Ivy that Dave needed help with a project. After smuggling the tandem bike here the other day, he'd collected all the materials he needed to repair it.

Dave's man-cave garage was equipped with every sort of tool they'd need. From the black-and-white checkerboard floor to the neon car signs on the wall, the garage was the perfect place to work on this surprise for Ivy. The scent of motor oil and pancakes filled the air. Wearing an old T-shirt and faded jeans, Bennett felt like he was sixteen again, working in his father's garage. Even the music was the same; Dave had turned on classic tunes they'd all grown up with.

Saturday mornings were his sister Kendra's specialty breakfast day—today, it was chocolate chip pancakes. His nephew was polishing off a second stack. Dave and his son were both tall with healthy appetites. Logan would likely be as muscular as his father.

While Bennett worked on the tandem bike, he smiled at the thought. "Did we ever eat like Logan? That kid is bottomless."

"I have a vague, blissful recollection of that," Dave said, patting his stomach. "Now it all goes right here."

"Those were good pancakes, though. She must have our mom's recipe."

Bennett tightened the wheel sprockets before stepping back to admire their handiwork. The old bicycle-built-for-two had new seats, tires, and gears. He'd added a wicker basket on the front that he thought Ivy would like. They had cleaned the frame, but it was clearly vintage.

"This was a real find," Dave said. "When Kendra sees it finished, she's going to want one, too."

"The upside is that you can eat more pancakes."

Dave scraped his scruffy beard. "That's an idea."

Bennett enjoyed spending time with his brother-in-law, who liked to tinker in the garage as much as he did. "Think we should paint this?"

"See what Ivy thinks. The vintage look is popular, especially at the beach. Paint would provide more protection, though."

"I'll give it to her first. She can choose the color she likes."

Dave grinned at that. "She's got you trained."

Bennett dusted his hands on his jeans and shook his head. "I wish I could get some training in mind reading."

"Oh, that's an advanced skill," Dave said. "Takes years to develop."

Kendra appeared at the kitchen door to the garage. "You know I can hear you." She slapped a large wooden spoon in her hand.

The two men laughed. Kendra was a scientist, and her

powers of observation were keen. Nothing got past her. Growing up, Bennett had tried.

She smiled. "But yes, I would like a bike like that. Let's look for one."

After cleaning the bike and airing the tires, Bennett and Kendra took it for a spin around the block. It was even more fun than Bennett had imagined. "Think Ivy will like it?" he asked his sister.

As she got off, her eyes were sparkling with laughter. "If she doesn't, we'll take it."

Bennett felt good about that. If Kendra enjoyed the tandem bike that much, chances were good that Ivy would, too. Still, he would like to have it painted for her. *Blue or green? Maybe red.* He wondered how he could find out what color she'd like.

Bennett drew a hand over the stubble on his unshaven face. "Can I park it here until I find the right time to give it to her?"

"You bet," Kendra said, hugging him.

Glancing at Dave's clock in the garage, Bennett saw he had just enough time to get cleaned up before meeting Boz.

Dave walked toward them, wiping his hands on a rag. "We're still on for later today?"

Shaking Dave's hand, he said, "You bet. I'll see you after lunch. Sure appreciate all you're doing for me this weekend."

Dave waved off his comment. "I like hanging with the guys."

"It gets him out of the house," Kendra said. "If Logan were a little older, I'd send him, too."

"Soon," Bennett said. Before he left, he went into the house to wash up and change into clean clothes for lunch—and say goodbye to his nephew.

. . .

As BENNETT PARKED his SUV near the Coral Cafe, his phone beeped. Looking down, he saw a message from his brother-in-law and one from his friend Axe Woodson. He breathed out with relief; his plan was unfolding well.

Bennett hurried from his vehicle and greeted Marina Moore, the proprietor and one of Ivy's good friends, at the entrance to the open-air patio.

The sun was out, and the weather was mild. Tall heaters positioned by the table would take off the chill of the evening air, but they weren't necessary at lunch. In the last couple of days, ocean breezes had ushered in warmer weather, so spring was officially underway.

"How's business?" he asked.

"Doing well," Marina replied. Wearing a beach print chef's jacket, she greeted him with a warm smile. "Are you here for a late breakfast or an early lunch?"

"The latter." Bennett had been up early getting supplies at Nailed It.

"Are you meeting anyone here today?"

Bennett lifted his chin toward a table where a man with a thick head of silver hair and a well-developed physique sat. "That would be Boz. I'll see myself over. Have any specials today?"

"Crabcakes on butter lettuce with a mandarin orange sauce. It's my grandmother's special recipe."

"Sold. Bring us an order to start with."

Bennett made his way toward Boz. Every couple of weeks, they met for lunch on the weekend to catch up on city business. As head of the planning department, Boz had one of the most demanding positions, especially at this time of year when homeowners began planning projects they wanted to complete before the summer season. He and Boz were friends, too, having worked together for years.

Today, he'd asked Boz to meet him for an early lunch. Bennett had a project he wanted to get started on.

Bennett greeted Boz and sat down. "How is your triathlon training going?"

"Great. A few aches here and there, but nothing I can't push through. You should join me."

"Maybe next year."

Boz grinned. "I've heard that promise before."

"And someday, I'll make good on it. Really," he added. "Goals—you have to have them."

The two men talked about Boz's plans and other events going on in the community. A few minutes later, Marina brought their appetizer course and took their order for lunch. Bennett placed a take-out order for several sandwiches. After she left, the two men dug into the crabcakes.

"These are delicious," Bennett told Marina when she passed by again. He knew she and her grandmother had developed all the recipes for the cafe.

As Marina sailed by, Boz gave her a thumbs-up, too, clearly enjoying the dish. "Summer Beach was lucky to get her and this new restaurant. We need to attract more unique places like this—not the chain restaurants that are just like everywhere else."

"That's been the plan all along." Bennett turned the conversation to the topic of the discount shopping mall on the old airstrip. Aaron had applied for a zoning change and had recently provided an impact study.

"How does Aaron's report look to you?" he asked.

Boz ran a hand along his chin. "It's professionally done, of course, and filled with positive economic impacts. Sales tax and property tax proceeds, mostly." He hesitated.

Bennett helped himself to another crabcake. "I sense a problem, though."

"Looking long-term, that project will cost the city in terms of increased infrastructure spend. Roads, traffic signals, lights, increased police patrol. The bridge will have to be widened to handle the amount of traffic, and that's costly."

"The village shopkeepers are worried about the impact, too," Bennett said. "On the other hand, a shopping center like that would bring more people into Summer Beach. That might be good for them. And people have to eat somewhere."

"I don't think so." Boz helped himself to the remainder of the order. "Aaron is proposing a food court on the property with quite a few national pizza and hamburger chains. My team has done its own impact study, and we came up with far different results. Beyond the financial aspects, we have to think about community needs. While tourism helps support shops, we should consider what Summer Beach needs in the long term. That project will change Summer Beach, and not necessarily for the better."

Bennett looked out over the ocean. "Now that more people are running online businesses and working from home, we've had more younger families moving to Summer Beach. They like the relaxed lifestyle and the small schools."

"So, what's your point about the airfield?"

"Other communities have sprawling designer outlet centers," Bennett replied. "Let them do that. Summer Beach is different. We have the farmers market, the new outdoor amphitheater, and the annual art show on the grounds of the Seabreeze Inn. Summer Beach is unique. Let's keep it that way."

"One of the airfield heirs is getting antsy to sell." Boz reached for another napkin. "If they can't get a zoning change, we could be looking at another lawsuit."

Bennett shrugged off that concern. The risk was low, in his opinion. "Not everyone gets their way," he said. "Their father had plans to renovate the airfield years ago when he bought it. I understand that's no longer economically feasible or desirable, but we need to look at different plans that would benefit our residents." He thought about what Ivy had said. Kids were already using the runway for biking and skating.

Boz nodded. "If the heirs had an ounce of their father's

drive and intelligence, they'd propose a project of their own. I've heard most of them don't need the money. They could buy out the instigator if they had to."

They continued talking over their main course about a range of uses for the airstrip, from a playground as Ivy had suggested to live-work uses. Some would take longer and cost more than others to implement. But the old airstrip had been an eyesore for a long time, and as the community grew, more services would be needed over time.

After they finished lunch, Bennett leaned back and laced his fingers behind his neck. Something Ivy had said about the property last night really stuck in his mind. So far, he'd managed to work on the tandem bike he'd bought for her without her knowledge. "What if the city sought donations to buy the property?"

"For what purpose?"

"A park or community center. A place for families to go—besides the beach. Maybe some local businesses, too."

Boz clasped his hand on the table and nodded. "The question is always how we manage to pay for that."

Behind them, laughter broke out at a table, and Bennett turned around. It was Poppy and the guests from the inn he'd met last night—Piper and Gayle—along with a couple of newcomers. He and Boz had been so immersed in conversation that he hadn't noticed when they'd been seated. They already had what looked like Marina's passionfruit lemonade.

"Ladies, you've chosen a great place for lunch."

"Marina has a special spa menu for us," Poppy said. "With all homegrown vegetables from her sister's garden."

Bennett noticed that Piper was sitting closest to them. She swung a thoughtful gaze between him and Boz. Had she been listening to their conversation? Not that it mattered; Bennett prided himself on being transparent with the public.

While the other women talked, Piper leaned over. "You're looking at plans to develop the old airfield?"

"That's right," Bennett replied.

"Ivy mentioned that, too. Mind if I talk to you later?"

"You'll find me at the inn," Bennett replied. "Ivy and I live in the unit above the garages."

Piper's mouth curved into a small grin. "That's cool. I'll find you." She turned back to the group.

Bennett was intrigued and wondered what Piper could add to the conversation. As mayor, he'd learned to be open to ideas wherever they came from.

Just as Bennett reached for his wallet, his phone buzzed. He paused, checked a message from Forrest, and smiled. "I've got a project this afternoon. Are you free?"

"That depends."

Bennett told him about his plan. "But don't tell Ivy or Shelly if you see them."

"Count me in," Boz said. "I'm happy to lend a hand. Meet you there in half an hour."

Bennett drew a hand over his jawline. "I was hoping you'd say that."

12

*A*s Ivy was setting up the music room for the afternoon, Piper poked her head in the doorway.

Fidgeting with a short curl, Piper asked, "Do you have time to talk about your idea to transform the airfield into a park?"

"Sure." Ivy placed a stack of cocktail napkins on the serving table. She was intrigued by Piper's question, and the younger woman seemed excited. "I wouldn't mind a second cup of coffee. Let's go into the dining room." Ivy kept coffee there for guests throughout the day.

"How was your lunch at the Coral Cafe?"

"Delicious. Gayle and most of the others stayed in the village."

After they settled at a table covered in a blue-checked tablecloth, Piper began, "I've been thinking about our conversation by the firepit. My dream has been to find a project that I could manage. I love San Francisco, but I really love the beach and the slower pace of small towns." She paused. "I'm thinking of staying here."

"Summer Beach is a wonderful community, but it's very different from a big city." Stirring vanilla creamer into her coffee, Ivy smiled at Piper's enthusiasm. "People are interested in everyone else's business. Could you deal with that?"

"I wouldn't mind. Even though everyone knows my family, I often feel lost in the city. People want more—more money, faster cars, bigger houses. I want to make a difference in people's lives. Does that sound crazy?"

"Not at all. And you think you could do it here?" Ivy imagined Noah had something to do this, too. In a positive way, she hoped.

"I'm pretty sure of it. I believe I landed on that airstrip for a reason."

"Noah?"

Piper nodded, and her cheeks colored slightly. "More than that, though. You're an artist; can you tell me what you would envision for that land?"

Ivy closed her eyes. "I can just imagine it in my mind, and I can see people in the community involved in it, too." She opened her eyes and told Piper about the two women she'd seen pushing strollers. "Older children could use a place to skate and ride their bikes. You'd want a variety of uses for people of different ages. Like a community garden, for example. Shelly could oversee that."

Piper pulled out her phone and began tapping notes on it. "Keep talking. I want to get this down."

As Ivy sipped her coffee, she painted a vision for Piper. "I'm not an architect, but I know what people like to do. Maybe you'd like to speak to Shelly and Poppy, and others in Summer Beach."

"I sure will." Piper seemed electrified over the idea.

"There's just one problem." Ivy leaned across the table. "You'd have to get the zoning changed for this."

"Could you help with that?"

Ivy shook her head. "It took a natural disaster for me to get the zoning on this old house changed to allow me to run an inn. Even if Bennett supports this, you'll need the city council's approval. I had a very hard time convincing a couple of old-timers on the council. I don't think they like out-of-towners."

"So, what should I do?"

"Talk to Bennett and Boz, and work on your plan."

"I plan to. I saw them briefly at lunch today."

Ivy wanted to encourage her, but she also needed to be realistic. "I'll help you any way I can. Still, it's going to be a tough pitch."

After Piper left, Ivy drained her coffee. If there was a chance to create a wonderful space for the community, everyone should support it. But she knew better than that. She hoped Piper wouldn't be too disappointed.

Still, Ivy would do what she could. A community park would be a wonderful addition to Summer Beach. If only she could help bring it to fruition.

IN THE LIBRARY, Ivy smoothed out a letter that Amelia had written to Gustav and peered through her leopard-print reading glasses. Although the date on the envelope was smudged, the letters appeared to have been filed in sequence. As she was reading, the door opened, and Shelly strolled in.

Ivy glanced over the rim of her glasses. "You're already back from Java Beach?"

"Mitch was gone," Shelly said. "His assistant said he'd been called away for the afternoon. Probably about that catering job he's been trying to land. I'll talk to him later." When Shelly saw the correspondence Ivy was going through, she brightened. "Find anything else here?"

Ivy waved her hand across the stack of envelopes. "These read like a soap opera."

"How so?"

Ivy picked up a letter. "Listen to this letter from Amelia." She began to read.

Just when I thought this would be an uneventful week, we have had a fair amount of excitement. Mrs. Keller reported that one of our maids, Doris, formed an unlikely liaison with a young man, a croupier, from the Lucky Lady. As such fraternization with guests—and he is a guest, regardless of how he came to be one—is strictly verboten, according to Mrs. Keller, Doris was promptly dismissed and escorted from her quarters.

Ivy lowered the yellowed stationery.

"How spicy," Shelly said, laughing.

"Wait, there's more. Evidently, an investigation of the *Lucky Lady* was underway. Once that barge floated toward the shore, it was illegal, remember?"

Shelly shimmied her shoulders in anticipation. "This is getting good."

Ivy continued reading from Amelia's letter.

However, I was unaware of this development at the time. A pair of private investigators looking into the unfortunate demise of the Lucky Lady *arrived to inquire as to whether I knew Mr. Diamond. As I hesitated to answer—who were they?—Doris and the roulette croupier were seen fleeing across the garden. The investigators gave chase, and that is the last we saw any of them. I am sorry to report the end of an era, my darling. Such a pity; our collection might not see any additions for the foreseeable future. Mr. Buckley will be quite distressed.*

Ivy lowered the letter and removed her glasses.

"A croupier is a dealer," Shelly said, creasing her brow. "But what collection was Amelia talking about?"

Ivy tapped a finger on her chin in thought. "Remember what the lower level was used for?"

Shelly snapped her finger. "I'll bet she was talking about their wine and spirits collection. Buckley was their multi-hyphenate employee—he also served as their sommelier, curating their collection."

"A Jack-of-all-trades, so to speak." Chuckling, Ivy folded the letter and slid it back into its envelope. "That must have dampened the Erickson's entertainment for a while."

"Maybe not. Remember what Arthur told us? They probably had a healthy inventory. Imagine the parties they must have thrown here. It sounds like they were no strangers to the *Lucky Lady*."

"He did say it was a popular venue."

"I wonder what happened to Doris and her croupier?" Shelly rested her chin on her hand. "Did they abscond to Mexico with Tony Diamond? Or did her croupier abandon her at the border? Poor Doris. I'll bet she was a fool for love."

"You should be writing screenplays," Ivy said, laughing.

Shelly gazed around the library, her eyes animated with imagination. "I wonder how many love affairs this old house has seen?"

"Past or present?"

"Well, we know of at least two, don't we?" A mischievous smile tugged Shelly's lips.

"And maybe a third taking place right now."

"Piper and Noah?" When Ivy nodded, Shelly laughed. "I thought maybe you meant Imani and Clark, but they predated our inn era."

Ivy liked seeing Imani with their police chief, and she wondered if their relationship would advance. Imani was quite discreet about that. Whether that was for Jamir's sake or Chief Clarkson's position, she didn't know.

Ivy smiled at her sister. "If Charlie hears about Piper and Noah, he'll have a new project in no time."

"It's such a beautiful, romantic old home. Maybe that's why Amelia never left."

"Stop that," Ivy said, suddenly rising. "You and Paige can talk about your hocus-pocus stuff, but leave me out of it. And don't let guests hear you."

"Geez, you don't have to be so sensitive about the former owner." Grinning, Shelly stood and stretched with one hand on her belly. "I think she really likes us."

Ivy blew out a puff of air. The idea of Shelly's supposed ghost was ridiculous. Still, Amelia Erickson had lived a fascinating life. Ivy quickly changed the subject. "How's the baby doing?"

"Quiet today. But she just started kicking again."

"They're more active some times of the day than others," Ivy said as she put the letter away and turned to the bookshelf. She didn't really have time to pore through old letters. With a sigh, she placed the carton on the bookshelf, hesitating as Shelly's words dawned on her.

Resting her hand on the top of the box, she raised her head. Had she heard correctly?

Did Shelly just slip?

Slowly, Ivy swung around, her eyes wide and her lips parted in surprise. When she met Shelly's gaze, her sister cried out and slapped her hand over her mouth.

"I said that out loud, didn't I?"

Joy welled up inside of Ivy until she thought she would burst. *A little girl!* "You sure did." She opened her arms to Shelly, and her sister sank into her embrace.

"I promised Mitch I wouldn't tell anyone. We made a pact."

Ivy stroked Shelly's thick chestnut hair, which was falling from its messy bun. Her mind was already racing with ideas. "You didn't tell me on purpose," she quickly assured her. "It slipped out. I just happened to be listening."

Shelly turned up her palms. "What? You don't always listen to me?"

"Come on, Shells. You've hardly taken a breath between words since you learned to talk." Dissolving into tears and laughter, Ivy hugged her, and as she did, she could feel the baby—*her niece!*—kicking against Shelly's tummy.

"Now you've got her going," Shelly said. "Promise you won't tell Mitch, and you'll act surprised when she's born?"

"Cross my heart," Ivy said, making the sign of an X on her chest as they had when they were kids. "Mom and Dad will be so excited."

"You can't say anything to them," Shelly said. "Mom will tell everyone she knows and even those she doesn't."

"That's because she's so proud of you—she always has been. But what does it matter? They're floating somewhere in the South Pacific right now."

Shelly clasped her hands in front of her chest. "Phones still work there. Please, I promised Mitch. It was his idea. He didn't want everyone criticizing our choice of names or drowning the house in reams of pink."

"Oh, please." Ivy let out a huff. "Do you think he'd feel that way about blue if it were a boy?"

Shelly threw up her hands. "See what you're doing?"

"You're right. I won't say a word." As Ivy spoke, she tucked her arms behind her back and crossed her fingers. Old habits between sisters were hard to break.

Noticing her sister's actions, Shelly spun her around. "Promise me."

"Okay, I'll try not to say anything," Ivy said, pressing a finger to her lips. And this time, she meant it because she knew how important this was to her sister. "Imagine how happy Mom is going to be. But she'd be thrilled if you were having a boy, too. And it's not going to be much longer." She grabbed Shelly's hands and did a little happy dance with her.

Her sister twirled around and laughed. "I'm sort of glad. That was so hard to keep from you. I've almost told you several times, but it's better this way. Technically, I didn't break my promise to Mitch. I didn't slip on purpose. But who could blame my pregnancy brain? At least, that's my story."

Ivy squealed with glee again, and Shelly joined her, hopping and twirling in a circle.

Just then, the door opened, and Poppy stepped inside. "What's going on in here? We could hear you two screaming with laughter as soon as we walked inside." She looked at her aunts expectantly.

Ivy and Shelly traded a look and burst out laughing.

Neither one of them could speak, and Shelly was laughing so hard that she had to sit down.

"I can't stand it," Ivy said, wiping happy tears from her eyes. "We'll tell you later."

"Much, much later," Shelly added, catching her breath.

Gayle and Piper peeked over Poppy's shoulder.

"I definitely want what they're having," Gayle said, waggling her eyebrows.

That line from an old film sent Shelly into another fit of laughter while Ivy tried—and failed—to regain a sense of decorum.

Poppy threw up her hands and turned around. "Well, if you can't beat them... Who's up for Sea Breeze cocktails by the pool?"

Shelly thrust her hands into the air. "Woo-hoo! Let spa week begin!"

"It's a virgin concoction for you two...unless you've already started," Poppy said, giggling. To Gayle and Piper, she added, "My aunts really love what they do. Just one more reason to come to the Seabreeze Inn."

Casting a look back at them, Poppy closed the door behind her.

At last, Ivy managed to draw a ragged breath. She'd laughed so hard her sides ached—and it had been a long time since that had happened. *Too long.* "We can always count on Poppy. Should we tell her about you-know-who?"

Shelly squelched her question with such a withering look that they both burst out laughing again, and Shelly slid to the floor, howling.

"Another time," Ivy managed to say.

She might have promised Shelly secrecy, but that didn't stop plans from forming in her mind. Shelly had to agree to a baby shower now.

13

*I*vy nestled into a slipcovered vintage wingback chair in front of the fireplace in the apartment above the garage and pulled a chunky sweater around her blue-and-white striped Breton top she wore with jeans. The days and nights were growing warmer, so this was likely the last fire of the season.

Spring often arrived overnight in Southern California. The rain ceased, clouds cleared, and the sun shone longer. Tomorrow was forecast to be warm enough for sundresses. Ivy missed the marked change of seasons in Boston, but there was just enough of a shift here to satisfy her. If not, the mountains were nearby, and she could trudge through snow all she liked without having to deal with it so often.

Checking the time, Ivy wondered what was taking Bennett so long. After helping Dave this morning and then meeting Boz for lunch, he'd called to say he was meeting his friend Axe Woodson about a project and wouldn't be home until much later. Still, it was unlike him to be out so late—not that it was that late. Guests were still lounging by the firepit, enjoying the ocean breezes and the lull of the waves. They would sleep well tonight.

She tucked her legs under her and reviewed the schedule. Tomorrow, after the beach walk, yoga, and breakfast with smoothies, she would swing open the doors to her studio and host a *Plein Air* painting class on the patio. Next to pampering massages, that was one of the most requested activities on the survey Poppy had sent out when they were considering the week-long event.

At noon, Shelly would lead a trip to the village for Rosa's fish tacos, followed by shopping at vintage and thrift stores for the Roaring Twenties party later in the week. Then, in the warmth of the afternoon in their heated pool, Poppy would teach water aerobics.

Ivy had made reservations at the Starfish Cafe for the evening, followed by a movie night. They would project a film onto the side of the house, set up speakers, and serve popcorn. With patio heaters, blankets, and hot tea, everyone would be cozy.

Ivy's phone buzzed, and she glanced at a message from Bennett. *We're at Shelly's house. Can you bring her by? Mitch is here, and he'd like to see her.*

Bennett was probably counseling Mitch about the situation with Shelly. She tapped a reply. *Be right there.*

After dousing the fire in the fireplace, she made her way downstairs and toward the fire pit group. Shelly was there entertaining guests with stories of her life in New York as a flower designer to the rich and famous. Weddings and parties had been her life there for years, and she'd received the most outrageous requests.

Everyone was laughing, and Ivy was glad to see their guests enjoying themselves. She perched on the edge of the chair, waiting for Shelly to finish her story before she motioned to her.

"Excuse me," Shelly said, rising. "Looks like I'm needed elsewhere." As their guests said goodbye, Shelly fell into step with Ivy. "What's going on?"

"I think the guys are up to something. Bennett texted me and said to bring you to the house."

"Did he give you any hints?"

"Bennett is probably going to help him with the construction. Mitch misses you, sweetie." Ivy put her arm around Shelly. She hoped that Mitch wasn't being obstinate. Bennett might have asked them to come to put more pressure on Mitch. Either way, it was a step forward.

"And I miss him. That room addition was a good idea, but the execution has been lousy. I wish I could help."

"You're not getting on ladders and hefting equipment at this point. Or inhaling paint fumes." Shelly had just a few weeks to go, and Ivy was worried about anything that might harm her or the baby.

"Relax, I've got this." Shelly wrapped a shawl over her roomy, floral-printed denim overalls, which had become one of her pregnancy staples.

As they walked toward Ivy's car, they talked about their plans for the Roaring Twenties party this week. "Did you decide what you're going to wear?" Ivy asked.

Shelly winked. "When I went on a pre-shop for our thrift shopping expedition in town, I found the perfect dress. Wait until you see it. It's wild. Our guests are going to love exploring the shops I've organized."

Ivy laughed. "I don't doubt it."

"You're still wearing the vintage dress we found?"

"That's what I planned."

"Good. I have something for you, too. It's going to be a fabulous party." Shelly tossed her shoulder with attitude. "It's just as well that I'm staying at the inn now. I can party as late as I want."

They slid into the old Chevrolet convertible and started toward the beach cottage. When they arrived, Ivy saw that their brother's truck was there, too.

Shelly noticed it as well. "I wonder what Forrest is doing here?"

"We'll soon find out." They got out and walked toward the front door. Vintage beach reggae music was blaring through the walls.

"Sounds like a party," Ivy said.

"That's a good sign. It means Mitch has been working."

As they approached the cottage, the door flew open. Mitch turned around and yelled, "Hey, could someone turn that down? They're here."

"What's going on?" Shelly asked as she stepped inside.

Mitch swept his arm around her and pulled her inside. The guys were clearly up to something. Ivy followed, and Bennett met her with a broad grin. He leaned over and whispered, "You're going to like this."

Mitch led Shelly toward the rear of the house and stepped outside. Their brother Forrest and two of his sons stood to one side, along with Boz and Axe Woodson, who'd enlarged the guest cottage and patio for Marina's Coral Cafe. Even Jamir, Imani's son, and Bennett's brother-in-law, Dave, were there. All the men wore jeans and work gear, and the yard had been turned into a professional construction zone.

The aroma of fresh-cut wood filled the air, and Ivy stepped over wood shavings with Shelly.

"What kind of party is this?" Shelly asked.

Forrest stepped to one side, revealing a multicolor polka-dot ribbon draped around the structure and tied in a bow.

Mitch hugged his wife. "The baby's new room is almost ready. They all pitched in. Sort of like a barn-raising." The neat structure featured large windows that would capture the sea breezes.

"Without the livestock, I hope," Shelly said. "Because they'd destroy my garden."

Forrest chuckled. "We have that planned out for you, too. I

knew that was important to you. We're building some raised beds that will be easier to work in."

"I'd love that." Shelly gazed at Mitch and took his hands. "I can't believe you let them help you. I'm awfully proud of you for that."

"Ah, that," Mitch said, looking slightly embarrassed. His face reddened against his sun-streaked hair, and he wrapped his arms around Shelly.

Bennett chuckled. "That wasn't easy, which is why I called in the reinforcements. Forrest is our specialist in the father-hood department."

"I should think so, after five kids." Shelly turned to Mitch. "So, how did he persuade you?"

"Actually, I couldn't stop him," Mitch replied. "Forrest started talking about how much he loved his kids as soon as he saw them, even if they were a pain in the you-know-what from day one."

"Hey," Forrest said, protested, but his boys, Rocky and Reed, only laughed.

Mitch went on. "While my new brother-in-law here was talking, he started working on one end and Axe on the other. Then everyone else showed up. I know a good thing when I see it, so I gave in." He threw back his shoulders, looking pleased with his decision. "Right away, they knew how to fix my mistakes. *Mahalo*, guys." He held out his fist, and all the men bumped knuckles.

"Glad you got over that hard-headedness," Bennett said, giving Mitch a high five.

"Is that all it was?" Ivy said, lifting her chin toward Shelly.

The tips of Mitch's ears turned even redder, and he wrapped his arms around Shelly. "The truth is, I missed my wife. When you moved out, I realized I'd driven you away, but you were right to do it. You and the kiddo needed the rest, and I was being an idiot about it all."

"You're forgiven," Shelly said, kissing her husband.

Ivy's heart went out to her sister. This is what Shelly needed, and Mitch finally delivered with help from Bennett and their family and friends.

Shelly bounced on her toes with excitement. "Can we look inside?"

"Watch your step." Forrest went inside, leading the way as he ticked off the steps of the process. "The drywall is up, and we taped and floated. Next is texture, then paint. Once the floor goes down, you're ready to move in furniture. We can do most of that this weekend."

Shelly's joy was almost palpable. "I can't wait to have our life back."

"I just want my wife back," Mitch said, grinning. "It's been pretty miserable around here. And way too quiet."

"Not with that music blasting," Forrest said.

Shelly looked up at Mitch. "Will you stay at the inn tonight?"

"We're working late, and I have to open early."

When Shelly's smile slipped, Mitch quickly took her hands. "I'll try."

"We'll kick him out," Forrest said. "Man, you've got responsibilities now. Happy wife, happy life—tattoo that on your arm. Or Shelly will do it for you."

The guys laughed, and although they were kidding Mitch, he was taking it well and seemed to enjoy having the other men around. They were becoming a replacement for the family he desperately missed having.

Ivy smiled at their easy camaraderie. She was relieved that her brothers got along with Mitch—and Bennett, too, who was their contemporary. Mitch was like a younger kid brother to them. In fact, he was only a few years older than Rocky and Reed.

The Bay family was growing, and Ivy couldn't be happier than to be in the middle of it all again. The only ones missing were their parents. She knew they were enjoying a spectacular bucket-list trip, but she missed them. Ivy swallowed against a lump in her throat. No one else called her *mija* but her mother. Shelly must feel the same way.

Ivy hadn't heard from them since she'd sent her message, but she was trying not to worry. Every day she prayed for their safety, but if anyone could manage an arduous voyage, it was Carlotta and Sterling. They were experienced sailors and had been thorough with their plans.

Shelly pointed toward a corner. "That's where I want to place the crib. We'll need a fan overhead and shutters on the windows to help control the sunshine. A baby's tender skin can burn easily. Even through a window."

"Are we painting it pink or blue?" Forrest asked, grinning.

Shelly glanced at Mitch before jabbing her brother play-fully in the ribs. "Yellow."

It was all Ivy could do to keep from bursting out laughing. Not daring to look at Shelly, she quickly turned to inspect the closet. But a warm, happy feeling grew within her.

Mitch was excitedly pointing out everything to Shelly, who was beaming at the work that had been done.

As Ivy and Bennett strolled outside, he put his arm around her. "Happier now?"

"Thank you for rallying everyone." Ivy swept her arms around his neck. She was so grateful that he'd taken charge of the situation with Mitch. "This will make such a difference to Shelly and the baby. Did you see how much calmer she looked? Excited but more confident. Her frame of mind will be so important when the baby comes."

Bennett gazed thoughtfully at her. "And I hope this helps ease your mind. I worry about your worrying. We have to take care of ourselves, too."

"Now you sound like my spa week brochure."

"So, you know this is true."

Ivy nodded, acknowledging this. However, she found it easier to promote self-care than indulge in it herself. She rested her hand on Bennett's cheek. "It's hard to take time for yourself when you're running a business."

Bennett folded his fingers around her hand. "Did you know that a lot of smart bosses insist that their employees take their holidays? People return more focused and creative. That's just good business. Remember that when you say you don't have time for yourself."

"Then maybe I need a spa day after spa week," Ivy said playfully, grazing her lips against her husband's.

A lazy smile turned up the corners of his mouth. "Maybe I have something planned."

"You're full of surprises, aren't you?" Ivy loved the thought, but she hoped it wouldn't take her away from Shelly for too long.

Bennett stared at her for a long moment as a grin spread on his face. Finally, he kissed her forehead. "You'll see soon enough, Ivy Bay."

14

*I*vy crossed the ballroom, checking the final details for the Roaring Twenties party before guests arrived. The week had passed quickly, and all the guests were enjoying themselves. Last night around the firepit, people were excited about the costumes they'd put together on the shopping extravaganza Shelly had led in the village.

Ivy turned at the sound of footsteps. Sunny and Jamir entered the room, and her daughter wiggled her fingers in a little wave.

Sunny had gone shopping with Shelly, too. She wore a short, black sequined dress, ropes of faux pearls, and a sparkly cloche hat that she'd tucked her hair under. Her lips were bright cherry red.

"Do I look okay?" Sunny asked, drawing up her brow.

"Just perfect," Ivy said, giving her daughter a hug. "Thanks for helping tonight."

"It's the family business." Sunny shrugged, although Ivy could tell she was excited.

Jamir appeared next to her in a smart in-striped suit with an ivory bow-tie. He wore a fedora at a rakish angle. He held out his hands. "This is the best I could do."

"I think it's very cool," Sunny said, laughing. She turned back to Ivy. "What do you want us to do?"

"You two will manage the bar." Ivy led them to a table she'd set up. "Shelly is bringing the Piña Colada and Sea Breeze cocktails—virgin and fully loaded. I've also printed recipes for a couple of 1920s cocktails."

Ivy tapped a print-out next to the bottles she'd lined up. "The Bee's Knees with lime juice and honey—gin optional, and the Mary Pickford with pineapple juice, maraschino liqueur or cherry juice, and grenadine. You can make them virgin with juice and soda for the health-conscious and nondrinkers, but if guests want alcohol, please go easy on it. We want them to relax and have fun, not get plastered."

Sunny looked at Jamir and burst out laughing. "There's an idea."

"Why do you sound just like Shelly?" Ivy pressed her palm to her forehead. "Jamir, please watch her."

"Oh, Mom, I'm kidding." Sunny poked Jamir.

"I'll see that she behaves," he said, nudging her back. "Might not be easy, though."

"Okay, you two. Have fun, but not too much fun, if you know what I mean. We're the hosts, and we have to look after our guests."

Ivy was glad that Sunny and Jamir were excited about tonight. They had become good friends—he'd shown her around the university campus when she'd arrived, and they often studied together. Jamir was a fine young man who would make an excellent, conscientious doctor someday.

Ivy continued checking the preparations in the ballroom. She had arranged for entertainment, including a dance instructor, who would be teaching dances popular in the twenties. She paused by the roulette wheel, which Arthur had thoroughly cleaned. Brass fittings and polished wood gleamed under a chandelier. The brass plate clearly read, *Lucky Lady*.

On a whim, she'd called Arthur and asked if she could

rent the roulette wheel for the evening. He refused to take any money for it, suggesting instead that people could make charity pledges to the school fund. He also volunteered to spin the wheel and take bets. Ivy agreed and was happy to include him and Nan at the party.

"Almost ready," Ivy murmured, rubbing her hands in anticipation.

A light buffet that her friend Marina had delivered was arranged on a long table—an assortment of appetizers, bowls of fresh fruit, roasted vegetable platters, curried rice, and chilled seafood towers with shrimp, clams, and mussels. Marina would tend to a carving station for roast beef.

For dessert, Mitch had supplied a tray of spa cookies, and Ivy had made orange sorbet in a fancy automatic ice cream maker her mother had given her.

Inside, everything was ready. Ivy flung open the French doors to let in soft sea breezes, lingering in the doorway to breathe in the fresh air. The surf provided a mesmerizing soundtrack, punctuated with crashing crescendos. She dimmed the vintage chandeliers, which cast faceted designs across the honeyed wooden floor.

As she plumped pillows in a seating area, Ivy thought about the parties this room had hosted over the decades. How many dancers had spun around that floor or basked in the moonlight on the patio and gazed over the sea? She could just imagine how the room might have looked with women in short, sequined flapper dresses and men in trim Gatsby-esque suits.

Shelly sauntered in wearing a short knit dress blazing with sparkling emerald sequins. She'd tossed a faux fur across one shoulder and wound their mother's pearls around her neck. Her lips were scarlet, and her hair was held in place with a sparkly feathered headband.

"Fancy," Ivy said, impressed with her outfit. "What a find that was. Love the headband."

"I made them." Shelly handed her one adorned with rhinestones and peacock feathers. "You look hot, but I thought you needed something extra for that dress."

"I'm so glad it fit." Ivy smoothed her hands over her sapphire-blue dress of liquid duchess satin. It was cut on the bias and gathered low on the waistline, effectively camouflaging her middle, which harbored a few too many muffins and glasses of wine. She and Shelly had found the dress months ago in a small, secret room behind Ivy's closet in her old bedroom, where Paige was now staying.

"I'll help you with the headband." While Ivy stood still, Shelly secured the feathered piece with hairpins. As she did, voices floated from the foyer.

A few moments later, Poppy guided a group into the ballroom.

"Our jazz singer arrived, and she brought some musicians with her." Poppy introduced the young woman, along with a few young men who carried instruments—horn cases and a bass. Ivy recognized them as high school students from Celia's musical program who had previously entertained at their afternoon mixers.

The teenage girl smiled shyly. "I usually bring my own playlist, but my friends wanted to get some practice, too."

"We're delighted," Ivy said. "I understand you know how to play the Charleston song?"

Another one of the teenagers grinned. "We've been practicing."

Poppy motioned to another woman beside her. "You remember Leah, the dance instructor."

"Of course. It's so nice to see you again." Ivy and Shelly welcomed the entertainers and showed them where to set up. Just as they were finishing, guests began to arrive. Besides the spa week guests, Gilda was there with her Chihuahua tucked into a pink backpack that matched her fringed flapper dress.

"I hope Pixie is welcome," Gilda said. "If I leave her alone, she just barks and disturbs everyone."

As if on cue, Pixie yapped, her eyes darting to Ivy's feathered headband. She strained in the backpack and whined for her freedom.

"Pixie is family, too." Ivy scratched Pixie's ears and wagged a finger at her little nose. "Just no stealing jewelry tonight."

Imani arrived right after Gilda. "So, what do you think?" She whirled around in a liquid-silver, dropped-waist flapper dress. Jeweled combs adorned her ornate updo.

"You look fabulous," Ivy replied, glad that everyone had gone to such effort.

"I barely had time to pull it together," Imani said. "Jamir and I were at the new house looking around. It's taken longer than we expected to finish it, but it's worth it. We'll have to throw a party once we're in."

"I'm so happy for you." Ivy would miss Imani. She was preparing to move into her new home on the ridgetop. She and her son Jamir had been living at the inn while their home was being rebuilt after the Ridgetop Fire.

Next, Ivy greeted Piper, who wore a sleek men's suit with heels and a hat, and Gayle, who wore a lacy gold-spangled dress. "You both look marvelous."

"Thanks," Gayle said. "I've always wanted to learn how to dance the Charleston. I remember my grandmother and her sisters whirling around the living room and having so much fun. That was from their era." She hummed a few bars and placed her hands on her knees, mimicking the dance.

Everyone standing around clapped at the move.

"Imani helped me find Leah," Ivy said, gesturing to the two women. "She knows all about the Charleston."

"Not many people know that tune dates from a musical that debuted during the Harlem Renaissance," Imani said with a smile. "It's based on an old style of dance my people brought with them from Africa. When they migrated from the south to the north, it became popular and spread."

The teenagers looked on with interest. The young singer spoke up. "Celia told us about that musical, *Runnin' Wild*. We've been practicing the music that James P. Johnson wrote for it. We're going to give some performances this summer."

"It's hard to believe that musical debuted a hundred years ago," Imani said. "There was a lot of good jazz and swing back then. Josephine Baker, Louis Armstrong, Duke Ellington."

"I love that music," Piper said, shimmying her shoulders. "It's retro, but it still sounds fresh and fun. A lot of my friends go to swing dance clubs. The competitions are so much fun to watch."

"Besides the Charleston, I'll also teach the Lindy Hop," Leah added. She also wore a fringed flapper dress. "It was named after Charles Lindbergh did his famous hop across the Atlantic. As soon as Ivy told me about the connection, I thought it would be fun to add it."

"What connection?" Imani asked.

"We're fairly sure the Ericksons knew the Lindberghs." Ivy knew that everyone in town was talking about Piper's incredible landing, but it seemed few people knew that the Lindberghs had often visited Southern California. She told her about the book Paige had found.

Piper's eyes lit up. "For his ground-breaking flight, Lindbergh took off from Coronado Island, just south of here, on an old airstrip that's now the Naval base. From there, he flew to St. Louis and then on to New York and Paris. I wish I'd been around then. It must have been amazing to be on the forefront of something so new and daring."

"Your landing had to be exciting, too," Gilda said. "What you did required a lot of skill. Very impressive."

"I'm just glad to be here." A look of relief washed across

Piper's face. "I've prepared for emergency landings but never thought I'd have to call on that training."

Ivy could hardly imagine what that was like. Sensing Piper had more to say, she added, "I'm glad you were ready for it. You've enriched our lives by your presence this week."

Piper's expression softened with thoughtful reflection. "I've learned that when you face what might be the end of your days, you begin to reconsider situations in your life—and what's really important." She added softly, "You've shown me that."

Ivy heard Piper's voice catch on her words. They'd had a heart-to-heart conversation last night on the beach. The younger woman had been spending a lot of time with Noah, the paramedic who'd tended to her, and she'd confided that she was falling hard for him. Ivy hoped he would be here tonight.

Gayle shared a smile with her friend. "No time like the present to make a few changes. You have all the support of your friends."

Hope flashed in Piper's eyes. "Maybe it's time to see what I can really accomplish."

Ivy gazed at the energetic young woman. "I have a feeling you have an interesting future ahead of you."

Piper dipped her head modestly. "Joan, the author who guided us in the break-through goal session—helped me realize that I have great potential for good. I have to put it to work. She told me, 'If not now, when?' It seems like everything I've been looking for in life is happening all at once."

"Sometimes it happens that way," Ivy said, thinking of the inn and Bennett.

She was glad the women had appreciated Joan's wisdom. She'd written a book that Paige carried in the bookshop, and she lived in Summer Beach. Joan taught and traveled extensively, and Ivy felt fortunate to have her on the spa week schedule.

Just then, Imani let out a whistle. "Would you look at that? Our mayor and police chief sure shaped up for the party."

Ivy turned around. Bennett and Chief Clarkson sauntered in wearing Gatsby-style suits. "Wow, you guys look amazing." She had asked Bennett to attend if he could, but she hadn't known he planned to dress up. She wondered where he'd found his snazzy garb.

Ivy shot a questioning look at Shelly, but her sister only shrugged, adding, "I'm just as surprised as you are."

Following them were Mitch and Noah, wearing oversized Zoot suits and black felt hats with white trim. Mitch wore a purple suit, while Noah was dressed in a shiny gray one. Ivy saw Piper's face light up. Things were still good between them, she thought with satisfaction.

Cheers went up from the crowd, and Pixie yapped at the sight of them.

"Where on earth did you get this gear?" Ivy asked as Bennett greeted her with a kiss on her cheek.

"We're resourceful in Summer Beach," Bennett replied.

Mitch tipped his hat to Shelly. "It's from Axe Woodson's cache of costumes for his outdoor theater."

"And where is he?" Ivy asked.

"Axe and Forrest kicked us out of the house," Mitch said. "They're the construction pros. I think we were in the way, so they'll finish faster without us."

Bennett elbowed his friend. "Speak for yourself. I'm pretty handy with a hammer."

"I'm better with a meat cleaver," Mitch said, looking slightly embarrassed, although he seemed to be handling it better now.

Shelly beamed at her husband. "You're staying here tonight. So, how about a Sea Breeze Cocktail?" Taking him by the hand, she led him to the table where she'd made pitchers of cranberry and grapefruit juice, along with the usual vodka accent—but not for her. She poured a glass and finished it with a squeeze of lime. "To my husband, for braving home improvement and knowing when to accept help."

"It's a lot harder than it looks on TV," Mitch said, sipping the refreshing cocktail.

A little later, when the performers took their places, Ivy introduced the musicians and the dance teacher.

Leah began to explain and demonstrate the Charleston. "You can dance with a partner or side by side. First, we'll learn in a line, and you can find partners later if you want."

Piper grasped Noah's hand, and the two of them began following Leah. Everyone joined in, and soon they were all deeply engaged in the amusing dance.

Ivy stood back, watching with pleasure. The evening was already turning out better than she'd planned. Music and laughter rang in the ballroom.

Bennett appeared next to her with an icy cocktail. "I think you've earned this."

"Thanks," she said, happy to accept a refreshing libation. "This week has turned out even better than I'd hoped. We have some fabulously talented people in Summer Beach."

"Starting with you." Bennett tapped her glass with his. As he gazed at her with admiration, the light of the chandeliers reflected in his eyes.

Magical, Ivy thought, taking a sip. Emboldened, she lifted her chin. "So, are you going to stand there like a pretty boy or ask me to dance?"

Quickly, Bennett deposited their drinks on the table. "You're on. Let's see what Madame First Lady can do."

Ivy laughed as he twirled her onto the dance floor. Between the vintage styles, music, and dance steps, she felt as if she were transported back in time. In Bennett's arms, she let her worries slip away.

Shelly and Mitch were dancing, too. Her sister was surprisingly light on her feet, and she was clearly having fun.

Soon, most everyone mastered Leah's simplified versions

of the Charleston and the Lindy Hop. Ivy couldn't remember when she'd danced so much. Guests were enjoying the food and music, and she heard several say they wanted to return for another spa week as soon as Ivy decided on a date. She was relieved; these theme weeks would see them through the lean winter months.

When the musicians took a break, Ivy steered people toward the food. Piper brought up the rear of the line with Ivy and Shelly. Bennett and Mitch fell in behind them.

"My great-aunt used to tell me stories about this place," Piper said, gazing around the ballroom while she waited. "When I got a little older, I realized Aunt Edna led a fascinating life, but I didn't make the connection with the Seabreeze Inn until Gayle mentioned it."

"And what was that?" Ivy asked.

"Aunt Edna knew this house as Las Brisas del Mar. It wasn't until I watched one of Shelly's videos online that I discovered one of my aunt's escapades had taken place here. She covered a lot of areas that weren't incorporated at the time. That was before she moved to the Bay area to be near her family."

"What did Edna do?" Ivy wondered if Piper's great-aunt was a friend of Amelia's.

Piper's voice rose with pride and excitement. "She was a private investigator, which was pretty rare for a woman back then. Aunt Edna used to tell me how she visited a beautiful mansion on the beach after the *Lucky Lady* wrecked on the shore."

Ivy and Shelly stared at each other while Piper went on.

"She used to tell me how she staked out the airfield, Seabreeze Shores, waiting for a gangster, Tony Diamond, to show up again. He'd left a woman behind in some sort of bind."

"Did she ever tell you the woman's name?" Ivy asked.

"She was one of the maids here. Her sister hired Aunt Edna to find Tony."

A tickle of intuition touched Ivy's neck. "Could the maid's name have been Doris?"

"That's it," Piper exclaimed.

Shelly raised her eyebrows. "Oh, no, that's not possible. Doris was with the croupier." She paused and held up a finger. "Unless it was a love triangle. Wow, do you think it might have been?"

Piper frowned. "What are you talking about?"

"We found some letters that Amelia Erickson had written to her husband." Shelly's eyes widened. "She wrote that Doris had fled with the croupier."

"Maybe that explains it." Piper grinned and went on. "Tony trusted Doris, and many thought she was hiding money for him. Maybe from the safe that had supposedly washed ashore. No one ever knew what happened."

"Maybe she hid it from him instead," Shelly mused. "Doris got the money and the hot young croupier."

Ivy laughed. "And how would you know that?"

"That's the way I'd write that story," Shelly replied.

Piper paused to pick up a plate and select from the chilled seafood tower. "I need to extend my stay in Summer Beach. Is there room at the inn? Because of the plane repair," she added quickly. "Noah has offered to help me, too."

"We're happy for you to stay, and I'm sure we could work something out for however long you need to stay." Ivy hoped Piper's relationship with Noah would continue to develop. They seemed well-suited, and Piper was hesitant to leave. Ivy didn't blame her; a lot could happen during a long-distance relationship.

As if reading Ivy's mind, Piper lowered her voice and glanced between her and Bennett. "I know it's barely been a week, but Noah and I instantly connected. Was it like that for you two?"

Ivy and Bennett traded a look, and they both laughed. "Not really," Ivy said, almost choking on her reply. It had been anything but that. "Still, it turned out pretty well."

Bennett smiled at Ivy. "Although we have yet to take that honeymoon."

"We'll manage it soon," Ivy said, squeezing his hand with assurance.

The serving line moved, and they stepped up to the table. Ivy inhaled; everything smelled fresh and wonderful. She gestured to her friend Marina, who had catered the event, waving her appreciation.

As Bennett heaped herb-roasted vegetables onto his plate, he said to Piper. "I'd still like to hear that idea you mentioned."

"It's Ivy's idea." Piper beamed at him. "I have to confirm a couple of details. Can we talk soon?"

Bennett looked at them both with interest. "I'll look forward to it."

Just then, Arthur approached them. "After people have finished eating, I'll begin spinning the roulette wheel if it's all right with you."

"I'll make the announcement." Ivy was looking forward to seeing the old wheel in action.

When Pixie barked her approval, Ivy laughed.

"How about a small wager on the spinning wheel?" Bennett asked, waggling his eyebrows. "I feel like giving some money to a good cause."

Ivy clapped her hands. "You're on."

She was pleased with how the evening had turned out, yet what Piper had said piqued her curiosity. Maybe the house had more connection with the shipwreck than she'd thought. As for the conversation she'd shared with Piper about the airfield, Ivy could hardly wait to learn what she was planning.

What a coincidence that Piper had landed on the abandoned airstrip. If not for that, she might not have met Noah, and Ivy and Piper almost certainly wouldn't have talked about the airfield.

As Ivy and Bennett made their way to the roulette table, she sent up a silent thought to Amelia. *You sure outdid yourself on this one.*

Quickly, Ivy straightened her shoulders. Not that she believed in that sort of thing, of course. But if she did, Amelia had.

Under a gleaming chandelier, people had gathered around the table. Among other guests, Imani and Clark stood next to Gilda. Pixie poked her head from the backpack carrier, intently focused on the chips on the table.

When they stepped to the table, Bennett turned to Ivy. "Red or black, even or odd?"

"Since red is my favorite color, I'll go with that." Ivy nodded toward the table. "You choose the number."

Laughing, Bennett said, "Two. Absolutely." He placed all the chips he'd bought on the table on the spot they'd chosen.

Arthur gave the no-more-bets hand wave over the table and moved to the roulette wheel. He spun the wheel and sent a small white ball careening in the opposite direction.

Clackety, clackety, clackety.

People around the table shouted their bets.

"Come on, red, come on two," Ivy called out, growing excited with everyone else.

Suddenly, Ivy saw something dart across the table.

Pixie!

As Gilda hovered over the table, Pixie leapt from the backpack and slid across the table, snapping at chips flying through the air. Snatching red chips in her mouth like a prize, she tore around the table as everyone tried to grab her.

"No!" Ivy stretched out her arms and dove for the little dog. "Got you!"

Pixie wriggled, yet she wouldn't let go of the chips.

"Oh, my poor baby-kins," Gilda cried. "I guess this is too

much excitement for her."

"Pixie has to get that kleptomania problem under control." Ivy plunked Pixie into Gilda's arms. "She's all yours. Except for those chips."

"Drop," Gilda said, giving a command.

With reluctance, Pixie deposited the chips into Gilda's hand. "See? Her therapy is working." Gilda stuffed her back into the pink carrier.

At the roulette wheel, the tiny ball bounced into a slot. Arthur called out the winning numbers.

"We won!" Ivy screamed with joy, but when she looked at the table, the chips on their spots were gone. "Why, you little thief," she said, glaring at Pixie, who burrowed into the backpack.

Bennett swept her from the table. "What would a party be without Pixie?"

"I guess you're right." She flung her arms around him and laughed. "This is yet another night to remember."

All around her, people were enjoying themselves, making new friends, or catching up with old ones. Feeling happy, she tilted her head back and gazed up. Just then, the chandeliers blinked once, twice, three times.

Bennett grinned. "Someone up there is winking at you."

Ivy heard Shelly break out in laughter behind her. She arched an eyebrow at Bennett. "Oh, not you, too?" Still, Ivy couldn't help but think Amelia would have enjoyed the party. Glancing across the ballroom, she spied Piper, who was also staring at the chandeliers.

Ivy looped her arms around Bennett's shoulders. "Have you noticed this old house seems to draw the right people at the right time?"

Bennett grinned. "I'll say. And it always seems to work out for the best."

For Piper's sake—and the rest of Summer Beach—Ivy hoped the old house wasn't mistaken this time.

*a*s Bennett showed Piper into a small conference room at City Hall, he gestured to a chair. "I know you're skipping the morning spa activities by coming to see me. I appreciate this, and I must say, I'm curious about your interest in the airstrip." At this point, Bennett welcomed a chance to deal with anyone other than the unpleasant Aaron, who was already making demands on the city.

"I didn't want to say much until I'd had a chance to talk to my parents and ask their advice. I've been working for my family's real estate company in San Francisco." Piper sat down and spread her hands on the table. "Old airfields are being transformed into a lot of other uses now. I think this one has potential."

"I've read about that," Bennett said. "Racetracks, housing…" He paused and grimaced. "And shopping malls. We need those, too. Just not in Summer Beach, I'd hoped. We want to keep the quality of life here high. And protect our small shops on Main Street."

"I agree," Piper said.

The door opened, and Boz entered and took a seat. Turning to Piper, he said, "I've heard all about your landing, and I must say, I'm impressed. Where did you learn to fly like that?"

Piper raked a hand through her short, curly black hair. "My parents are aviators, and my grandfather was a pilot during the Second World War. I grew up thinking that flying was as natural as driving a car."

Bennett leaned back in his chair. "As I mentioned, Piper has an idea for the old airfield."

"Ivy got me thinking about it." She began to outline the idea. "Instead of a shopping center, how about a park that would serve the community?"

Bennett recalled his conversation with Ivy. "That would be a fine addition to Summer Beach, but the city doesn't have the funding to acquire or maintain it."

"My mother worked in nonprofit organizations, and I've helped her raise funds for a variety of community causes. Children's museums, wild animal parks, and green belt renovations. I think this would be a great location for a multi-use park. I plan to spend more time in Summer Beach, so I could oversee the redevelopment."

"How would you go about raising money for this project?"

Piper began, ticking off points on her fingers. "We can raise money through family foundation offices that want to do something good for the community and the state. Do you know how much money has been made in technology in the Bay area alone? Billions."

"Why would they want to come here?"

"Who wouldn't?" Piper said, motioning toward the view of the beach and the ocean through the plate glass window. The city offices sat atop a rise, and the views were spectacular. "They might visit only a couple of times a year. It's better than having hordes of cars clogging your narrow streets into Summer Beach for a bunch of discount merchandise."

"The streets have kept the community small," Boz said. "But you'd have to act fast. Another developer is pushing for approval, and a couple of city council members think that something should be done with the property. They want to see our tax base grow."

Piper tilted her head. "You don't agree?"

"We represent the community," Bennett said. "Therefore, it can be a juggling act. Some people want the shopping center, while others are dead set against it. But we'd be interested in alternate plans that would elevate the lifestyle here for residents."

Nodding with enthusiasm, Piper said, "I think we could secure the property pretty quickly. My dad knows Aaron and how he operates." She grinned. "Kids are already using the pavement for skating and biking. You could keep that part and break up other areas for playgrounds and water features. The old structure there could be turned into a local history museum to showcase the origin story."

Boz laughed. "Prohibition and rum-running?"

"And early flight history," Piper said eagerly. "Important pilots landed here; I'm sure of it. Ivy has some letters about the Lindberghs. I've heard about Amelia Earhart and Bessie Coleman landing here, too. But people would love to know about the casino barges and Prohibition. All that is part of Summer Beach's history. Ivy volunteered to contribute some letters and other artifacts. She has some great ideas."

Bennett hadn't realized they'd talked so much about this. "And what others did she have?"

Piper blushed. "The bike path is her idea, too. Shelly liked the idea of a community garden for people who don't have much space to grow food. And a children's playground, of course. Poppy liked the skating aspect, and she's up for promoting it."

Bennett realized the whole crew was in on this. "You have been busy. What do you need from the city?"

"My dad told me there should be an assurance that the space would be used for the community, and that there is money to maintain it. But I can help with that. All we need is a zoning change."

Piper looked at Boz, who cleared his throat. "Piper, have you ever done anything like this?"

"Not exactly," Piper replied, hesitating.

Boz caught Bennett's look, so he tried again. "How exactly?"

"I've seen what my family's company—and others—have done," Piper replied. "I know I could manage this. I really want to stay in Summer Beach. All I have to do is get the right people together. That's what my father does. 'Put the right people in the right place.' That's what he says. I can use his connections, and I have some of my own—right here in Summer Beach, too. Wouldn't you want as many local people working on the project as possible?"

Piper was persuasive, and she seemed eager to do this project. But why in Summer Beach? Bennett steepled his fingers in thought. "Would this have anything to do with Noah?"

Piper's face flushed. "Not really." Her voice drifted off.

"What if things don't work out between you?"

"This has little to do with him," she insisted. "I've been looking for a place like Summer Beach for a long time. Where people are real, and I can make a mark on the community." She shook her head. "My parents gave my brothers and me everything we could want growing up, but all I want is to be accepted for who I am, not what my father owns. Besides, he's decided to give away most of the money he's made in his lifetime when he dies."

"That's admirable," Boz said. "Must have been a tough decision."

Leaning forward, Piper went on earnestly. "My brothers and I have to carve out lives of our own. Dad says it's best for us. Where we come from, if you don't have money, you're no one. I don't agree with that. I want to do something that matters to other people."

Bennett thought about the ramifications of her plan. "You won't get rich off this."

"You've seen my plane," Piper said, grinning. "I don't have to have the best, but I do want to be the best. I've been saving money to do something else with my life. I'm sure this is it."

"Maybe the first of many things," Bennett said, intrigued by Piper's thinking. Her drive reminded him of Ivy.

He looked at Boz. "What do you need from Piper for the city to consider this idea?"

Boz tapped a pencil on the pad in front of him. "I'll make a list for her."

"Good." Bennett stood and stretched his hand to Piper. "Let's see what you've got as soon as possible."

THE NEXT MORNING, Bennett strolled through the marina, greeting boat owners on the way to check on his craft. With spring officially here, he needed to assess repairs and plan for the busy summer season ahead when he and Ivy would take the boat out more often. He'd been thinking about Piper's proposal, too. If she could pull it off, a new park and community area would be good for Summer Beach.

And Ivy seemed to be behind it all. She never ceased to amaze him.

Whistling, Bennett continued through the marina, intent on accomplishing what he needed to do this morning. After Ivy left the house after breakfast today, he had an important meeting at the house.

"Good morning, Tyler," he said, waving to his neighbor on the ridgetop. "Celia sure is doing well with the music program. We had some amazing young talent at the inn for our Roaring Twenties party." Bennett always made sure to tip the kids well. Many of them planned to make music their career.

"Morning, Mayor," Tyler replied. Dressed in cream trousers with a beige sweater, Tyler certainly wasn't there to work on his boat as others were.

Sure enough, a work crew emerged from his galley.

Must be nice, Bennett thought with a chuckle. But then, Tyler had put in years of hard work in technology in the Bay area in order to retire young. Now his problem seemed to be having too much time on his hands.

Tyler gestured to him. "If Celia asks, you didn't see me here."

The muscles in Bennett's jaw tightened. He nodded toward others in the marina. "Are you going to ask the same of all of them? I won't lie for you, bud."

Immediately, Tyler's face flushed. "Look, I wouldn't ask if it weren't important."

"Where is Celia?"

"At the school working with the kids."

"In the music program?"

Tyler shoved his hands into his pockets and nodded.

"My advice to you is to go help her," Bennett said.

"Music isn't really my thing. And she's nothing like Ivy."

"Ivy isn't perfect, and neither am I. Or you and Celia. When you agreed to fund the music program at the school, did you have any interest in it at that time?"

"Not really. It was something for Celia to do."

"You need something to do as well. Those kids could use your encouragement and connections. Some of them don't have fathers in the house, and they could use the proper sort of male guidance." Over Tyler's shoulder, he saw a leggy redhead in a short dress strutting toward them. She didn't even have the right shoes on for a boat.

Everyone at the marina turned at the sound of her heels tapping across the wooden planks. Tyler noticed that, too.

"You're busted, Tyler." Tamping down his anger, Bennett said, "Why don't you make that your project with Celia—instead of whoever you'd planned to take on your boat."

Tyler started to protest, but then the young woman called out to him. "Sorry, I'm late."

"You can start working on your marriage right now." Bennett put his hands on his hips.

"Look, I don't know." Tyler threw up his hands. "Okay?"

"Listen to me. Celia deserves better." To get through to Tyler, Bennett had to speak his language—the language of money. "And she'll get it if you keep this up. More than half, I'd say."

"Hi," the woman said brightly to Bennett. "Are you coming with us? I could call my friend."

Bennett shook his head. It wasn't any of his business, but he had to take a shot. "I was asking Tyler for his help on an urgent matter. I'm the mayor of Summer Beach, and Tyler and Celia mean a lot to this community." He turned to Tyler. "Can you come with me now?" His friend was free to decline, but he was giving him a way out of the mess he was about to get himself into.

The woman's sunny smile dimmed. "And who is Celia?"

Tyler didn't answer the question. Instead, his face flushed. "I'm sorry, Dawn. The mayor needs help right now. I have to go. You understand, right?"

Dawn's gaze fell to Tyler's left hand and the tell-tale white band on his finger where he'd removed his ring. "Oh, I understand, all right. It was too dark to see that at the bar last night. What a jerk." She spun on her heel and strode away from them.

Bennett let out a sigh. He didn't like being pushed into such situations. "You know I had to do that, don't you?"

"Yeah, I do." Tyler's shoulders slumped like a defeated prizefighter. "Guess I should go see Celia."

Bennett clenched his jaw. He felt like knocking some sense

into Tyler, but that wasn't his style. "No, buddy. You *get* to see Celia and some promising young talent. Go make a difference in their lives and watch what happens to yours in return."

"You sound like my dad."

"Maybe you should listen to him, too. Good choice today, though. Now, stop looking like a sad sack and go. Teach those kids about the determination you had to build your company. They're going to need that. And stop off at Imani's flower stand and pick up a bouquet for Celia."

"There's no special occasion."

This time Bennett felt like strangling him. "Do it because you cherish her."

"Maybe you're right. I've tried everything else. She threw a diamond bracelet back in my face the other day."

"Stop being a jerk. You're a good guy underneath all that. You just feel a need to prove yourself. A real man takes care of his responsibilities. I know you can do that." Gesturing toward Dawn, he added, "But you need to fill your time with something else."

"Got any other ideas?"

Bennett thought of Piper's project. "Maybe I do. We'll talk later."

Tyler slunk off, and Bennett watched him until he climbed into his Land Rover alone and took off.

Bennett rubbed his neck. Technically, nothing had happened here, other than Tyler had made an earlier error in judgment that he corrected of his own accord. Still, he felt sorry for Celia. As mayor, Bennett was often privy to things he'd rather not know. If Tyler didn't clean up his life, he wouldn't blame Celia if she left him—and took his boat. But he hoped they could still make a go of it.

Bennett had done what he could.

Shaking off the ill feelings, he started toward his boat, which was in the last slip. He would have to give it a quick inspection because he wanted to beat Ivy back from the village, where she'd taken people shopping after breakfast. He had a delivery planned, and he had to be there for it.

While he and Ivy were becoming more accustomed to each other's peculiarities—and he was the first to admit he had some—he thought they could benefit from some time alone. Since their marriage, there'd hardly been a day without guests at the inn. Financially, that was good for Ivy, but he saw the strain building on her—even though she pushed through it every day with a smile.

Very simply, he wanted to take care of his wife. Mitch and Shelly had the opportunity to take their honeymoon in Baja, and he saw the difference it had made in their relationship. He and Ivy needed that, too.

Stepping onto his boat, he pulled out a notepad and began to make notes for supplies and maintenance. Tyler had taken up too much of his time. He hoped it was worth it. Barely fifteen minutes later, Bennett was in his SUV. On his way back to the inn, he took the advice he'd given Tyler and stopped off at Blossoms.

"Hey, Mr. Mayor," Imani sang out. She wore a turquoise sundress with a matching sweater tied around her shoulders. She was creating a springtime arrangement with tall stalks of sunflowers. "Any special occasion?"

"Does there need to be one?"

She laughed. "That's what Tyler just said. You should have seen the bouquet he had me make for Celia. Almost made me think he'd been up to no good again."

"Or he's learning to appreciate Celia." Bennett was pleased that his friend had followed at least part of his advice. He hoped Tyler would join Celia at the school today.

"She deserves it." Imani swept leaves off her counter. "Something for Ivy?"

"Those sunflowers look mighty cheerful. What else do you recommend?"

"These glossy monstera leaves will give those a tropical vibe. Shelly uses this combination at the inn a lot."

He gestured toward pink peonies and ranunculus. "These look romantic. Let's go with them."

"Ivy loves those." Imani gathered a range of colors from delicate shell pink to a deep mauve and wrapped trailing ivy around them. "She has plenty of vases. Unless you want me to arrange them for you."

"Thanks, but I have a delivery at the inn pretty soon." After paying for the flowers wrapped in paper, Bennett cradled them and stepped back into his vehicle.

He turned into the car court just ahead of the delivery van and motioned for the driver to park near the kitchen steps.

Running ahead, Bennett bounded into the kitchen and deposited the flowers in the sink in a bowl of water. No one was there. "Perfect," he said to himself.

As he swept back through the kitchen, he heard a voice behind him.

"What's going on?" Sunny had wandered downstairs. Her hair was mussed, and she wore a pair of faded jeans and a cream-colored sweater.

He'd thought she was out, but she must've been sleeping late. That was okay.

"I wanted to surprise your mother," he replied. He still had the bike, but he'd decided to have it painted now. *Red is my favorite color,* she'd said at the roulette wheel. He smiled to himself. She looked good in the old cherry-red Chevy convertible, too.

After living with the trainwreck that was Jeremy, Ivy deserved every good thing Bennett could do for her. Her feelings had to be complicated after Jeremy's death. Bennett knew she was having some difficulty adjusting to living together now, but he was determined to shower her with love and thoughtfulness.

Sunny rubbed her eyes. "Surprise her with what?"

Bennett gestured outside. "You'll see in a moment. Did you sleep late?"

Sunny stretched. "I had an early exam this morning. Since I studied late with Jamir, I came home and passed out." Standing on her tiptoes at the window, she peered out. "Is that a dishwasher?" She let out a little squeal.

"Two, actually. We have a lot of dishes to do every day after breakfast and the afternoon gathering."

Sunny broke into a wide grin and launched herself at Bennett, wrapping her arms around his neck. "You're my hero," she cried. She planted a kiss on his cheek before dashing to the door to watch a pair of men wheeling two dishwashers from the truck.

Bennett chuckled at Sunny. Her response alone was almost worth it. He couldn't wait to see Ivy's reaction. Every once in a while, a man needed to feel like a hero to those who mattered most in his life.

He thought about Tyler and his need for attention. If his friend could become a mentor to kids who would look up to him, that might feed his ego. Yet, Tyler would need to earn their respect first, and modesty wasn't his natural mode.

"Right over there, just as we'd planned." Bennett pointed to two cabinets he'd determined could house these two snazzy models he'd found at an appliance store in Summer Beach. The large kitchen had been built for a staff of kitchen help and had numerous cabinets that Ivy wasn't using. Surely, she'd love these new additions.

He checked the time, figuring he had just enough before Ivy returned.

Sunny was hopping around the kitchen with glee. "I never thought I'd be so excited over kitchen appliances. Don't let any of my friends know how geeky I am over this. When I was growing up, we always had a dishwasher in the house, and I took it for granted. I didn't even know how to turn it on."

"I'll keep your secret." Bennett laughed, remembering how important it had been to look cool at that age.

"Mom is going to love these. We'll all use them, but it will really make her life easier." Sunny bumped her knuckles with his. "This is way better than candy or flowers—even though those are gorgeous, too." She nodded toward the bundle in the sink.

"I like taking care of your mother—and helping out everyone."

A slow smile grew on the young woman's face. "You're good for Mom. My dad would never do anything like this. He left everything up to her."

"Your mother is extremely capable," Bennett said, side-stepping a discussion about her father.

"Want me to put those in a vase for her?"

"That's thoughtful of you, thanks."

"About time, right?" Sunny grinned and reached into a cabinet for glassware.

Ivy's youngest daughter was becoming more real by the day. Summer Beach had that effect on people. Besides, Ivy was a remarkable mother and role model. Bennett respected her for that because he knew she'd had a difficult time with Sunny's behavior after Jeremy's death. He was no fan of Ivy's former husband; Jeremy had bought this old house with the intention of tearing it down and building a hotel tower with his new girlfriend. When Ivy's children discovered that, it had been a sobering lesson.

Misty had consoled her mother, but Sunny had acted out her grief and disappointment. At first, she had refused to accept that their financial circumstances had changed and continued to run up her credit cards. Her father had spoiled his daughters—especially Sunny—by choosing lavish spending over quality time. For that reason, Bennett avoided trying to buy Sunny and Misty's love. Instead, he focused on listening and helping them.

Now, Sunny's appreciation for something as mundane as dishwashers was a sign of her emerging maturity. Bennett was proud of her for that.

The workmen began disassembling the lower cabinets near the sink. Old wood splintered and gave way to make room for progress.

Bennett's phone buzzed, and he looked down. Recognizing his sister's number on the phone, he stepped into the butler's pantry so he could hear over the demolition. "Hey, Kendra."

He was listening to his sister tell him about her plans for her son's birthday party when he heard a commotion in the kitchen. Quickly, he told Kendra they'd speak later. Bennett pushed through the kitchen door.

Ivy was standing over the workmen, who had stopped working and were watching a heated exchange between Ivy and Sunny.

"I see what's going on here," Ivy said. She pressed her lips into a thin, angry line and glared at Sunny. Then, pointing toward the appliances, she gestured toward the door. "My daughter might have ordered those, but I am not accepting delivery. Take them away, and put my cabinets back together. Right now."

"But, Mom—" Sunny slid off a stool and spread her hands wide.

"Just because you got tired of washing dishes by hand didn't give you the right to order these. I thought you were past shenanigans like this." Ivy whipped out her hand. "I want your credit card right now."

"You don't understand." Sunny darted a look at Bennett.

"Hey, things aren't always what they seem," Bennett began.

Ivy whirled around to face him. "Don't you dare stick up for her. This is unacceptable, especially to pull this stunt when the inn is full. I can't believe she thought she could get away with this. A little dish soap and water never hurt anyone." She shot a withering look at Sunny. "Just for that, you're on dish duty for the next month."

Sunny smothered a laugh. "Sure, why not?"

"Ivy, calm down," Bennett said, chuckling.

"You need to rephrase that," Ivy said, fury snapping in her eyes. "You're both minimizing this. I'm appalled at your impertinence. Both of you." She snatched her purse and stormed from the kitchen.

16

*B*arely able to contain her anger, Ivy strode across the car court. A couple of guests were lounging by the pool, so with the windows in the kitchen open, they'd heard everything. Cringing inside, she crossed the car court, desperate to get away from everyone.

Just when Ivy thought the week was going well, her daughter had to pull this trick.

Footsteps sounded behind her.

Bennett called out, "Ivy, wait up."

Gritting her teeth, she stopped. Lowering her voice, she whirled around and said, "I am not having this out in front of our guests. They've heard enough."

Bennett held his arms wide in an appeal. "The dishwashers are a gift from me. I wanted to surprise you."

"Why didn't you say something?" The anger coursing through her quickly dissipated, replaced with embarrassment. She heard the women at the pool gasp and laugh.

"You didn't give me a chance." Gingerly, he placed an arm around her.

"We don't need to spend that kind of money." Why hadn't he consulted her?

"It's my treat. My contribution to the effort here."

Now thoroughly embarrassed, Ivy felt terrible about what she'd said to her daughter. She covered her face with her hands. "I can't believe I tore into Sunny like that. No wonder she was laughing at me. You could have told me."

"I was on the phone with Kendra when you came home, and frankly, I was a little in awe of you." Bennett kissed her cheek. "You're pretty formidable. Shall we start over?"

She heaved a sigh. "I think we'd better."

Bennett folded her hand into his and the warmth emanating from his skin coursed through her. Even when she was angry, her attraction to him remained.

"Good things often come in three," he said with a smile curving his lips. "First, let's check out the new pair of twins in the kitchen. You can name them whatever you'd like."

Ivy smiled at that, though she was still irritated—only now with herself over her assumption. They returned to the kitchen, where Sunny was talking to the workmen, who cowered by the door when they saw her.

Was she really that formidable? She'd never thought of herself that way. Passionate about her work, perhaps. But formidable? She slid a glance at Bennett. She sort of liked that description.

She pulled back her shoulders and lifted her chin. "I'd like to go inside for a better look at these modern marvels."

Bennett took her hand. "This way, my love."

On the second viewing, gratitude surged through Ivy. Bennett had seen a problem—all of them spending too long in the kitchen—and sought to solve it. From his budget, too. And these would make her life easier. Her heart softened toward him.

Approaching the appliances, she nodded at the devices. "These can stay," Ivy said, reassuring the workmen as she ran a hand over the cool stainless steel. Bennett had chosen well; these were quite state-of-the-art.

The workmen looked relieved and hurried back to work.

Grinning, Sunny flung her arms around her mother. "I wish I'd recorded that. Your reaction was priceless."

Finally, Ivy had to laugh at her own foible. "Forgive me for jumping to a conclusion?"

Sunny laughed. "If that were an Olympic event, you'd have the gold medal, Mom."

"You can't blame me for that. You hate washing dishes."

Sunny's shoulder's slumped a little. "Okay, I minded, but I was trying not to."

"Me, too," Ivy said, bumping her shoulder. "Sometimes, you have to roll with the dice of life."

"Does that mean I'm officially an adult?" Sunny flashed a grin. "You're always asking me when I'm going to grow up."

"Am I?" And then, Ivy's often exasperated words floated back to her. *When will you ever grow up?* She hugged her daughter. "I have no doubt you're on a good path now."

With his hands in his pockets, Bennett rocked on his heels. "I'll let you in on a secret, Sunny. Everyone—regardless of age—is trying to act grown up. For some, that's easier than others."

Ivy cradled Sunny's face in her hands. Paraphrasing a line she recalled from Anne Morrow Lindbergh's book, she smiled at her beautiful young daughter. "*A woman must come of age by herself.* But everyone's timeline is a little different. You're doing well, darling."

Sunny beamed at her, and Bennett rubbed his hand across Ivy's back. These small actions of connection were what Ivy needed. Having the forgiveness and support of those she loved meant so much to her. And Bennett's thoughtfulness was truly touching.

"Maybe it's better this way," she relented, admiring the shiny stainless steel. "If you'd suggested this, I would have found a thousand reasons not to buy them. I have so many other repairs earmarked in my budget before I would have bought these."

"That's why I did it," Bennett said. "And I'm pretty handy with a hammer, remember? I'll handle some of those repairs."

"You know me well." Ivy looked at the brand. "They're so much nicer than what I would have chosen."

Putting his arm around her shoulder, he said, "On certain investments, you can't go wrong with choosing the best because you hope to have them for life." He squeezed her shoulder.

As Sunny watched them, she laughed. "I think he means you, Mom."

Ivy felt her cheeks warm. "That's a good philosophy. Now, who is going to pick up the detergent for these dream machines?"

"I will," Sunny replied. She inclined her head toward the flowers resting in the sink. "I'll also put these beauties in a vase for you." She disappeared into the butler's pantry.

"They're so lovely," Ivy said, turning to Bennett. "This means so much to me."

"You have one more surprise coming," he said, leading her from the kitchen.

Bennett swept her into the ballroom and onto the front patio that overlooked the beach, where they were alone. Ivy breathed in the scent of the ocean and Shelly's sweet jasmine, which was winding with wild abandon on trellises she'd placed in pots near the doors. With the ocean lapping on the shore, she thought it was a beautiful setting for his third surprise. A shiver of anticipation coursed through her as they sat on a teak loveseat facing out to sea. But this wasn't all about her. She wondered what she could do to surprise him, too.

Holding her hands, Bennett gazed into her eyes. "We've been talking about taking a special trip…"

Ivy began to sigh, then checked herself. "You mean our delayed honeymoon?" She struggled to keep a defensive note from creeping into her voice. Bennett knew she didn't want to leave Shelly for a long trip.

"Before you say anything, hear me out. I'm thinking about a mini-trip, like a honeymoon appetizer. We could plan the main course later."

She had to laugh at the meal analogy. "I can hardly imagine what the dessert might be."

"I think we need a short getaway—just the two of us for a long weekend," Bennett said. "Now that the dishwashing load is lighter…"

"Oh, I see how your mind works. Very clever, Mr. Mayor. Is this the way you win over people at City Hall?"

"I didn't mean to plan it like that," he said, dipping his chin. "But it will help. What about a few days in Palm Springs? We can drive there in a couple of hours, and it's beautiful this time of year. Now that Mitch has almost finished the house, Shelly will move back in a day or two."

"That's true," Ivy said, considering the offer. The team of Forrest and Axe had worked miracles. Shelly wasn't due for another four to six weeks. *What could a long weekend hurt?*

As Bennett waited, she thought about the inn schedule ahead. After the current guests departed, the inn would likely be slow for a couple of weeks before the spring break crowd arrived. Once the weather was predictably warm in Summer Beach, the tourist season would be underway. If she was truthful with herself, she and Bennett could really use a few days alone to reconnect. And he was trying so hard, the least she could do was meet him halfway. She allowed him a small smile. "How about one of those mid-century-modern inns in Palm Springs?"

Bennett's eyes lit with hope. "I know of some I think you'd love."

"Do you now?" Ivy asked, teasing him a little. "With a pool and a view of the mountains?"

"I'm sure I can find one like that."

"And a sweet little patio with hummingbirds?"

"If I have to bring the hummingbirds with us, I will."

Ivy laughed. "It sounds wonderful."

"Is that a yes?"

"Absolutely," Ivy replied, sealing the agreement with a kiss. "Now I have to find a new swimsuit." She'd always had plenty when she was younger, having grown up on the beach and worked as a lifeguard as a teen. But now was different. Her suit from last summer was a bit small and faded.

"I'll take you shopping if you want."

"Absolutely not." Ivy swept her hands apart. She wasn't twenty anymore when everything looked good on her. No, this would take some time. But then she remembered what Shelly once said. *He thinks you're hot and loves you just as you are.* Her sister was right. Ivy wouldn't minimize herself in his eyes anymore. Summoning her confidence, she added, "I'd rather it be a surprise."

"I'm so happy you agreed," Bennett said. "I was starting to worry that you didn't want to be alone with me anymore."

"How can you think that?"

Bennett placed his hand along her cheek. "I don't, but let's not lose ourselves in the busy minutia of life. I've seen it happen to others."

Ivy had, too. "That's the last thing I want," she said.

LATER THAT AFTERNOON, Ivy gathered the spa week guests on the terrace. Poppy had just returned with the group after a walk to the Hidden Gardens, where owners Leilani and Roy Miyake led a walk around the nursery and discussed spring gardening.

Today was the final evening, and after dinner, she and Poppy were planning an afternoon book discussion, followed by an evening swim and hot tub party. Shelly would offer a relaxing yoga session before bedtime. Most of the guests would leave tomorrow.

Only Piper had decided to stay on. Ivy was excited about the young woman's ideas for the old airfield and how she could offer input. Summer Beach needed this park. Plus, it was close enough to the inn for guests to enjoy. She hoped Piper's meeting with Bennett had been fruitful.

Bennett was right to insist they escape for a long weekend. She smiled at his term for it: *An appetizer honeymoon.* She liked that—it implied more ahead.

Once guests were seated around the patio tables, Ivy passed out a questionnaire. "Since this is our first spa week, we'd love your thoughts on what you enjoyed, what we could have done better, and what you'd like to see for future specialty weeks."

Gayle raised her hand. "How about another week added on?"

"We could do that," Ivy replied.

"Or a coastal excursion by boat," another woman added.

Ivy thought of Mitch and his charter boat service. "We could arrange that, too."

"I like doing absolutely nothing," added another guest. "Massages, naps, and a good book—that's what I came for."

Ivy smiled. Each guest seemed to have gained what they needed, whether it was a restorative visit or a getaway with new friends. After their discussion, Poppy led the group to the lower level, where Paige was ready for the book discussion.

The older woman welcomed the group, and then she held up a slim volume. "Did anyone read *Gift from the Sea* while you were here?"

Almost all the ladies nodded.

"Like the author, I felt the draw of the ocean," Gayle said. "How she analyzed phases of women's lives was thought-provoking. I often feel like I'm in the busy oyster bed of life, juggling my work with my children's schedules and my husband's needs. And those of my family and friends."

Several other women agreed.

Paige acknowledged them. "And who identified with the Argonaut, or the vacated shell—the empty nester?"

Two women raised their hands, and a lively discussion ensued. Ivy had enjoyed the book, too. Soon her nest would be nearly empty as well. Sunny would leave one day, so Ivy felt pressure to make the remaining time with her daughter count.

While the women talked, Ivy slipped out. Shelly was leaving in the morning, and Ivy wanted to share a cup of tea with her before she left. Bennett was at Mitch and Shelly's home, helping with a few final details.

When Ivy entered the kitchen, the dishwashers were purring in the background, and Shelly had put on the kettle.

Shelly brought out a pair of cups from the cupboard. "I think we should celebrate a successful week."

"You did a great job," Ivy said, easing onto a stool. "How are you feeling?"

"Pretty good. Since I caught up on sleep, I feel like I could run a marathon. Except for this excess baggage I'm carting around." She patted her belly. "You hear that in there? Don't get too comfortable. Your eviction notice is coming soon."

Ivy laughed, happy that Shelly was regaining her spirit. "Bet you're looking forward to going home."

"I am, but I'm awfully thankful we had a spare room here." Shelly paused thoughtfully. "After this kiddo makes an entrance, we won't have much time like this anymore. Just the two of us talking over tea in the evening like we used to. I'll have a little one hanging onto me like a monkey."

"Life is always changing." Ivy smiled at her sister. "You have an exciting new chapter ahead of you. One you always wanted—and with a sweet little girl." When Shelly pressed a finger to her lips, Ivy quickly added, "I haven't told anyone else about that."

Shelly looked relieved and happy. "I used to worry that the life I yearned for would never be mine. I'd almost accepted that, but I hoped another path was meant for me. As for Mitch, even though we have our differences, I know we're right for each other. Had I not left New York, I never would have found him."

"I couldn't imagine you two in the big city."

"Neither can I." Shelly twisted her lips to one side and grinned. "In Summer Beach, we don't have to fit in. We can be ourselves."

Ivy appreciated Shelly's quirky ways, and Mitch was right there with her. "I'm glad you found each other."

They settled in with their tea and talked a little more. Shelly was warming to the idea of a party to celebrate the baby. "Does it have to be called a baby shower?"

Ivy sipped her tea and thought about what was right for Shelly and Mitch. "How about a welcome party? Or a celebration of a new life?"

Shelly's lips parted with delight. "Or a welcome to planet Earth party!"

Laughing, Ivy nodded. "Sure, why not?"

"Now, this might be fun," Shelly said, her demeanor shifting. "Mitch could really get into that."

"Then let's do it. I'll talk to Poppy to get some more ideas."

As they were putting up the tea, Shelly rubbed her back and stretched. "I'm going to need a bucket and some old towels. That leak I mentioned under the sink in my room might get worse tonight. I don't feel like tackling it now. I'm a little achy from you-know-who punching me in the ribs all day."

"I'll take care of that. Have you looked at it?"

"Not really, but the wall is damp now. The leak might be coming from the room above. This time, we might need a professional."

Ivy frowned with concern. "Sounds expensive."

After grabbing a bucket and towels, Ivy set off for the guest room with Shelly, who'd picked up her tool bag on the way. Once inside, Ivy peered at the wall. From the faint lines on the wall, it was clear to see it had been patched before.

"I don't like the look of this. There must have been a leak in the past." She pressed her hand against the soft drywall. "Water might have come from the window above on the second story. We had that hard rain."

"That's been a few days. But moisture is coming from somewhere."

Ivy shook her head. Leaks could cause a lot of damage in a short period of time. "I hope there's no mold under that squishy old wallboard. The insulation probably needs to be upgraded anyway."

"Only one way to find out." Reaching for a chisel in her toolkit, Shelly stepped closer. "This will have to come off anyway." She dug in and peeled back the soft wallboard.

At once, the wall bulged. "That's odd."

Even though they'd meant to wait until tomorrow, Ivy couldn't resist investigating. She reached over Shelly's shoulder and pulled the damp part of the wall back. Something that Ivy assumed was insulation was lodged behind the wall, but it didn't look like any she'd ever seen. "What's this they used? It's sort of like felt."

Shelly tugged on the wall. "That's not insulation. It's a bag." She jerked on a corner of the fabric. As the wall gave way, Shelly tumbled backward.

"Be careful," Ivy cried out as something clinked. She knelt beside Shelly to help her up. "Are you okay?"

Shelly pushed herself from the floor. "Just a bit unsteady with my little helper on board." She shook the small, wet pouch she clutched. *Clink, clink.* It was so old that it began to disintegrate in her hands. After ripping it open, Shelly spilled the contents onto the floor.

Large coins tumbled and spun like tops. Shelly stared at them before breaking out with laughter. "For a moment, I thought we'd finally found my pot of gold. This stuff is filthy, but it looks like some kind of fancy gambling chips or tokens."

Ivy picked up a tarnished coin. "Maybe Amelia's maids had a gambling problem. I'll get a towel and see what's under all this grime."

She returned from the bathroom with a white washcloth. "Thank heavens for bleach." She rubbed the large coin. As she did, a word appeared from beneath the grime. "It says *Liberty*."

"That seems familiar…" Shelly peered at it.

Soon, a woman's profile appeared with a spiky crown. Ivy turned over the coin and rubbed harder. "An eagle." Ivy paused and stared at Shelly. "I don't think this is a casino chip."

"Let me see that." Shelly scraped off dirt with her fingernail. "1920. And look, on the other side. *One dollar*."

Shelly's gaze darted to the small pile on the floor and back to the wall. "Think there are any more?"

"Only one way to find out. There's a crowbar in the garage." Ivy grinned. "We'll have to repair this wall anyway."

"This time, let it wait until tomorrow." Shelly sighed and closed her fingers over the coin. "Even if we find a hundred of these in the wall, that would hardly be enough to buy a stroller or keep a kid in diapers."

"You have a point." Ivy gestured to the wall. "And it's going to cost a lot more than that to fix all this. But whatever is in there is yours for the finding. That's the least I can do."

"I'll say." Shelly laughed and nudged her.

"Hey," Ivy said, poking Shelly back.

Shelly shook her head. "I'll bet this was Doris's room. Couldn't she have stashed gold bars instead?"

Ivy looked at her sister, and they both burst out laughing.

Wiping tears of laughter from her eyes, Shelly said,

"Wouldn't you know it? My pot of gold turned out to be silver dollars."

The irony of it all was simply too much.

Ivy touched Shelly's shoulder, soothing her. "Maybe your pot of gold is this new life you wished for. Remember that?"

Stroking a hand across the curve of her belly, Shelly leaned into Ivy. "I guess what I've been looking for is already here. Almost, that is." As she spoke, a tiny limb poked her in the ribs. "Oof, that smarts, kiddo."

Ivy wrapped her arms around her sister. "I'm going to miss you."

"I'm not going far."

"But it won't be just the two of us out to prove ourselves anymore."

Shelly smiled at her sister. "I think we still have a few things to prove—if to no one but ourselves."

"Well, you're going to be the best new mother ever." Ivy kissed Shelly on the cheek. "My new baby niece will love having fun with you and Mitch."

"I still wish—" Shelly hesitated. "I'm so glad you'll be with me when the baby is born."

"Me, too." Ivy knew what Shelly had started to say—*Mom*—and she felt a pang of sadness for her sister. No matter how much she did for Shelly, she was no replacement for their mother. Ivy didn't resent Shelly for that; it was simply the reality of their situation.

Ivy missed their mother, too. Yet the fact that Shelly wasn't whining or lamenting about that was another sign of her increasing maturity. Motherhood did that to a woman. This was only the beginning of that lifelong path for her sister.

Ivy brightened. "Why don't we call Mom tomorrow? She'd love to hear about your pot of gold."

Shelly beamed. "Silver, that is."

Laughing at that, Ivy said, "Who knows? Maybe they have historical value."

"Or notoriety." Shelly grimaced. "If they were stolen from a dead gangster's ill-gotten gains, who gets to keep them now?"

"This time, I think they're ours," Ivy said, rubbing the back of her neck. "We should ask Arthur and Nan about these old silver dollars."

17

*S*hielding her eyes from the morning sunshine, Ivy held out the phone to Shelly. "Straight to voice mail again."

Shelly adjusted the strap of her floral-print overalls and leaned on the patio table near the pool. "I hope nothing has happened to Mom and Dad."

"They're likely just out of range." Ivy couldn't let herself imagine anything else, or she'd never stop worrying. She and Shelly and Poppy had been writing up a debriefing memo on their first spa week—what worked, what didn't, and what they could add for the next one. Overall, guests had been enthusiastic; they'd left rested and rejuvenated. Even with additional costs for the events, the inn was profitable that week.

Ivy put down her phone. "We'll keep trying."

"I will," Shelly said. "You'll soon be on your honeymoon."

"A starter honeymoon," Ivy said. "Or, as Bennett says, an appetizer." Still, she was thrilled to be going away with him. "Three blissful days of being nothing more than a guest at an inn."

Wearing shorts and a T-shirt, Bennett stepped up beside her and kissed her cheek. "Make that a pampered guest."

"Yes, please," Ivy said. "How was your run?"

"Short," he replied. "I'd like to leave on our mini-break as soon as we can."

"Where are you staying?" Shelly asked.

"At the Ingleside Inn, one of my favorites in Palm Springs," he said. "An old friend of mine, Mel Haber, owned it for years. We got lucky. They have an opening for a couple of days. After that, they're sold out for the next month."

Winter and spring months were the high tourist season in the Palm Springs desert, so Ivy wasn't surprised. A frisson of excitement sizzled through her. She loved traveling, yet as an innkeeper, she seldom had a chance anymore.

Touching Bennett's hand, Ivy rose from her chair and slid her phone into the pocket of her navy and white sundress. "While you're showering, Forrest can look at the guest room damage."

Shelly looked up. "Before you go, Piper wants to meet while you guys are gone to talk about her proposed project. I think it's pretty cool, but do you think it's good enough to get past the city council?"

"I can't speak for the council, but it's an attractive plan that would be good for Summer Beach," Bennett replied. "Piper gave my wife most of the credit, though." He squeezed Ivy's shoulder. "Well done, sweetheart."

She smiled, pleased that Bennett liked her ideas. "As my father often said, ideas are cheap..."

"...it's the execution that matters," Shelly finished.

"Wise man," Bennett said. "Were you able to reach your folks?"

"Not yet," Ivy said. "Shelly will try calling later."

"I wouldn't worry too much," Bennett said.

"Of course not," Ivy said, even though she had a gnawing feeling that something had shifted in their itinerary.

Her brother was walking around the edge of the house. "Here's Forrest. Scoot into the shower, and I'll see you soon."

Ivy showed Forrest to Shelly's guest room, and she followed them. "We made a mess last night, but all this will have to come down anyway." She opened the bathroom door.

Forrest held a device to the wall that beeped where it detected moisture. "Pretty big job you have here. How about I put Reed on it? The boy needs some experience leading his own job."

Ivy stepped over the damp drywall that she and Shelly had swept to one side. "Will it be expensive?" At least they didn't have reservations for this room. Not right away, that is.

Forrest shook his head. "Let's call it training, and I'll kick the cost in for you. Just keep hosting family dinners here."

"That's a deal."

Shelly closed her suitcase on the bed. "It seems I'm one step ahead of every construction crisis."

"I'll get that for you," Forrest said, hoisting her luggage. "Can't take a chance with you."

"Thanks." Shelly beamed at her older brother. "And I really appreciate your help with the baby's room. I can hardly wait to start decorating."

"It's what I do." Forrest grinned. "I haven't had the chance to help my sisters until now. Think of it as payback for all the teasing Flint and I heaped on you when we were younger."

Shelly folded her arms. "In that case, I'm thinking of another addition." When Forrest looked surprised, she laughed. "Just kidding. There's no more room to add on. I need my gardening space. We'll just pile the kids in bunk beds if we have to. Or stash them in the attic rooms here."

Ivy told him about the silver dollars they'd found. "There might be more in the walls."

"It's not the first time we've found things stashed in walls during remodels." Forrest gestured to the faint outline that Ivy had discovered. "Looks like this section was cut out, filled in, and painted over a long time ago. People did all kinds of crazy things back then. They didn't always trust banks."

"Maybe the money was siphoned off from the casino," Ivy said.

"Or it washed ashore from who knows where," Shelly said. "Either way, a dollar was worth a lot more back then."

Forrest carried Shelly's bag to the car court, where Mitch was waiting for her. He'd insisted on escorting his wife home, and Ivy thought that was sweet. He was driving Shelly's old Jeep—the one every Bay sibling had learned how to drive in. When he saw his wife, he raced to her, enveloping her in a huge hug.

Ivy smiled at their reunion. Shelly and Mitch needed each other, and their time apart seemed to have brought them even closer.

After seeing Shelly off, Ivy made her way upstairs. She made a fresh cup of coffee and waited on the balcony for Bennett. Thinking back over the last few years, she decided her life was something of a minor miracle now. She never would have dreamed that all this—Bennett, the house, the inn business—would have been possible. Happiness welled up inside of her.

After dressing, Bennett joined her outside. He'd brushed his damp hair back and put on a crisp white shirt with casual blue slacks and tan loafers.

"You look very Palm Springs," she said. "And very handsome."

Bennett beamed at her. "I had to shape up for you."

She laughed. "Ready to leave our work behind and go have fun?"

"I sure am. Boz and Nan will handle everything at City Hall for a few days." Bennett paused. "Did I tell you to bring your hiking boots?"

"My what?" Ivy had packed a new swimsuit, sundresses, and sandals. "Are you sure hiking is on the itinerary?"

"There's a romantic place I'd like to show you. We can picnic by a waterfall and take a dip to cool off."

"That part sounds good, as long as there's a massage on the schedule somewhere."

"I promise it's not too arduous," he said, drawing her into his arms. "I know my wife."

"Then you know I'm more of a glamping kind of woman, but I'm up for a hike with you."

Bennett grinned. "I like that you're not afraid of trying new things."

Ivy started to say that she wasn't new to hiking, but she thought better of it. Her father had once planned a family hiking adventure to a nearby lake. As a know-it-all teenager, she'd disregarded her mother's admonitions about sunscreen, insect repellent, and sturdy shoes. During the hike, she'd suffered a sprained ankle, a sunburn, and a mosquito swarm attack. Her father and brothers had taken turns supporting her as they navigated the trail back. That outing had become the stuff of family legend, but that had been many years ago. Since then, she'd invested in a good pair of hiking boots that had seen little use beyond cold winter wear on the flat streets of Boston.

Ivy kissed his cheek. "Glad you warned me. I know just what to take."

"That's the adventurer I love."

AFTER MAKING the drive to the desert area, Ivy and Bennett pulled into the Ingleside Inn, a historic Palm Springs land-mark that had been a Hollywood hideaway for years—first as a private estate and then as a secluded inn. At the end of a narrow street tucked against the San Jacinto mountains, bungalows were shrouded by softly rustling palm trees and rambling bougainvillea laden with pink and purple bracts.

Ivy and Bennett checked in and then wound past sun

loungers that lined a private pool. No one else was there, and Ivy felt like it was all theirs.

When she stepped into the villa Bennett had reserved, she felt as if she had been swept back in time. A brick fireplace anchored the sitting room, and polished terracotta tiles gleamed underfoot. White linens, dark antiques, and desert landscape artwork created a serene ambiance.

Bennett swung open a pair of French doors, revealing a private patio surrounded by more bougainvillea, birds of paradise, and a trickling fountain. A hummingbird feeder was nestled among tree boughs, and one of the tiny birds with iridescent wings fluttered nearby. White gardenia flowers scented the air with their delicate perfume.

"What do you think?" he asked. "I made a special request for the hummingbird feeder."

"I love it all," Ivy said, stepping outside. "I'm so happy we're finally doing this."

"I only wish this trip hadn't been delayed." Bennett wrapped an arm around her. "We'll take a longer trip in the fall—a proper honeymoon."

Feeling tension draining from her limbs, Ivy rested her head on his shoulder. "It doesn't matter what we call it. Getting away together is what's important."

She'd had so many things she had wanted to talk about with Bennett, yet now that they were here, none of it seemed that important anymore.

Simply being together was all the magic they needed.

Everything had fallen into place for them to get away. Sunny and Poppy could manage without her as Piper was the only guest who had stayed on. By now, Shelly and Mitch were probably happily furnishing the baby's room. Expecting photos from Shelly, Ivy had checked her mobile phone when they arrived, but she didn't have much of a signal.

Not that she needed to check messages. Ivy couldn't remember when life had been so placid. With the high summer season ahead, that wouldn't last, but for now, this is just what they needed.

Bennett kissed her forehead. "How about a swim first? Looks like we might have it to ourselves."

"I'd like that." Ivy had found a flattering new swimsuit and coverup at a village boutique on sale. At the inn, she seldom had time for a swim. "We should swim more at our place. Maybe in the evenings once the weather gets warmer. Most of the guests are out having dinner then."

"Should I remind you of that?"

"I wish you would. I get too wrapped up in my daily chores. But half an hour after dinner would be relaxing. We could create a new routine for ourselves."

Bennett smiled at the idea. "Sunny could join us, too. Family swim time to relax and talk."

"I don't know how much longer she'll be around," Ivy said. "With Misty on her own, I think Sunny is aching to have her own place, too."

"We'll always have room for them at the inn."

Ivy laughed. "At least in the attic."

"I've been thinking that we need to add a bathroom up there."

"That's a lot of work, and the cost—"

"I can take care of that," Bennett insisted. "You have a partner in life now. Let me pitch in."

Ivy let out a breath. "Thank you," she murmured, resting her head against his chest and feeling a heart beating in rhythm with hers. He was right. She'd forgotten how to ask for help—or even expect it. Jeremy had mastered the art of disappearing whenever she needed assistance.

She raised her head and smiled. "Ready for the pool?"

"You're on."

After changing, they slipped into the refreshing water and paddled around, laughing and enjoying the warm sunshine like they had when they were teenagers. The day turned out to be everything that Ivy had hoped it would be, from a relaxing afternoon to an exquisite dinner at the intimate restaurant on the property, Melvyn's, and the nightcaps they shared on the patio.

The evening breeze was crisp, and Bennett started the fire that had been laid in the fireplace. As Ivy lay in Bennett's arms, she thought it was the sweetest night she had ever known.

THE NEXT DAY, Ivy dressed for their hike. She put on her swimsuit under her shorts and T-shirt and laced up her hiking boots. She and Bennett had bought canvas hats with chin ties that made them look like they were going on a safari. Knowing the desert sun could be scorching—even if it wasn't terribly hot—Ivy slathered on sunscreen.

Bennett was prepared for their hike. He spread a map on the table and pointed out where they were going. "We'll have lunch once we reach the waterfalls. You'll love it there. Do you have your swimsuit?"

"I'm wearing it underneath my clothes." A part of her preferred to laze around the inn, but marriage was a compromise. If Bennett thought this would be an easy hike for her, then she was a willing participant. Besides, swimming in a natural pool in the mountains was appealing.

"We'll take our time," Bennett said, folding up the map and tucking it into his pocket.

Once they reached the trail, they started off. Ivy was glad that Bennett was leading the way. The elevation was a little steeper than she'd thought it would be, but her old boots were holding up well as they followed the creek. They stopped to admire unusual cactus or watch mule deer and bighorn sheep in the distance. Despite rocky mountainous slopes, sycamore, cottonwood, and willow trees proliferated near the creek.

Bennett paused to take a photo of her against the rugged

terrain. Lifting her arms to the sky, she smiled for him. Despite her initial trepidation, she was enjoying being surrounded by such awe-inspiring scenery. She took photos, too, and thought about how she could capture this scene in a painting.

As they hiked on, Ivy couldn't help but wonder what was happening at home. Shelly had teased her about her relentless worrying, which had become a habit she wasn't proud of. Why couldn't she leave that behind? She drank in the fresh air, trying to get rid of the gnawing feeling.

Yet, the sense persisted. She shrugged it off and forged ahead, determined to have fun. This was her honeymoon appetizer, and she was going to enjoy it.

When they reached a bend in the creek, they wound their way under stands of fan palm trees on its banks. Ivy heard the waterfall before they reached it.

"We're almost there," Bennett said, gripping her hand to guide her along a rocky portion of the path. "Isn't this incredible? Native people lived in this area long ago, and a local indigenous group still owns this land." He pointed out artifacts as they neared the falls. "This property belongs to the Agua Calientes Band of Cahuilla Indians."

Ivy enjoyed listening to Bennett share the history of an area he'd visited often. Soon they stopped, gazing at a waterfall that rushed down a face of granite rock into a sparkling natural pool below. After walking around it, they shed their outerwear and waded into the cool water in their swimwear.

Taking a breath, Ivy plunged in. The water felt so fresh and natural.

They enjoyed swimming for a while before stopping to nibble on a gourmet picnic the inn had prepared for them— assorted cheeses, bread, salad, and fresh fruit.

Ivy stretched in the sunshine, letting her hair dry naturally.

"Hey, beautiful." Bennett smiled and kissed her. "I like this carefree look on you."

Ivy laughed and looped her arms around his neck. "You were right about us needing this trip—I'm so glad we came."

Bennett's hazel eyes shimmered in the sun. "I love a good appetizer."

"Me, too." Even as she relaxed, the gnawing sensation within her grew. Unable to resist it, she reached lazily for her phone. "I wonder how things are going back in Summer Beach?"

Bennett frowned at her. "Do you really have to do that? They're all adults."

Ivy paused, thinking about what he said, but she still clicked on her phone. "It will only take a moment." She smiled sheepishly. "You win anyway. There's no signal up here." Smiling at her lapse, she tucked her phone into her lightweight jacket. "I'm a mom; old habits are hard to break."

"We'll be back at the room soon enough," Bennett said. "You can talk to Sunny before dinner. I made a reservation at a restaurant I think you'll love. It's one of my favorites."

Once they finished eating and exploring the area, they packed their remains, taking care not to leave anything behind that could spoil the natural habitat. The downhill hike was easier, and by the time they reached the SUV, Ivy felt tired yet invigorated from the exertion.

They climbed into the vehicle, and Bennett set off toward the inn. As they neared the community of Palm Springs, both of their phones began beeping.

At the wheel, Bennett groaned. "I'm tempted to ignore that, but we'd better check to see what's so urgent."

Ivy picked up her phone—and immediately caught her breath.

"It's a message from Mitch." Quickly, she tapped the voice mail. Mitch's voice sounded strained, and she could hear Shelly in the background.

Frowning, Bennett slowed the vehicle. "What's up?"

Pressing a hand to her heart, Ivy could hardly force out

the words. "They've gone to the hospital. I think…something happened."

Mitch had left another message, and as Ivy listened to it, panic rose in her throat. "He sounds pretty shook up. I'll try to reach her." With her heart racing, she sent a call to Shelly's phone, but the connection went straight to voice mail. "Shelly, I just got Mitch's message. Please call, I'm worried—" She stopped and glanced at Bennett, who nodded grimly and motioned ahead. "We'll be there as soon as we can." She hung up and shook her head.

"I should have been there with her," Ivy said mournfully.

"You couldn't have known this would happen," Bennett said. "Let's trust that she's in good hands."

Ivy closed her eyes in agony, wishing she hadn't left Summer Beach and willing support toward her sister.

Bennett turned in the opposite direction from their romantic lodging. "I'll ask the inn to send what we left in the room. Call Mitch. Let him know we're on our way." He pressed the accelerator to the floor.

Ivy was grateful for Bennett's decisiveness. She tried Mitch's phone, but it went straight to voice mail as well. "I'll call Forrest—maybe Mitch reached out to him."

But Ivy's brother was unaware of what was happening, though he promised to find out. Ivy hung up and checked the time, biting her lips as she calculated their driving time. "We're going to hit traffic on the highway, and it will take us forever."

"Not if we cut through the mountain. But we might lose cell service in areas."

Blinking against the sun, Ivy thought rapidly. She needed to reach Shelly. "Let's take the mountain road."

18

*I*vy's nerves had been on edge during the entire drive from Palm Springs. Due to the poor cell service on the mountain road shortcuts Bennett took, she hadn't been able to reach Mitch or Shelly—or Poppy or Sunny. No one at all. Finally, Bennett had suggested she stop trying and just breathe. There was nothing they could do until they arrived anyway.

"I almost wish Shelly was using that kiddie pool to give birth right now instead of being rushed to the hospital," Ivy said. "That's what she and Mitch would have wanted. She has a doula she really likes, too."

"You don't always have that choice," Bennett said. "What's important is that she's getting the care she needs right now."

Ivy couldn't help but imagine that he was thinking of Jackie. She breathed slowly, willing good vibes and prayers in Shelly's direction.

When they arrived at the hospital, the receptionist immediately waved them to a waiting area where Sunny, Poppy, and Imani were waiting.

"How is she?" Ivy asked as Sunny fell into her arms.

"I'm scared for her, Mom," Sunny said, wiping tears from her eyes.

"Aunt Shelly handled it really well, though," Poppy said, joining them in a hug. "Imani volunteered to drive us, and Gilda and Pixie are watching the front desk for us."

The thought of a Chihuahua announcing new guests with a yap brought a smile to Ivy's face. "That's fine. We're not expecting any new guests."

Imani drew a hand over Sunny's back to comfort her. "Shelly was complaining about a fierce backache and thought she'd overdone it in yoga, but as it turned out, she was probably in the early stages of labor. Mitch arrived a little while ago; he's with her now."

Sunny's eyes widened. "We were joking around on the patio one minute—Shelly was drinking tea and eating dates—and in the next minute, her water broke. I didn't know what had happened, but all of a sudden, Shelly freaked out. I'd seen Noah with Piper on the beach, so I ran to get him."

"That was quick thinking," Imani said. "Noah checked her out but recommended going to the hospital."

Just then, a physician entered the area. She was a tall, striking woman with short gray hair and sculpted cheekbones. "Are you Ivy?"

Praying that Shelly was okay, Ivy bit her lip and nodded. "Can we see her?"

The doctor smiled. "She's been asking for you."

"Go," Bennett said, squeezing her hand.

Imani put her arm around Sunny and nodded toward Bennett. "We'll look after Indiana Jones for you."

It was then that Ivy realized they still wore the clothes they'd put on early that morning to hike to the waterfall in Palm Springs. She had on her hiking boots, and Bennett still wore his khaki hat with a chin strap slung around his neck.

"Today has been quite an adventure." Ivy hurried after the doctor, who showed her into a room where Shelly and

Mitch were. With her brow beaded with perspiration, Shelly looked tired but exuberant, while Mitch looked on in awe.

When Ivy perched on the edge of the hospital bed, Shelly gripped her hand. "Ow, that labor pain was a strong one. You almost missed all the fun, Ives."

"You have plenty of fun ahead." Feeling relieved to see her sister, Ivy smoothed Shelly's hair from her forehead as monitoring machines winked around her. "Especially when you hear that first little cry."

"Mitch just got here, too," Shelly said. "Piper and Noah brought me in, and Imani brought Sunny and Poppy. It turns out Piper knows a lot about first aid, too. She and Noah are pretty amazing together." She turned a loving smile toward Mitch. "Like us, babe."

"I'm so glad everyone was with you," Ivy recalled being in labor by herself in a hospital in Boston. For Misty's birth, Jeremy had been away on a business trip, and for Sunny's birth, he was in town but stayed with Misty. The truth was that her husband never wanted to be involved with the birthing process. Childbirth had been joyful, yet without her husband, it was a lonely experience for her—even though the nursing staff had been caring and supportive.

For Shelly's sake, she was glad Mitch was there, even though he looked slightly shocked. His eyes were wide with excitement, and his spiky hair seemed to vibrate on an electrical current.

"It all happened so fast," Shelly said, drawing out her words. "I was drinking red raspberry leaf tea and eating dates by the pool because I read that helps prepare your body for labor. Wowzer, that sure worked. So, we came here." She threw a grin at Mitch. "Besides, we hadn't disinfected the kiddie pool yet."

Mitch's face reddened with embarrassment. "I should have—"

"No need now, right?" Shelly reached for her husband.

"Maybe we'll try that with the next one…with my doula and some meditative music. She's coming soon, though. Piper called her on the way here."

"I can put on some music for you," Mitch said, brightening as he fumbled for his phone. "The nurse brought me a charging cord, so I have battery power now."

So that's what happened, Ivy thought, smiling. She could just imagine the panic that must have ensued in getting Shelly to the hospital.

"That would be cool," Shelly said, her eyes glazing. "Maybe I'll use that pool as a water feature or planter in the garden. I'll think about that later." She rolled her face back to Ivy, her words tumbling out. "I'm sorry I interrupted your mini-honeymoon, but will you stay with me, too?"

"Of course. How about some of that acupressure you've been telling me about?" Ivy pressed her thumb on Shelly's hand. "You might have to refresh my memory." Ivy would stay with her sister as long as she wanted. "Mitch, why don't you pull up a chair on the other side of your wife?"

Shelly gestured to him. After tapping a song on his phone, Mitch rushed to her side. The sounds of beach reggae filled the air, and Shelly shook her head. "Seriously? *Don't Worry, Be Happy?* Couldn't you find something else?"

Just then, a nurse entered. "If you'd like, we can move you to our new birthing center," she said. "The water labor is very popular with our new moms."

Shelly and Mitch shared a look and then burst into grins. Shelly's eyes brightened with excitement, and she placed a hand over her belly. "Woo-hoo! We get to go swimming, kiddo!"

Relief washed over Ivy, and she grinned at Shelly's delight. Her sister was getting her wish after all.

. . .

A LITTLE WHILE LATER, Ivy emerged into the waiting room, eager to share the news. Their brothers, Forrest and Flint, had arrived, and Bennett, Sunny, Poppy, and Imani were playing cards.

Ivy cleared her throat for the announcement. "We have a new baby girl in the family. And Shelly is doing just fine."

Her sister had been in good spirits and determined throughout her labor, which had been relatively brief. Witnessing the birth had been a miracle for which Ivy felt privileged for being included. The baby was beautiful—a little lean like Shelly due to being early, but she was well-formed and strong enough to go home with Shelly and Mitch in a few days Like her mother, she was a real fighter with a gutsy cry that made Ivy laugh and weep with relief.

Everyone cheered, and Sunny asked, "What's the baby's name?"

"Shelly and Mitch will announce it together." Neither one of them would reveal the name, and Ivy hadn't pushed them. She couldn't help wondering if they'd decided yet.

"Can we see her?"

"Soon," Ivy said. The baby was undergoing routine tests, and Shelly was resting from the exertion. "Mitch will let us know."

A short while later, the family crowded into the room where Shelly held her tiny, swaddled baby in her arms. Her face was wreathed in a sweet smile brimming with love.

Mitch perched on the bed next to her, and Bennett gave him a warm, brotherly hug that brought tears of happiness to Mitch's eyes.

"I'm really glad you guys came back," Mitch said, emotion thick in his voice.

Bennett bumped his fist to Mitch's and grinned. "We couldn't miss this."

Shelly motioned to Ivy. "Want to say hello?" She lifted her

small bundle. "You can hold her." She motioned to Poppy. "Would you take some photos for Mom and Dad?"

Ivy waited as Poppy took some of Shelly, then she moved closer and shifted the small child into her arms. "Hi, little one. Welcome to the family. I wonder what lovely name your parents have picked out for you?"

Shelly took Mitch's hand. "This is Daisy Bay Kline. We wanted to make sure her name fit her. Look at her sweet, sunny smile. And she seems to like it, don't you, Daisy?"

Everyone smiled at their choice.

"Daisy," Ivy murmured, her heart growing full with love for her new little niece.

This small child reminded her of one of her own, and in a way, she was. Daisy was part of their tribe. Her tiny lips curved into a quirky little smile just like Shelly's, and her spiky hair resembled her father's. But Ivy could see Sunny in the curve of her cheek, and Misty in the shape of her brows.

"She's a baby Bay, alright," Flint said. "Just look at that nose."

"At least she got my hair," Mitch said, grinning. "Look at that blond tuft on top."

Ivy passed Daisy back to Shelly. She was looking forward to hearing this child babble, seeing her first steps, and watching her grow.

Her heart clutched with love for the tiny girl. As little Daisy squinted at the faces surrounding her, she blinked in confusion and stretched her neck beyond them, as if she were looking for someone she sensed was missing.

Just then, footsteps sounded behind them. Ivy turned and gasped.

Carlotta smiled and held out her arms. "And who is this new addition to our family?"

"Mom!" Shelly clamped a hand over her mouth while tears of joy sprang from her eyes.

With her cotton turquoise skirt swishing around her and

silver bangles tinkling, their mother crossed to Shelly and enveloped her youngest daughter in her arms. "My darling, *mijita*. I tried to surprise you before your baby arrived, but you were always an impatient girl who did things your way."

"I know, Mom, but this time it was Daisy." Shelly smiled up at her mother.

"Daisy," Carlotta said, her melodic voice giving the name a magical lift. "What a marvelous name."

"Did Dad come with you?" Ivy asked.

"Sterling stayed with the boat. We'd just arrived in Australia, so Sterling is sailing on to see Honey and Gabe in Sydney. But the morning we made land, I had such a feeling of urgency—I knew I had to come right away, especially when I saw your email. After all these years, your father is accustomed to my crazy feelings, so he put me on a plane without a second thought."

Ivy glanced at Bennett and smiled. He'd done the same for her in Palm Springs.

"Will he join you here?" Flint asked.

"In a week or two," Carlotta replied. "He'll need to see Honey and Gabe, who are taking the boat out while we're gone. Even though your older sister sails, she needs instruction before they set off. But he sends his love to all of you."

"Will you fly back to continue your journey?" Ivy asked. "And I want to hear all about where you've been."

"We'll continue, but in a more leisurely fashion than we'd originally planned," Carlotta replied, gazing at the newborn infant as she spoke. "From Mexico, we followed the Milk Run. The Galapagos Islands were intriguing, as well as the Marquesas, the Tuamotus, and the Society Islands. But now, we want to spend plenty of time between excursions with this precious little one."

Ivy was glad to hear that. Although she supported her parents' journey, all of their children missed them.

Shelly held Daisy to Carlotta, who swept the baby into her

arms. "My darling little love. *Que linda, mi amorcita.* You look so much like your mother did—with a little dash of Mitch mixed in as well." She winked at him. "There are a lot of Bays on this shore."

"And one I adore in particular," Mitch said, kissing Shelly's forehead.

Bennett stood beside Ivy, and they watched the family gather around Shelly and Mitch. Encircling her shoulders, he whispered, "This sure turned out to be an interesting day. I'm so relieved we made it back for Shelly and Mitch."

Ivy loved that he hadn't even hesitated to return. "May I have a rain check on that appetizer honeymoon?"

Bennett's eyes warmed to hers. "You can have as many appetizers as you'd like. As long as you leave room for the main course and dessert."

Ivy leaned into her husband. Babies might be unpredictable, but they brought such joy to families. This wouldn't be the first time Daisy might upset plans, but Ivy couldn't be happier with the new arrival.

Watching Bennett, she saw his face fill with emotion, and she wondered if he were thinking about the baby he'd lost when his first wife passed away. That had been a double tragedy for him. Ivy was nearly past the age of having children, yet a wild, crazy thought crossed her mind again.

Reflexively, she smoothed a hand over her stomach. Not that she would act on it, but there it was. And it was a topic they should discuss sooner rather than later.

Because, as she'd learned in the last couple of years, anything was possible.

19

The next few weeks after Daisy's birth passed in a whirlwind. She helped Shelly as much as she could, and she was grateful that their mother had returned to help Shelly with her new baby.

Piper had stayed on at the inn, and she and Noah had become even closer. He was helping her enlist support for the abandoned airport project, and the inn had become a lively center for Piper's planning meetings.

Ivy had pitched in with ideas, but she wanted this to be Piper's project. Between caring for her husband, a new niece, and her guests, she had plenty to do. Yet, she would support Piper as she could. She'd learned that she couldn't do it all. Now, she was beginning to ask for help.

Today, the spring weather was so beautiful—sunny and calm—that Ivy had opened all the windows in her art studio overlooking the patio. With the new dishwashers reducing her workload in the kitchen, she had been determined to put that time toward her painting.

Perched on a stool with a view of the ocean, she brushed paint onto a canvas, fastidiously recreating the delicate glint of sunlight on the ocean waves. In the foreground was an orange umbrella on the beach. She was so engrossed in her work that her mother's voice startled her.

"I was worried that you wouldn't find time to paint after your marriage."

Ivy dabbed at the crest of a wave. "What gave you that idea?"

"Your past history, I suppose. I'm glad to see you're developing your talent now." Carlotta spoke gently, but the message wasn't lost on Ivy.

She swiveled on her stool. "Bennett is different. If he knows that I haven't been painting in a while, he scoots me off to the studio. He doesn't need me by his side every minute."

"I can see that you're inspired." Carlotta nodded her approval of Ivy's work. "Your painting has such energy. I can practically feel the sun on my shoulders when I look at that. Your technique is progressing quite well." Lifting her face to the sea breezes, she gazed through the open windows. "This view is so inspiring. It's a true gift from the sea for you."

Ivy smiled at her mother's choice of words, recalling the book she'd just finished reading. "This painting is a special commission for a client. It will occupy a spot above the fireplace in their beach house." Ivy stepped back to take it in. Satisfied with her work for the day, she set about cleaning her brushes.

Carlotta gathered her full, yellow ruffled skirt and slid onto a stool, her matching jade bracelets clinking on her wrists. Ivy paused, taking in the sunlight glistening off the silver strands in Carlotta's dark hair. The effect was a soft halo. Ivy took in every detail, noting her mother's softly burnished skin, the result of spending months on the boat. Carlotta's face shimmered with serenity and happiness.

"Hold that for just a moment." Ivy snapped a quick shot to jog her memory.

"You're not going to paint me, are you?" Carlotta asked, crossing her legs and clasping a knee.

Grinning, Ivy took another photo. "What do you think?"

Carlotta laughed. "I'd love a painting of your father."

"Consider it done." Ivy unbuttoned her painting smock and hung it on an antique coatrack she'd salvaged from the lower level. Underneath it, she wore a bright floral shift paired with sandals. "I want to surprise Shelly with a painting, too. I've started some sketches of her and Daisy. Maybe for Christmas. I don't have time for much painting in the summer months."

"That would be a sweet surprise," Carlotta said. "Daisy is such a treasure, and Shelly seems to be settling into motherhood."

Ivy smiled at that. "She told me she has new respect for you. Five children. Neither of us can imagine how you managed that."

Carlotta waved a hand. "Back in those days, we made sure you knew how to swim and turned you loose on the beach. You all looked after one another."

"Shelly came along later," Ivy began.

"Seven years. She was our surprise baby."

"You weren't too much younger than I am now." As soon as the words left her mouth, she could feel her mother's gaze boring into her—and her cheeks warming under the scrutiny.

"Are you considering another child with Bennett?" Carlotta touched Ivy's forearm. "Or have you told him yet?"

"What? No, I'm not, I mean, I don't think...no, that's impossible."

"Few things are actually impossible," Carlotta said. "You simply look...happy. That must be it."

"That's all. Besides, we hardly have room for ourselves in that flat above the garage. He thought I'd want to move into his home on the ridge top, but I wanted to stay here." Ivy was stumbling over her words—her brain tangled over a crazy idea that she probably had no business even considering.

"What we have is enough, isn't it? Just the two of us…with Misty and Sunny, of course."

"Only you can be the judge of that. But this is quite a good-sized home." Carlotta swept her hand around the room.

Ivy pressed fingers to her temple. "You're not much help, you know."

"Every child is a blessing. But nothing says you must have children. Have you and Bennett talked about this?"

Ivy bit her lip. Last summer was a blur now. Superficially, perhaps, but had they really talked seriously? She didn't think so. "I don't know if I want to offer the possibility unless I'm sure I could follow through."

Carlotta leveled a gaze at her. "Most couples discuss these things in depth before they marry."

"We did, a little." Ivy knew she sounded too casual about this, but they'd had a ceremony on a whim before her parents left. Not that she wasn't sure of Bennett—she was even more certain now than the day they'd married.

"He assumed I wouldn't want more children, which was true then. And I think he figured he was too old to become a father."

"That sounds vague." Carlotta arched an eyebrow. "You're not as young as you were when you had Misty and Sunny."

"No." That single word of truth hung in the air. Should she even consider the potential for endangering her health at her age? And yet… She sighed. "Daisy is adorable."

Carlotta tossed her hair back and laughed. "Now you know why I had five children. Every time I thought we were finished, one of my friends had a precious baby. That cuteness weakens one's resolve." She paused, her eyes twinkling. "And, as you know, I have a very handsome husband."

Ivy grinned. Her parents were still very much in love—perhaps even more so after this long voyage. "Was Dad always okay with having more children?"

"He adored each of you and would have loved having

even more." Carlotta tucked her hand through the crook of Ivy's arm. "Have a chat with your good man. Whatever you decide will be right. You won't hear me pining for more grandchildren. Forrest and Flint gave us more than we ever imagined. And I daresay one of our grandchildren might be having a playmate for Daisy before too long."

That took Ivy by surprise. "Who?"

"Haven't you met Reed's girlfriend?"

"I didn't even know he had a serious one."

Carlotta smiled. "Neither does he. But she's the one, mark my words. Now, about this baby shower for Shelly...do you need help with invitations or anything?"

"Not a thing. It's more of a beach party than a baby shower. Poppy has been planning it with Darla, Imani, and Gilda. Darla also circulated word at Java Beach, so half the town will probably show up. I'm expecting beach ball instead of baby games."

"What fun," Carlotta said. "Shelly isn't the frilly-dress-and-tea-cakes sort anyway."

"Speaking of which, we need to leave for Shelly's cottage soon. I like to be here in the afternoon when guests check in."

When Ivy and Carlotta arrived at Shelly's beach cottage, her sister had placed Daisy in a portable bassinet outside under a shade tree. She was tilling another patch of ground for her garden.

"Hey," Shelly called out. "I thought you were Darla and Gilda. They're coming over soon to talk about the party."

"We came to help you with Daisy." Ivy picked her way past the daisies Shelly had planted along the walkway and the tomato plants she had started in the greenhouse at the inn.

Shelly drew a hand across her forehead and tucked a few strands of hair into her messy bun. "Daisy is on autopilot right now. I had to get out of the house. I was going crazy in there, and the garden needed tending." She tucked a small plant into the hole she'd dug and covered the roots with care.

"Did you finish decorating Daisy's room?" Ivy asked.

"With Mom's help." Shelly stood and brushed her hands on her denim overalls. "Come on, I'll show you."

She scooped up the bassinet by its carrying handle and headed toward the door. "Daisy is amazingly portable," Shelly said over her shoulder. "Being outside seems to help her sleep better, too. She's an eating-sleeping machine right now."

Ivy followed Shelly inside. The baby's new room was decorated in yellow and green, with colorful daisy designs bordering the walls and curtains. Suddenly, a realization came over Ivy. "All these daisies...you were hiding her name in plain sight all along, weren't you?"

Shelly laughed. "I wondered how long it would take you to figure that out. Mom was pretty quick, too."

"The place looks great," Ivy said, admiring the cheerful room. She could see evidence of her mother's handiwork around the house. The furniture Shelly had been meaning to paint now stood pristine and white against bright new cushions scattered about. At last, the cottage was turning into a home for Shelly as well as Mitch.

"The surfboard coffee table is going next week," Shelly said, casting a smile at her mother. "Not far, though. Mitch is mounting it on the wall in the garage. He can put anything in there—he claimed it as his man cave."

"It will be good for him to have a space to call his own," Carlotta said. "Children have a way of overrunning a house."

"I thought so, too," Shelly said. "I was going to cash in the silver dollars at the bank to cover the cost of some of what I'm doing around here, but Nan told me they could be worth a lot more because they're pure silver." Shelly shrugged. "Or more genuine silver."

"Maybe those really are your pot of gold," Ivy said.

"I'll have to find out more, but I just haven't had the time."

"That's motherhood," Ivy said. "I'll ask Nan or Arthur the next time I'm in town."

They returned outside and gathered around a second-hand table Shelly had placed outside under the shade of an old willow tree.

Shelly swept her hand across the backyard. "Next week, I plan to create graveled paths around these raised planters and add a few new fruit trees. I'm planning a play area for Daisy near the house on a soft carpet of grass."

As Shelly spoke, Daisy stirred and cried out. "It's feeding time."

Shelly lifted her baby from the bassinet, unfastened a strap on her overalls, and lifted her T-shirt. Daisy latched on, instantly comforted. Shelly grinned at the ease of it. "This sure beats making formula and washing bottles."

"You're truly fortunate," Carlotta said, stroking the soft crown of Daisy's head.

As Ivy watched her sister, she recalled the trouble she'd had trying to breastfeed Misty. She never did manage it, and later they'd discovered that Misty had a tongue-tie that made it difficult for her to latch on. In comparison, Sunny had been a breeze. Ivy wondered if she could still manage that.

When Ivy felt her mother's gaze, she glanced away. Her mother was right. Babies were far too cute, even though Shelly told her that Daisy had a set of lungs on her that had set off the wild coyotes on the ridge one night. She wondered what guests would think of that. Of course, there was always Bennett's house on the ridge.

She surprised herself with that thought. Could that be what he'd had in mind? She swept a hand across her brow. What was she thinking? She was nearly like the Argonaut shell, the keeper of an empty nest.

"So, this is where you are," Darla said, trudging around the corner of the house in her Birkenstock sandals. Her sparkly visor caught the sunlight.

Gilda followed her with Pixie perched in her backpack. When she saw Shelly, she paused and pressed a hand to her chest.

"This is the sweetest, most bucolic setting I've ever seen. Just look at you in this garden with your sweet Daisy." Gilda sank onto the chair next to Shelly, and Pixie poked her head out.

"We came to talk about Daisy's first party," Darla said. "Half the town is coming. They want to know what they can bring you."

"There's no need for gifts," Shelly said. "We couldn't fit them in the house anyway."

"Nonsense," Darla said, cutting her off. "I've told everyone they can bring diapers. Cloth or disposable?"

"I should say cloth," Shelly said, darting her eyes to one side. "How about both? I'm already tired of washing clothes."

Carlotta placed a hand on her daughter's arm. "Oh, honey, you're just getting started. I'll help while I'm here."

Pixie stretched her nose toward Daisy. The baby's toes were curled up, and Pixie inched out until she could reach her. Darting out her little tongue, she licked the baby's feet.

Daisy jerked a foot back, and Pixie yapped in surprise. At the sharp bark, Daisy wailed back.

"Oh, no," Gilda said, trying to shush Pixie, who was now barking at the strange alien creature.

Kicking and screaming, Daisy clearly thought the same of Pixie.

While Ivy cooed to her little niece and stroked her forehead, Shelly cradled Daisy and rocked her back and forth until she finally calmed down. Shelly shifted her to her other side, and Daisy quickly found solace again.

"Whew," Shelly said, stroking her baby's cheek. "You can tell people I need earplugs. My gosh, she can scream."

"Just wait until her lungs get stronger," Ivy said with a knowing look. "I can hold her after you finish."

Once again, Ivy felt her mother's eyes on her, and she remembered what she'd said. Daisy wasn't making her yearn for a baby...or was she?

Darla and Gilda went on to talk about party plans with Shelly. "This will be a good chance for you to meet other young mothers in Summer Beach," Gilda said, making sure that Pixie stayed quiet in her lap.

Darla leaned forward at the table. "Since there will be so many people, we thought we could have it on Main Beach near the playground and volleyball courts. We could have barbecue and music, too."

Shelly laughed. "What did I predict about a beach party?" When Darla looked surprised, she quickly added, "I love this idea. It's perfect. I want everyone to feel at ease and not worry about bringing gifts or playing silly baby shower games."

"Hey, I love that stuff," Ivy said.

"You would," Shelly said, poking her.

Carlotta interrupted them. "Now, girls. Don't you think you're a little old to squabble?"

At their mother's admonition, Ivy and Shelly broke out laughing. "We're way past that, Mom," Shelly said. "Although Ivy always starts it."

Ivy started to protest, but instead, she just grinned. She and Shelly had been through a lot these past couple of years. And through it all, they'd become more than sisters. They'd become the best of friends, too.

Ivy could see that motherhood was changing Shelly and her relationship with Mitch—both for the better. Once again, Ivy glanced at Daisy and felt a familiar stirring in her core. Her mother was right; she needed to talk to Bennett.

"Will you be there?" Gilda asked.

Blinking, Ivy said, "At the beach party?"

"At City Hall," Gilda replied. "For Piper's project. The airstrip."

"Oh, yes, of course. I'll be there." Clearly, she'd missed part of the conversation.

As Ivy fanned herself, she caught Carlotta gazing at her with a knowing look. Ivy sat up straighter in her chair; she couldn't let her mind wander like that. Was she delusional for having such thoughts at her age?

Yet, Ivy didn't feel her age. When she was in her twenties, a woman in her mid-forties seemed old. Now, here she was—and somehow, she was feeling younger and less burdened than she had in years.

A baby would sure fix that. Ivy laughed at herself.

Carlotta cleared her throat. "Piper's project would be good for Summer Beach. The old airstrip has been an eyesore for years."

The conversation shifted to the projects they'd proposed to Piper for her pitch regarding the renovation of the airport. However, she still needed city approval and private funding. Ivy knew Bennett supported the idea, but the decision wasn't his alone to make. Residents would have a chance to speak for or against it, and then there would be a vote.

They talked about the council meetings, and when there was a lull in the conversation, Darla said, "I wouldn't be surprised if we had another marriage soon in Summer Beach."

"And who might that be?" Carlotta asked.

Gilda traded looks with Darla and blurted out, "Piper and Noah. I'm betting they elope. I don't think her parents would be happy with her marrying a paramedic over a fellow gazil- lionaire. Six months. I'm calling it right now."

Darla nodded emphatically. "I'd take Noah over half of the suits in San Francisco. Not that there's anything wrong with a good-looking man in snazzy garb, but Noah is solid and talented. He's as good as they come. That is, he's up there with Bennett and Mitch," she added quickly.

"Sure glad you tacked my husband onto that last part,"

Shelly said, chuckling. "And Gilda, I hope you're not placing that bet with Charlie at Java Beach."

Gilda looked a little sheepish. "Did I say anything about Charlie?"

Shelly laughed. "You didn't have to. Old Charlie was taking bets on Mitch and me, and on Ivy and Bennett, too."

"I want you to know I didn't bet against either one of you," Darla said, raising her palm. "In fact, I made out pretty well by believing in you two." She nodded with satisfaction.

Ivy forced a smile. She recalled the fracas that bet had caused between her and Bennett. "Can't the Java Beach crowd find another way of welcoming Piper to Summer Beach?"

"We don't mean any harm," Darla said. "That just means she's one of us now. Any woman who can land a plane like that is sure worth knowing."

"Is that what it takes?" Shelly asked, fastening her overalls. "I'm kidding," she added with a wink.

Gilda and Darla chuckled along with her.

They're laughing now, Ivy thought. Yet, she remembered how tough Darla and some members of the city council had been on her when she was seeking a zoning change for the inn. Of course, Jeremy's dreadful reputation in Summer Beach had preceded her, but she hadn't known the extent of that until later.

"I'll be there to support Piper," Ivy said. She had a feeling the young woman would need it.

20

*I*n the meeting room at City Hall, Bennett looked out over the chattering crowd that had gathered to discuss the potential use for the abandoned airfield. Ivy was sitting next to Piper, who was looking around in nervous excitement.

He couldn't help noticing how nice Ivy looked in a coral-colored sundress. She and Carlotta had gone shopping, and he was glad to see that his wife had splurged on a new dress, although he suspected that her mother might have bought it for her. The shade brought a radiant glow to Ivy's face, almost as if—he cut off that thought. Thinking about the loss of Jackie and their baby was always sobering, even though it had been years. And he and Ivy were beyond that phase of life anyway.

Boz took a seat next to him. "Ready when you are, boss."

Quickly, Bennett composed himself. "Looks like everyone is present." He saw Mitch and Shelly with their new baby seated near an exit, along with Carlotta.

Keeping his thoughts off Ivy was difficult. When she was in a room, she drew his attention like a magnet, but he had a job to do here.

The only person missing was Aaron Macallan, the developer who had presented his proposal for the sprawling discount shopping mall at the last meeting. That was just as well. This was a competing project, and Aaron could be a real jerk.

Bennett called the meeting to order and invited Piper to speak. As expected, most residents and shopkeepers appeared in favor of Piper's project, but Bennett knew there was opposition among council members.

Piper stepped up to the microphone, which was hardly needed in the small setting except for people who spoke softly. Piper was not one of those. She tapped the microphone and leaned toward it. "Can everyone hear me?"

Her voice boomed across the room.

"I'll say, and probably in Toledo, too," Darla said, covering her ears. Noah grinned and gave her two thumbs-up from the front row.

Piper stepped back a little. "First, I want to share some history about the Seabreeze Shores Airfield." She tapped a key on her laptop to begin a visual presentation projected on a screen behind her.

Noah dimmed the lights and returned to his seat.

"Tony Diamond might have built the airfield for his offshore casino, but it also has a noteworthy history. Many famous aviators landed there—some by invitation from Amelia and Gustav Erickson, others brought in by Mr. Diamond to stage airshows and bring people to his casino." She read a list of early aviators that included Amelia Earhart and Bessie Coleman, among others.

"And Piper, too," a resident from the audience called out.

Piper grinned and went on. "According to historical records that Arthur and Nan supplied, the airstrip continued to provide a safe landing area even after the casino washed ashore and Mr. Diamond disappeared. Ivy Bay found information that the Ericksons contributed to its upkeep while they were in residence. Situated as it was between San Diego, the home of Ryan Air, and other emerging airplane manufacturers in Los Angeles, including Hughes Aircraft, Seabreeze Shores was an important airstrip in the early days of aviation."

"That was then," Piper said, looking up. "Now, since the community has grown up around the airfield, we have a chance to reclaim this prime piece of land to benefit residents." She clicked onto a photo of a rendering that Ivy had drawn for her. "Several people here will talk about their vision for the space, too."

Bennett looked out over the audience. Most seemed supportive, but he was concerned about two council members who had business interests in the area. Bennett called up the next person on the list.

Shelly passed Daisy to Mitch before making her way to the podium. "I'll have to make this quick before little Daisy wakes up, so here goes." She tapped on a key on the laptop that Piper had left on the podium.

"This is what I envision for the community gardens. A place where people can have access to land to grow food and share gardening expertise. I can help oversee the development, and Leilani and Roy of Hidden Garden nursery have agreed to offer educational classes there. We can work together on implementing a project landscaping plan that a landscape architect can provide. If you want to see a working version of this, Ivy and I have a friend on Crown Island who runs one. If anyone wants to see it, we can drive there or take the ferry."

Bennett made a note of that. He'd met the mayor of the nearby island community at a conference he'd attended recently.

The next person to speak was Mitch, who outlined his plan for what he called a Beach Hut—an outpost food stand with healthy options catering to families. "It would be cool to have it staffed and run by high school students interested in learning restaurant and service businesses. Not everyone wants to go to college, and even if they do, Summer Beach needs to maintain good local restaurants. Several foodservice owners here will help train the next generation of restaurateurs in Summer Beach."

"Sounds like that would create a few jobs," a council member said grudgingly, making a note. "Though not as many as the shopping center. And generate far less sales tax the city could collect."

Several hands in the audience shot up. Bennett knew a heated discussion would follow, and they still had more people who wanted to present. "Let's hold questions and discussion until after the presenters have finished. You'll all have a chance to ask questions then." Despite grumblings in the crowd, Bennett continued. "Now we'll hear from Antique Times proprietors, Arthur and Nan. I think most of you know them."

As peopled nodded, the couple took the microphone. They spoke about transforming the existing structure on the property into a museum staffed with volunteers from the Summer Beach historical society.

Arthur pulled up images of various antiques to display on the screen, including old photographs of the airfield in its heyday with noted pilots and Hollywood celebrities.

"And that's Tony Diamond," Arthur pointed out. "We have a lot of artifacts that come through our shop that are a rich part of our community's history, such as these casino-branded dinner sets and barware. We've put aside items of historical significance, and we'll reach out to residents for more ideas and donations."

Darla called out, "What about that roulette wheel?"

"Nan and I would be happy to put that on display, too."

Bennett tapped his pen on the table. "What about old newspaper articles and letters about the airfield and the floating casino?"

"Absolutely," Nan replied, her red curls quivering as she nodded. "We'll also include the history of early aviators who used the airstrip and offer tours for teachers and their students. Efforts can be supported by modest donations."

As they sat down, one of the other council members leaned forward. "Isn't there any plan for a park or other activities?"

Sunny's hand shot up, and Bennett gestured for her to speak.

"I'll help create a dog park, and I'm sure we can find someone to run the bike concession—rentals—if people don't have their own. And my cousin Poppy can organize the skating part. We've already asked my uncle Forrest to build a playground. My cousin Reed is going to oversee that."

A council member laced her fingers and leaned forward. "Is this a Bay family affair?"

Piper stood to answer. "I've been staying at the inn, and they've been very generous with their suggestions and offers. But I welcome everyone's participation and ideas."

Just then, Aaron Macallan sauntered into the meeting. Acting with importance, he made a show of settling his long, angular frame into a seat at the front. He turned a smirking face toward Piper. "Don't let me interrupt you. Finish your little plan, and then we'll get down to real business." He nodded toward a couple of council members as if they had a done deal.

Here we go, Bennett thought. Was Piper up for this fight?

While Piper glared at the developer, Ivy suddenly stood. Bennett could see the flush in her cheeks, and he knew what was coming. Instead of stopping her, he said, "Piper, I believe Ivy wants to say a few words. Will you recognize her?"

Piper lifted her chin. "Yes, I will."

"How incredibly rude of you," Ivy said, gesturing to Aaron. "This accomplished woman has put forth an important plan for the community. How dare you belittle her efforts

—and those of our community. You don't know anything about Summer Beach. All you want is to come here and make money at the expense of our longtime shopkeepers and restaurant owners. And for what? Discount goods people can order online or buy fifteen minutes away in the next community? Summer Beach is different, and that's why people choose to live here and visit."

"Well, well." Aaron chuckled. "Do you think I haven't heard that before? You can have your sweet little ideas, but my shopping mall will bring real progress and prosperity to Summer Place."

"You mean Summer Beach." Ivy planted her hands on her hips.

The council member seated next to Bennett suddenly perked up. He was one who had voted against Ivy's request for a zoning change for the inn. Bennett knew he was all about the bottom line, but he was dedicated to the community.

"That's what I said," Aaron insisted.

Darla sprang to her feet, incensed. "Aaron Macallan, you should be ashamed of yourself. You don't care enough to learn the name of our town."

"Don't be ridiculous," Aaron huffed. "I know what it is. But what does it matter if the city goes bankrupt?"

Another resident frowned and spoke up in a worried tone. "We're not in a bad financial position, are we?"

"Not at all," Bennett said quickly. Aaron's ploy was to seed doubt in people's minds and make them think they needed his development more than he needed them.

"Until the property heirs sue the city for standing in the way of this deal," Aaron said smoothly. "Remember what happened the last time Summer Beach tried to stand in the way of development? You could have had a world-class resort, but instead, you have a ramshackle inn by the beach that's not carrying its financial weight for the community."

Ivy stood again. "I pay my share of property taxes, and we do a lot for the community."

"Thank you, Ivy, and that's enough, Aaron," Bennett said. He was pleased that Ivy was speaking up. "We didn't come here to discuss that matter tonight, which has been settled to the satisfaction of the community. The Seabreeze Inn is also a historical landmark."

"Funny that your wife runs it." Aaron smirked at another council member, who quickly looked away. "And you're living there now, are you not?"

"That's not relevant to this discussion." Bennett clenched his jaw, determined not to succumb to the other man's trickery. Aaron was trying to push his agenda by intimating that the city had been playing favorites. That couldn't be further from the truth. When Ivy came before the board to ask for a change in zoning, it was long before they formed a relationship. Most of the people in the community knew that, so Aaron wasn't gaining any points by bringing that up. Quite the opposite; Ivy had the community on her side now.

Aaron rose from his chair, adjusting the lapels on his dark suit, which looked entirely out of place in Summer Beach. "Look, this is very simple. My company builds the shopping center, and we lease it to retailers we already work with. Summer Bay gets more property taxes and sales taxes. Everyone wins. What's the problem?"

Some people in the audience laughed, and Bennett passed a hand over his face. The guy still couldn't get the name of their community right.

Ivy shot back, "Is that the best option for Summer Beach long-term?"

"And what about roads and infrastructure to support increased traffic?" Piper turned to the audience. "You have a chance to improve your community, not congest it and drive shops and restaurants out of business, because that's what will happen."

Aaron laughed. "And you know that because your father has done just that in many communities, right?"

Though Piper's cheeks flushed, she continued undeterred. "He has also built community centers and roads to offset impacts. But yes, I've seen that happen. It shouldn't happen here. He might be my father, but that doesn't mean I agree with him."

Aaron stepped toward Piper. "Or is this a ploy to get the property for your dad?"

Ivy charged to the front. "Just because you don't have any integrity doesn't mean others don't." She turned to the audience. "Who is in favor of Piper's plan?"

"Wait a minute," a council member said, but it was too late. Almost every hand in the audience went up, and the noise level ratcheted up several notches.

"And how are you going to buy that property?" Aaron said, raising his voice over the din. "I doubt your father is backing you."

Piper bristled at that comment. "I've arranged other resources."

Just as Aaron waved off her comment, Tyler stood and raised a finger to speak.

Bennett swung his gavel for order, which surprised people and swiftly silenced the room. He didn't use it often. "Tyler, did you have something to add before we move to a vote?"

"I do." Tyler cast a look at Celia, who sat beside him.

Her long black hair was pulled back in a simple, chic ponytail, and she wore a pink silk blouse with white jeans and kitten-heeled sandals. She nodded her approval for him to proceed.

"Since we moved here, my wife has been contributing her time and our money to Summer Beach's music education program." Tyler hesitated, scuffling a foot. "Look, everyone knows I've been a jerk, but I discovered something recently. Each of us can make a difference here, even if it's helping just one person. You can't buy what folks here have created, which is a real community where we care about each other. I've finally realized that."

"You tell him," Shelly shouted, raising her fist.

People around them chuckled at that, but Tyler continued. "If you're afraid that Summer Beach might get sued for blocking the sale of the old airstrip to Aaron, don't worry about it. I'll offer more." Gesturing toward Aaron with contempt, he added, "Believe me, I've got a bigger boat than that clown."

"Don't forget the frat pack," Celia said.

"Oh, yeah," Tyler said with a self-conscious grin. "I'll get my tech buddies to donate to the cause, too. They might only come here a couple of times a year, but they're good for it. See, there's no place like Summer Beach." As he finished speaking, Celia reached for his hand and smiled up at him.

Bennett nodded at Tyler. Maybe some of what he'd said to Tyler at the marina had sunk in. He and Celia were acting more like a couple than he'd ever seen.

Next to Bennett, one of the council members who'd voted against Ivy jiggled his leg and drew his hands over his jaw, clearly contemplating the issue.

Aaron threw up his hands in exasperation. But before the developer could say anything else, Bennett called for the vote. He just hoped he'd read his fellow council members correctly.

21

"*H*ere's to the success of a new playground for Summer Beach." Ivy clasped Piper's hand and raised it high in victory before the crowd that had assembled early on the cracked pavement of the airfield.

She looked out over the small gathering. Bennett had a client meeting this morning, but Shelly and Mitch were there with Daisy, who was sleeping soundly, along with Imani and Chief Clarkson, Nan and Arthur, and Gilda and Pixie. Other residents had gathered as well, eager to meet Piper and hear more about the new community park.

"Thank you all for coming out this morning," Piper said. "I'm so happy to bring this project to you." Her dark curls blew around her face, and her deep blue eyes were filled with joy. "This is really your project. I'm just here to see it through."

"She'd being modest," Noah said as he stood proudly beside her. "Piper might be new in town, but she's dedicated."

The love in their eyes was obvious, Ivy thought. She was happy about the small part the inn had played in bringing them together. They weren't the only couple brought together there. She thought about Nick and Rosamie, who'd fallen in love over the Christmas holidays. She still heard from them, and she'd noticed a reservation for them this summer.

Piper brought Tyler to the front of the crowd. "And let's have a big round of applause for our benefactor."

Celia stood at the front of the crowd, clapping and beaming at her husband.

Ivy noticed that Celia was gazing at him with real admiration. She had never seen her friend look at Tyler like that before. There was hope for their marriage after all, she decided, feeling relieved for them.

The drawing Ivy had created for Piper's city council pitch stood on an easel next to a folding table that held a jug of lemonade and soft drinks. The property was overgrown, but it clearly had potential. Beyond the dunes she and Bennett had scrambled over when Piper's plane had landed, the ocean views were spectacular. This would be a beautiful place for generations to enjoy. It would be their little Central Park in Summer Beach.

Piper's vintage aircraft was still parked to one side. She was waiting for parts to repair it.

After answering a few questions from residents, Piper began to circulate with Noah.

"Lemonade?" Bennett held out a paper cup.

"You came," Ivy said, surprised. Bennett had gone to meet a real estate client early this morning. "Did you meet that guy who's looking for a house?"

"I guess he changed his mind. I'd rather spend the day with you anyway."

Ivy sipped the lemonade. "You're welcome to help me decorate at the beach." Shelly's big party was later this afternoon. "Poppy and Darla are there now getting ready."

"I heard Mitch is cooking," Bennett said. "Everyone will come for that."

"It's just what Shelly wanted. No baby games, but plenty of food and fun."

They talked a little more, and then Bennett glanced at the crowd that had gathered. "Piper might be spearheading this project, but it's your ideas that made up the foundation."

Ivy shrugged with modesty. "I didn't have time to handle this, and Piper was looking for something to do. It worked out well."

Bennett took her hand. "I meant to tell you how impressed I was with you at the City Hall meeting. You were ferocious, and the way you defended Piper was inspiring. I believe that what you added to the conversation truly influenced the council."

Ivy thought about that meeting. "I had faith in Piper's ability to pull that off. But the one who really surprised me was Tyler." She nodded toward her friends. "Celia told me he's been acting differently."

Bennett grinned. "How so?"

"Like he's discovered a new purpose."

"Maybe he had an epiphany." He squeezed Ivy's hand. "I'm glad you spoke up in defense of Piper at the meeting. She needed that—and so did the community. The vote could have easily gone against her proposal. I was watching my colleagues. A couple of them had doubts about her, but they saw the strong community support."

"If I'd thought about it, I might have hesitated," Ivy said. "But Aaron upset me. He and his massive shopping center didn't belong here. He couldn't even remember the name of Summer Beach. Honestly, it's not that hard. And did you see the way he was dressed? Like an undertaker, for Pete's sake. As Shelly would say, read the room, dude."

"Hey, that's pretty good." Bennett laughed at her imitation. "It's great to see people here excited to pitch in. Just like we do at the inn."

Just then, Arthur and Nan made their way toward them. "We have some incredible news for you," Arthur said. "Nan was combing through our archives, and she found a newspaper article on this airfield."

"From the 1920s?" Ivy asked.

"Much later," Nan replied. "This was from the 1950s, not long before Amelia Erickson left Summer Beach. She stated that she planned to buy the defunct Seabreeze Shores Airfield."

Ivy felt a peculiar energy course through her. "For what purpose, I wonder?"

Clearly thrilled at their discovery, Arthur and Nan grinned. She said, "Her intention was to dedicate the land for a future park for Summer Beach."

"You didn't know anything about that?" Bennett asked Ivy.

"Not at all." At a loss for words, Ivy gulped her lemonade. She knew exactly what Shelly was going to say about this coincidence. Was she on some sort of strange wavelength with Amelia? Not that she believed in that. This was purely happenstance.

"Sounds like this was meant to be," Bennett said.

"I'd call it serendipity," Ivy managed to say, and they all laughed. Whatever it was, Amelia certainly would have been pleased at this turn of events.

Ivy and Bennett spoke to others who were equally excited about the upcoming park and activity areas. When the small crowd broke up, Bennett clasped Ivy's hand.

"How about taking the beach route back to the inn with me?"

"Sure," Ivy said. She had walked here by herself, leaving Sunny in charge at the inn. Yet, strolling on the beach never grew old, especially with Bennett. There was something about the ocean breeze and the rhythm of the waves she found endlessly soothing.

They crossed the dunes and took off their shoes when they reached the water's edge, dangling sandals from their fingers.

Ivy looked out over the ocean, catching sight of boats in the distance and seagulls overhead. The sea was calm today, and cool water lapped their ankles as it rushed in and stole out along the sandy shore.

As they walked, they talked about the upcoming beach party. When they reached the inn, a new sight caught Ivy's attention.

"Wow, would you look at that," she said, stopping to admire a gleaming red bicycle for two parked in the car court. It looked like a vintage bike that had been restored to mint condition. "I wonder if Piper or Noah brought this here?"

Bennett stuffed his hands into his linen shorts and rocked on his heels. "They're still at the airfield, aren't they?"

A playful feeling welled up inside of Ivy, and she wiggled her eyebrows.

Bennett laughed. "They'd never know if we took it for a ride."

"We couldn't do that," Ivy said, although she longed to ride it. A tandem bike like this was way out of her budget, but thinking about it was fun. Hiking up her white cotton capri pants, she slid onto the first seat, which was set at the perfect height for her.

Bennett held it steady for her. "You look great on that."

She glanced around. "Why don't you try it, too?"

He rested his hands on her waist as he settled onto the seat behind her. A second set of bars was right behind her seat.

"How does that feel?" she asked over her shoulder.

"It's just right. I think we should try it out."

Ivy was so tempted. "Let's see how it is in the car court."

"There's not enough space here to really see what it's like. Let's take it out onto the road in front of the house."

"What if they come back?"

"Do you think they'd care?" Bennett laughed. "You've changed Piper's life. No way would she be upset."

Testing the bike with Bennett would be so much fun. And

he was right. Surely Piper wouldn't mind. Unless she wrecked it, which she wasn't planning on doing.

"Let's go," she said, pushing off and feeling like a kid again.

A moment later, they were sailing along the street. Ivy loved having the wind in her hair. "Wow, this is fun! Keep pedaling back there."

"I'll catch you yet," Bennett called out.

Just then, Ivy spotted Noah's car turning onto the street. Instantly, she felt a little self-conscious for having borrowed the bike, but there wasn't anything she could do now. She waved at Noah and Piper.

As Noah pulled nearer, he slowed the car. Ivy stopped beside him.

"We couldn't resist borrowing it. I hope you don't mind." When Noah looked perplexed, she said, "Isn't this yours?"

"It's not," Piper said. "But what a great idea. We should get one, too."

"Then whose is it, I wonder?" Ivy said.

"Surprise number three." Bennett waggled three fingers by her shoulder.

"What?" She whirled around, hardly daring to believe what he was suggesting.

"The house didn't count." Bennett smiled. "It's yours. To use anytime you like."

"Oh, my gosh, I love it," she cried. "And this cherry-red color is my favorite. It matches my car. How did you know?"

"Red or black, even or odd." Bennett tapped her nose.

The roulette table. Her heart filled with love for him. "This is so thoughtful of you." She threw her arms around him. As she did, the bike wobbled, and they both stumbled.

"Whoa, watch it," Bennett said, catching the bike before it fell.

Piper and Noah laughed and waved. "We shouldn't distract you. We'll see you at the inn after your ride."

"Where did you find this?" Ivy asked, still hardly believing it was theirs.

"I saw it in the window at Antique Times. It didn't look anything like this at the time, in fact, it was pretty beat up. I took it to my sister's house, and Dave and I restored it. New gears, new tires, new paint job. New seats, too." He grinned and bounced on his seat.

"It's spectacular. I've always loved these. Once, I even looked into getting one, but I didn't have anyone to ride with."

"You'll never have to worry about that again."

Ivy was so thankful for Bennett and that they were now smoothing out the bumps in their marriage. Adapting to each other had its challenges, but the good times were far outweighing any minor inconveniences. "Let's cruise down Main Street and show it off."

"I'm right behind you," Bennett said, laughing.

With a ring of the bell mounted on the handlebars, Ivy stepped on the pedals and took off, shaking her hair back in the ocean breeze. Life really was better in Summer Beach.

LATER THAT AFTERNOON, Ivy and Bennett rode the new bicycle to the beach for Shelly's party. When they arrived, their family and friends gathered around them to admire the tandem bike.

"This is amazing," Shelly said, carrying Daisy as she stepped closer to look at the bike. She turned toward Mitch, who was cooking over a grill on the beach. Darla was standing next to him, handing him paper plates for the food. Shelly called out, "Hey, babe. We should get one of these, too."

Mitch waved at them with a long-handled spatula. "We'd have to put a third seat on the back, and I don't know if I'd feel too comfortable with that."

"Spoken like a new dad," Ivy said. "Congratulations

again, you two. Just leave Daisy with us, and you can take the bike out. I think that's a fair trade."

"You're on." Shelly rubbed Daisy's back. "Park that contraption and come join the party."

Ivy reached into the basket on the front of the bike. "I know this isn't a baby shower, but I brought something I know you like." She handed Shelly a bright yellow gift bag.

Shelly looked inside, and her eyes widened. "Cake pops! You remembered. And they have daisies on them. How cute." She pressed a hand against her heart. "I have something for you, too."

Ivy stepped off the bike and adjusted her fluttery floral top. "Darla was right. It looks like half the town turned out." Music spilled into the air, and the scent of barbecue and suntan lotion mixed on the ocean breeze. Ivy inhaled the familiar smells of the summer ahead and smiled.

Everyone who had been at the airfield that morning was here now, along with many other people from Summer Beach. Jen and George from Nailed It, Leilani and Roy from Hidden Garden, and Louise from the Laundry Basket. Even Paige had joined them. She was seated under a broad umbrella where Shelly had been sitting with Daisy, protecting them from the sun.

Ivy knew Poppy and Darla had set up the umbrellas, brought the food, and supplied the tiki torches and decorations. One banner read, *Welcome to Planet Earth*. Ivy smiled, wondering who had created that for Shelly. A nearby table held a mound of packaged diapers that was spilling onto the sand.

"What do you think about it all?" Poppy asked, waving her hand.

"It turned out perfect." Ivy laughed at the diapers. Shelly had indeed gotten just what she'd asked for.

"It's so good to see everyone again," Carlotta said, waving to friends. Dressed in a white sundress, her mother looked happy and animated. "Ginger Delavie asked all about the trip. She has visited many of the same places we have." Ginger was Marina's fascinating grandmother.

Carlotta went on, her silver bracelets glimmering in the sunshine. "As much fun as it is to sail around the world, I can hardly wait until Sterling returns. We'll have a proper reunion here in Summer Beach."

"We should do that," Ivy said. "Don't we have a lot of relatives who'd love to see Daisy?"

"I should think so," Carlotta replied.

"Oh, no," Shelly said, cutting between them. "I don't want any sort of fuss over Daisy. It's likely to go to her head."

Ivy and her mother burst out laughing. "She'd probably sleep through it all," Ivy said, touching Daisy's soft crown of hair.

Shelly gestured toward the table. "I have something for you and Mom. Come with me."

Ivy followed her sister and mother, and they gathered under the colorful, patterned umbrella. Still holding Daisy, Shelly sank onto a folding chair. She was wearing her pre-pregnancy clothes again, with a short denim skirt and a loose top that Ivy knew she'd worn so she could easily nurse Daisy.

Carlotta reached out to her. "Shall I hold her for you, *mijita*?"

"I'd love that. For such a little bag of beans, she sure gets heavy after a while." Shelly kissed Daisy's pink cheek and handed her to Carlotta. She shook out her arms before reaching for two pouches on the table.

"I talked to Arthur and Nan about the silver dollars we found," Shelly said. "Because the coins had been in circulation and they're pretty scuffed up, they're not worth as much to collectors as if they were in pristine condition. However, due to the high silver content, they're worth more melted down than as currency." She opened one of the felt pouches. "But I had another idea." She withdrew a necklace with care.

Ivy gasped. "You made pendants of them. How lovely!"

Shelly's eyes sparkled with pride. "I thought these would be something to remember our crazy times together at the inn. All the treasures we've found—and returned to rightful owners—and the fun we've had. Nan had some vintage silver chains at the shop, and I found a silversmith in the village who crafted these unique bezels. I sketched what I wanted and told her they should look like palm fronds."

"They do," Ivy said, admiring how the coins were cradled in feathery palm tree leaves rendered in silver.

"I made them for you and Mom and Poppy." Shelly blushed. "And one for myself. We've all been on this journey together." She looped a long necklace over Ivy's head and carefully fastened one around her mother's neck, hugging each of them as she did.

Their mother touched the handcrafted pendant. "These are exquisite, *mija*. Have you thought of selling necklaces like these?"

"You have plenty of silver dollars," Ivy said. "You might find even more once Forrest opens the wall."

A broad smile bloomed on Shelly's face. "Actually, I filmed the entire process, and I'm going to upload the video on my channel and take orders for a limited quantity." She took Daisy back from her mother. "And I made one for this little monkey, too. She won't get it until she's older, but she's part of our tribe."

"This is a wonderful surprise," Ivy said, touching her heart. "I'll cherish this."

The three women sat around the table and talked, and Ivy realized how much she had missed doing this with their mother. Yet, her parents were entitled to their lives, too—just as Ivy's daughters were. Misty was living her life in Los Angeles, and Sunny might soon follow her.

Life had an ebb and flow of people and events, as sure as the ocean that stretched out before them. Touching the pendant nestled against her chest, Ivy vowed to appreciate every moment she was granted with those she loved. Reaching out, she took their hands in hers. "I love that we're all together today."

Carlotta kissed her cheek. "And I love all my girls."

Before long, the scent of barbecue filled the air, and Ivy realized she was hungry. She was sure Bennett was, too. Glancing around, she saw Forrest and Flint arrive with their families, along with a lovely young girl beside Reed—the one Carlotta had mentioned, no doubt. She caught her mother's eye and she nodded. Another generation was in the works.

Bennett poked his head under the umbrella. "Can I bring some food to you ladies?"

"I think we'll join the party now," Shelly said, rising.

"Thanks for offering, sweetheart." Ivy took Bennett's hand in hers. "Looks like the Bay family is out in force. Are you ready for all this madness?"

Mitch was calling everyone from the beach volleyball court to get food. "Come get your burgers—veggie and old-school style. Same for the hot dogs. Step right up, folks. And virgin Sea Breezes all around."

"We'd better get one to cool off." Bennett put his arm around Ivy. "I have a feeling we're going to have a hot summer ahead."

Ivy had the same curious sense. This spring had brought more changes at the inn, new friends, and a new family member. "Perhaps I'll have some surprises for you. It's my turn, after all."

"I'd like that," Bennett said. "But you're more than enough for me."

Looking toward the marina, Ivy put a finger to her lips. "This party shouldn't last too late. How about a date later? I'll drive."

Bennett laughed. "You're on, gorgeous."

22

Stretching onto a fluffy faux sheepskin on the bow of Bennett's boat, Ivy gazed at the stars in the clear night sky. Her floral top fanned out around her and fluttered in the light breeze.

"We should have this kind of date night more often," she said lazily.

The champagne that she and Bennett had bought at the market after going to Shelly's beach party was going to her head, but she didn't mind. With Bennett, she felt safe. They were alone at the far end of the marina, the boat bobbing gently in the waves. Moonlight cast a glow on everything around them.

Bennett sat next to her, strumming the guitar he kept on the boat and softly singing, *The Way You Look Tonight*.

"Mmm, even better than Frank Sinatra."

"Look at my inspiration."

She smiled up at him. "Way cuter, too. Do we have any more of those strawberries?"

"So that's what you're after." Bennett put his guitar aside and dangled a ripe red berry above her mouth.

"Maybe you, too," she teased him. She took a bite and moaned. "Berries definitely taste better this way."

Laughing, Bennett kissed her nose. "So noted, sweetheart."

She looped her arms around his neck, and he pulled her into his lap. "More champagne?"

"Just a splash. I still have to pedal."

"I can get you home. Or we can sleep on the boat." He tapped his glass to hers. "That tandem bicycle was one of the best investments I've ever made. Aside from the dishwashers."

"I love those, too. You've surprised me in so many ways. What have I done for you?"

"You surprise me every day," Bennett said. "Sometimes I wake in the morning surprised—and thrilled—to find you in my bed. I never thought I had a chance with you."

Ivy gave him a small smile; she'd had the same thought. Bubbles tickled her lips as she sipped. She couldn't help herself; she still giggled like a teenager with him—as she had so many years ago. "Did you ever imagine that we'd be cycling around Summer Beach like a couple of mid-life lovers?"

"That's exactly what we are, and I'm pretty happy with that status." Bennett laughed and reached for her glass. "Maybe I should finish this."

"Not a chance." She sipped her champagne and pressed the cool glass against her cheek. "You're the one who said I needed to unwind tonight."

"And I'm glad you are. What a month it's been." He clasped her hand in his and brought it to his lips.

Ivy stretched out her legs. "From shipwrecks and spa weeks to a new baby and a new park. For such a small town, life is never dull here."

"Not with you around." He planted a kiss on her forehead.

And she never felt lonely anymore. A widowed woman of a certain age could get lost in a big city, but not in Summer

Beach. She counted herself fortunate to have found Bennett again and made many new friends.

Ivy looked up at him. "I've been thinking about our place."

"Oh, really?"

She eased onto her side, supporting herself on her elbow. She'd given their living situation a lot of thought. "The other day, I walked around the rear of the garage. There's plenty of room to build a deck off the back. It wouldn't be costly construction. If Forrest got us started, I bet we could finish it. I'm better at demolition, but I'm sure I can learn to build. What's so hard about wielding a hammer and nails anyway?"

Bennett almost spewed his champagne. "You want to learn the building trades now?"

"Why not? I can hang pictures, and I've gotten pretty good at creaky doors and plumbing repairs. Forrest gave me plenty of tools and gizmos. Or I can watch some videos online and figure it out. Really, how hard can it be?"

When he didn't answer, she went on, growing more excited about her idea. "Imagine the bedroom opening onto a long covered porch. The palm trees would shade it, or we could put a roof on it and add ceiling fans. With a few extension cords or a laptop, you could have a workspace out there. Like a *Swiss Family Robinson*-style treehouse with an ocean view."

"Why do I think it might turn out more like *Gilligan's Island*?" he said, chuckling.

Ivy gave him a playful swat on the arm. "I'm serious about this."

"So am I—and it might be an interesting addition." He smoothed his fingers on his chin. "If you're set on building it, I could teach you a few things. With a little guidance from Forrest or Axe, we could probably manage it. Or at least do the finish work."

Ivy's mind was whirring again. "We could also add storage

beneath the deck off the back of the garage for your outdoor gear."

"More storage is always good."

She could tell that she was appealing to him. "If you wanted, we could screen in the porch and add a pot-bellied stove for winter." The addition was taking shape in her mind's eye. "We could also hang roll-up bamboo shades and throw grass mats on the floor. There is some antique patio furniture stored on the lower level. I could make colorful cushions from outdoor fabric to withstand the sun and occasional rain that might blow in."

More than anything, she knew he needed his space. "This would give us more room to spread out. What do you think about bumping out the bathroom wall and adding a larger cupboard and dressing area for you?"

"That's a good idea." Bennett sipped his champagne and nodded thoughtfully. "A deck facing the ocean would get plenty of sunshine, too. We could probably use it most of the year."

"I'll sketch it for you, and you can add whatever you'd like. This could be our autumn project after the summer rush." She held her breath, hoping he would agree.

"It might be a viable solution to our space problem." Slowly, he nodded. "My current tenants are pretty excited about the house I found for them to buy. And there is another family interested in leasing my house. That is, if you're sure you don't want to move into it. This could be your last chance for a while. Not that I'm pressuring you," he added quickly.

Ivy hesitated. They'd already talked about this, and he knew how she felt. "I really want to stay here and build our treehouse."

He smoothed her hair from her face. "Then I like that idea, too."

Even though he said that, Ivy had to make sure. She

pressed her fingers lightly against Bennett's cotton shirt. "You won't be upset about leasing your house again?"

Putting his arm around her, he pulled her close. "I like meeting the guests and helping around the inn when I can. And if we want to get away, we can always come here or take the boat out."

"It is peaceful here." Ivy peered into the distance, spying seals splashing in the water—probably on a nocturnal hunt for fish. Somewhere, a baby cried in the night. Bennett heard it, too. "That could be Daisy."

He chuckled. "I was thinking the same thing. I'm really happy they both got the family they wanted."

"Mitch wasn't sure about having children at first."

"Guys might say that, but kids always melt our hearts." Falling silent, he stared out at the far horizon.

Sensing where his thoughts had drifted, Ivy waited. Silences were comfortable between them now. After a while, she cleared her throat.

As if pulled from a trance, Bennett turned back to her. "Are you okay?"

"Sure. But I was wondering about you." When he looked perplexed, she decided to plunge into the conversation they needed to have. "I wondered if you had another reason for wanting to move back into your house. It would have given us more room. Sort of like the room that Shelly and Mitch needed."

Slowly, her meaning dawned on Bennett. "That wasn't the reason, although it could have been. Just so you know, I wouldn't have minded."

Hesitating for a moment, Ivy pressed her lips together. "Neither would I."

Bennett snapped his head up. His eyes shimmered in the moonlight. "Are we...expecting something?"

She shook her head. "Still, since seeing Daisy, I've been having this feeling." She pressed a hand against her stomach.

"I would hate for you to feel like you've missed an important part of life, especially after what you went through with Jackie."

Bennett clasped a knee and nodded. "I've thought about that, but I came to terms with it a long time ago. My nephew has been like a son to me."

"Only he isn't," Ivy said softly. "It might not be too late."

"I love him just the same." Bennett took Ivy's glass and put it down before sweeping her into his arms. "I couldn't let you take that risk. Not at your age."

"I've had two children, so it's not as difficult. If you wanted…"

A pained expression filled Bennett's eyes. "For years, I felt like I had killed Jackie—"

"No," Ivy said, shaking his arm. "That wasn't your fault."

"I thought if she hadn't been pregnant, she wouldn't have died."

"Each of us has a time," she said gently.

Bennett clenched his jaw. "I know, but I had a hard time believing that, even after years of therapy. Please promise me you won't take such a chance. Please."

Ivy drew a breath, searching for the right words. When she didn't answer right away, he gazed at her with alarm.

"Yesterday, seeing how you looked when you arrived at the meeting—you were glowing, and it reminded me of…" He stopped, cradling her face in his hand. "Are you sure you're not pregnant?"

Taking his hand, Ivy kissed it and folded it in hers, pressing their twined hands to her heart. For all the strength and wisdom that Bennett had, he also harbored the scars of deep loss. At once, she understood the wellspring of his compassionate nature.

Blinking, she lifted her face to his. "I'm quite certain, and I would never do anything without discussing it with you first."

"Unless it were an accident."

She smiled. "There's always that chance."

"It's a romantic idea, but the reality could be devastating." Bennett drew his fingers along her cheekbone. "Had I missed out on you, I would be a poorer man. If we were chosen to be parents, I have no doubt that we would rise to the challenge. I didn't think we needed to seek out that experience—and responsibility—but do you feel that you want one more?"

Ivy heaved a sigh. His words held the answer she needed to hear. "While a part of my heart yearns for another child with you, I'm old enough to recognize the hormonal tug—" she balled a fist and pressed it to her stomach, "that can feel as strong as the tide. The difference is that waves sweep out to sea, leaving little behind on the shore. Not so in the case of a baby."

Bennett grinned. "Are you saying that another child would be like a wave crashing over us?"

"A tidal wave," Ivy said, smiling back at him. "If you're not aching for a baby, then we certainly don't have to entertain the idea."

She hesitated, feeling a great sense of relief edged with a sliver of loss. A part of her would have loved to have had a child with Bennett. In the future, there might be an infinitesimal chance of an accidental pregnancy—but a child wasn't necessary to their life together. Bennett wanted *her*, and he was looking out for her health.

That meant everything to her.

She had to trust that she was in just the right phase of life for her now. Her shell might soon be an empty nest, but it could still be filled with love. This was the gift she cherished most of all.

Bennett wrapped her in his arms and peppered her face with kisses. "Ivy Bay, you're a wonder. I never know what's going on in that beautiful brain—and heart—of yours. What a date night this turned out to be. For a moment, I thought you were going to tell me I would be a father soon."

She laughed. "Let's leave parenthood to Shelly and Mitch." And she meant that. But then, anything could happen.

Picking up her champagne, she tapped the glass against Bennett's and drained the last drop. "Who's ready to see if we can balance that bike back to the inn?"

"I love you, but I'm definitely steering." He stood and scooped her in his arms. "Off we go, Ivy Bay."

Laughing, she nabbed her sandals as he carried her off the boat. "What will people think about the mayor carrying his wife through the marina?"

Bennett kissed her softly. "I think they all need to see what love is really like."

AUTHOR'S NOTE

Thank you for reading *Seabreeze Shores*, and I hope you enjoyed the spa week excitement at the Seabreeze Inn. Be sure to read the next story in the Summer Beach series, *Seabreeze Reunion*. When the unexpected occurs at a family reunion at the Seabreeze Inn, can Ivy and Shelly manage the new challenge, or will this change the family forever?

If you've read the Coral Cottage at Summer Beach series, join Marina and Kai and the rest of the Delavie-Moore family in a beach wedding to remember in *Coral Weddings*.

Coming soon...the first book in a new series! You'll love making new friends on *Beach View Lane*.

Keep up with my new releases on my website at JanMoran.com. Please join my VIP Reader's Club there to receive news about special deals and other goodies. Plus, find more fun and join other like-minded readers in my Facebook Reader's Group.

More to Enjoy

If this is your first book in the Seabreeze Inn at Summer Beach series, I invite you to revisit Ivy and Shelly as they renovate a historic beach house in *Seabreeze Inn*, the first book in the original Summer Beach series. In the Coral Cottage series, you'll meet Ivy's friend Marina in *Coral Cottage*.

If you'd like more sunshine and international travel, meet a group of friends in the *Love California* series, beginning with *Flawless* and an exciting trip to Paris.

Finally, I invite you to read my standalone family sagas, including *Hepburn's Necklace* and *The Chocolatier*, 1950s novels set in gorgeous Italy.

Most of my books are available in ebook, paperback or hardcover, audiobooks, and large print. And as always, I wish you happy reading!

RECIPE: TIRAMISU CHILLED COFFEE

In *Seabreeze Shores*, when Mitch creates new summer coffee drinks at Java Beach, he serves this delicious concoction to Shelly and Ivy.

The key to a mild cold brew coffee is to simply let the coffee steep naturally. Aficionados say the coffee is smoother that way.

In a hurry? No problem. You can also make fresh coffee in a pot or Keurig coffee machine. When I brew coffee, I often keep leftover coffee in the refrigerator for chilled pick-me-ups in the afternoon. Here's a way to transform that into a tasty summer cooler.

Makes 4 servings
Ingredients:
4 cups cold brew coffee (below) or regular coffee, chilled
2 cups ice cream (coffee, mascarpone, vanilla, or chocolate)
1 pint heavy cream (for whipping)
2 Tbsp. powdered chocolate (for dusting)
Optional: 1 Tbsp. chocolate chips
4 to 8 ladyfinger cookies (*savoiardi* in Italian)

Instructions:

Cold Brew Coffee

Place 1 cup coarse grind beans (not fine) into a bowl. Pour 4 cups of filtered water over the beans. Cover. Let steep for 12 hours. Strain and chill.

Tiramisu Coffee Drink

Whip heavy whipping cream until creamy. Set aside.

Pour 1 cup of cold brew into a tall glass. Add a scoop of ice cream and a dollop of whipped cream.

Dust with chocolate powder and/or sprinkle with chocolate chips. Serve with 1 to 2 ladyfinger cookies to dip into the coffee as you drink. Enjoy!

ABOUT THE AUTHOR

JAN MORAN is a *USA Today* bestselling author of romantic women's fiction. A few of her favorite things include dark chocolate, fresh flowers, laughter, and music. She loves to travel to places rich with history and mystery and set against snowy mountains, palm-treed beaches, or sparkly city lights. Jan is originally from Austin, Texas, and a trace of a drawl survives, although she has lived in Southern California near the beach for years.

Most of her books are available as audiobooks, and her historical fiction is translated into German, Italian, Polish, Dutch, Turkish, Russian, Bulgarian, Portuguese, and Lithuanian, and other languages.

Visit Jan at JanMoran.com. If you enjoyed this book, please consider leaving a brief review online for your fellow readers where you purchased this book or on Goodreads or Bookbub.